Still Life with Volkswagens

Still Life with Volkswagens

Geoff Nicholson

The Overlook Press
Woodstock · New York

First published in the United States in 1995 by
The Overlook Press
Lewis Hollow Road
Woodstock, New York 12498

Library of Congress Cataloging-in-Publication Data

Nicholson, Geoff
Still Life with Volkswagens / Geoff Nicholson.
p. cm.
I. Title
PR6064.I225S75 1995 823'.914—dc20
95-17593 CIP

First published in the U.K. by Quartet Books Limited

ISBN: 0-87951-616-X
Manufactured in the United States of America

First American Edition

I

Gentlemen Prefer Volkswagens

He is dreaming. It is an erotic dream of sorts. It happens. The bombs go off. The balloon goes up. The car is blown apart from within. It is all slow-mo and freeze frame, a carnival of special effects, brightness dancing and hanging in space, shimmering, spinning tinsel, particles that curl and leapfrog, fragments of vehicle that shuffle and reshuffle, furling and unfurling in the dented air; electrical components, shards of glass, slices and slithers of upholstery and optional extras, tatters of fabric and machine. It is all fallout. There is a great levelling, a loss of organisation, a bringing down to size.

He stirs. He wakes up. He is not sure who he is. He is not sure who is the owner of the dream.

At the Milton Maynard Mercy Seat – one of the home counties' more discreet and unostentatiously fashionable asylums – a group consisting of a dozen or so inmates is playing I Spy. They are a varied though unexceptional group of patients. They display a predictable set of symptoms. There are few medical or psychological surprises to be found in their amalgams of depression, schizophrenia, neurosis, compulsive, obsessive and self-destructive behaviour. A couple of them claim to be receiving messages from other planets, but that too is par for the course.

1

The only one who looks out of place is Mr Charles Lederer, but he does not look that way because he is displaying signs of some new or unusual mental condition, rather the reverse. He cuts a sane, dapper figure amid the pyjamas and dressing gowns. He is wearing a blazer and a wide-brimmed Panama. None of the other inmates recognises his tie as that of the Garrick Club, but it is a tie he is perfectly entitled to wear. His shirt is a freshly laundered white and his flannels have razor sharp creases. Only the lack of a belt for his trousers and the fact that he's wearing tartan carpet slippers without socks, reveal anything of his situation.

He would tell you, if you asked, that he used to be a well-respected figure in English public life; a back-bench Tory MP and director of a handful of extremely profitable companies. But it all changed when a man in a Volkswagen stole his daughter, slept with his wife, invaded his house, turned the media against him and caused his incarceration. You would probably listen politely to these colourful fantasies. They might sound like the all too typical ramblings of a disordered mind. In Charles Lederer's case, however, they are nearly all true.

A large, shapeless, sad-faced woman called Magenta, whose hormones are severely out of control, is currently leading the game. 'I spy with my little eye something beginning with b,' she says enthusiastically. Once such obvious contenders as basket, book, bristles, biro, button and bulbs have been eliminated and everyone has admitted defeat, Magenta tells them that the b in question stands for 'bare bottom'.

'But we can't see anybody's bare bottom,' Charles Lederer reminds her gently but authoritatively, and even as he says it he realises his error.

'Oh yes you can,' Magenta shouts and she stands up, drops her loose, white, sexless pyjama trousers and reveals an almost equally loose, white, sexless bottom. A flurry of sniggering, schoolyard mirth flushes through the group, and, not for the first time, Charles Lederer wonders if playing I Spy is really a valid form of therapy. But he doesn't have much time to think about it since the group has decided it's now his turn to spy something. He accepts graciously.

'I spy with my little eye something beginning with v,' he says.

The group agrees that's a tough one. Vase, Vaseline, Vimto and Valium are all suggested.

'No,' says Charles Lederer. 'You'll never get it.'

'In that case there's no point guessing, is there?' says Magenta, and Charles Lederer agees.

'It's a Volkswagen that I spy with my little eye,' he says triumphantly.

'Where?' asks Magenta.

'Yes, where?' the others all demand, keen to know where there might be a Volkswagen lurking.

'I spy it with my *mind's* eye,' he answers.

That throws the rest of them into confusion. They have to think about that, and thinking is not necessarily their strong suit.

'Well, I can't see it,' says a short, middle-aged, baby-faced bruiser of a patient.

'Yes you can,' Charles Lederer insists. 'It's a fairly early model, black in colour with white wall tyres. You *can* see it if you try. You can see it's humped back and those headlamps like nasty, slitty eyes.'

And Magenta says, 'Yes, I can see it now. I can see it with my inner eye.'

'Of course you can,' says Lederer.

'Me too,' says another patient, then another, and before long the whole group has focussed its various inner eyes on some phantom Volkswagen of their collective unconscious.

'Yes,' Charles Lederer continues, 'just look at that evil, sloping front end, and hear the horrid death rattle of its air-cooled engine. And smell those clouds of noxious exhaust fumes. Terrible, isn't it?'

3

The others tend to agree. A couple of them choke on the imagined fumes.

'But wait,' he continues. 'What's that sitting on the passenger seat? It's a package. A suspect package. I wonder what's in it. I wonder if it contains a couple of pounds of highly unstable plastic explosive. And could that ticking noise be coming from some sort of timing device? Yes, I think it could. Look, on the seat right beside the package there's an alarm clock, and wires attached to a detonator, and you can hear the seconds ticking away. When the big hand gets to twelve it'll be all over for that cursed Volkswagen Beetle. There'll be an almighty bang. There'll be fire, flames, black smoke. Metal and glass will be sent flying like so much filthy dandruff.'

Several of his listeners gasp. They are all becoming tense and agitated. Charles Lederer's verbal picture has cut right through their placid, generalised sedation.

'Look at the clock,' he says. 'Only ten seconds to go now. Let's count them down together, shall we? Ten, nine, eight . . . '

They recite the countdown in unison, but the feeling is not of a downward motion, rather of a steep ascent, of a spring being tightened. 'Seven, six, five . . . ' One or two have their eyes closed by now, and one or two others have their fingers in their ears waiting for the big bang. 'Four, three, two . . . ' Only Charles Lederer remains impassive, his head high, both his lips commendably stiff. 'One . . . '

There's a half moment of hesitation, of sweet but frightening anticipation, a sense of simultaneous horror and joy at what will be unleashed when the dreaded word zero is said.

'Zero,' says Charles Lederer.

Volkswagens explode violently and picturesquely all across a dozen disturbed psyches. Mania and hysteria gush out of the patients. There is screaming, mayhem, the tearing of clothes and hair, a certain amount of foaming at the mouth, and Magenta decides to beat her head repeatedly against an electric radiator. It takes several hours, the use of half a dozen straitjackets, some strong arm tactics by the hospital staff, and a whole sweetshopful of drugs, before order is again imposed. Only Charles Lederer has remained calm throughout, and that's because he knows he's in a lot of trouble.

Here is Barry Osgathorpe sitting on the steps of his eighteen foot 'Homemaker' caravan, on a site not far from Filey, in Yorkshire. This is an award-winning site. The shower blocks and laundry facilities are first rate, and it is in all the best guide books. Barry looked at quite a few residential sites before choosing this one, but spurned them because they were all full of old hippies. This one does have a handful of longterm residents like himself but they are a neat, well-mannered group, mostly retired and very caravan-proud. But the site caters mostly for mobile holidaymakers who stay a couple of nights, or a week at most, then travel on. Barry likes this. He likes the transience even if he personally remains firmly fixed.

The owner of the site, a bald, avuncular, only intermittently competent man called Sam Probert, quite likes having Barry there as a sort of eccentric in residence. Once in a while Barry will attempt to perform some odd jobs around the place, and in return Sam Probert makes a small reduction in the rent.

A car is parked next to Barry's caravan. You cannot see the car properly since it is wrapped in one of those fitted car covers, but there can be no doubting from the shape that it's a Volkswagen Beetle, rather a special one actually, one with the nickname 'Enlightenment', although Barry hasn't driven it for a few years, not even removed the cover for some months. In recent times Barry has rather changed his feelings about Volkswagens and life on the road.

As he sits outside his caravan he is surrounded by a small

crowd of children, the offspring of the holidaymakers at the site. This is not an unusual occurrence. Barry enjoys something of a reputation as a harmless eccentric and quite a good storyteller. The kids gather round and he talks to them.

'Don't call me Ishmael,' he says. 'That's not my name, not any more. I was called that once but it was a long time ago. It was a good enough name for a Zen Road Warrior, as I then styled myself, but now I'm my old self again, Barry Osgathorpe, and that's a good enough name for me.'

And then he tells some rather tall and lurid stories about his life on the road, tales of car chases and petrol bombings, of violent confrontations with police and other members of 'straight' society, of crowds of people who briefly followed and worshipped him, of strange practices with sex and drugs, of a woman called Marilyn whom he loved and lost, of how he had once very nearly had his own chat show on television.

The kids eat it up, and indeed he does tell the stories with an undeniable flair. Whether any of the kids believe the stories to be true is debatable, but that doesn't spoil their enjoyment. However, having told these action-packed adventures he always says, 'And let that be a lesson to you kids. Remember that speed kills. Remember that the motorcar is not our friend. And be sure to tell you parents to drive with care.'

Generally the kids let him get away with this. They are perfectly accustomed to having inappropriately worthy morals tagged onto the end of stories they hear. But on this occasion, as the troop of kids wanders away, one of them stays behind to ask Barry some questions, and Barry is initially rather pleased by this.

'What's so wrong with motorcars?' the kid asks directly.

He is a cheerful but serious, red-haired little tyke, no more than ten years old, with dirty knees and a blue American football shirt.

'Well,' says Barry very patiently, 'for one thing they use up the earth's precious resources.'

The kid thinks for a moment and says, 'But my Dad says that these days motorcars are designed to be recycleable. Almost every part can be melted down and reused.'

'I don't know about that,' says Barry.

'Well, my Dad does. He says from that point of view they're one of the most ecologically friendly products we have.'

'Well, I'd want to see some chapter and verse on that,' says Barry, 'but in any case they emit toxic gases and contribute to the greenhouse effect and global warming.'

'My Dad says it's not quite as simple as that. Did you know for example that Roger Revelle, the only begetter of the theory of the greenhouse effect, changed his mind shortly before his death?'

'Er, no,' says Barry.

'He recanted. He said, and I think I'm quoting accurately, "The scientific base for greenhouse warming is too uncertain to justify drastic action at this time. There is little risk in delaying policy responses." Basically he was saying, play it cool.'

'How old are you?' Barry asks.

'Nine and a bit,' says the kid.

'What's your name?'

'They call me the Ferrous Kid.'

'Do they really?'

'Well no, but I wish they would.'

'Okay Ferrous,' says Barry, 'I'll try to make it simple for you. Look at it this way; we've only got one planet. We must share it with all the animals and trees and birds, and with every other living thing.'

'Well, my Dad says that wildlife thrives alongside every stretch of motorway in the world.'

'Does he indeed?' says Barry. 'Well you tell him from me

that motorways are evil, ugly things that scar and mutilate the landscape.'

The kid thinks for a while before replying, 'I think my Dad would say "not necessarily". I think he'd say go take a look at some of the freeway architecture in Los Angeles, and tell him if some of that doesn't constitute a brilliant work of art.'

'I think I can answer that for him without going to Los Angeles, thank you very much,' Barry says tartly.

'And my Dad would certainly say that some cars are works of art. He'd say look at a 1938 Talbot Lago T150SS with the Figoni and Falaschi body, look at a Rolls-Royce Silver Ghost Piccadilly Roadster, even look at a perfect example of a humble Volkswagen Beetle, and tell him if that isn't a thing of beauty. And then he'd say isn't it worth a bit of pollution for the sake of beauty? Okay, he'd say, certain problems attach to the motorcar but it's not exactly the work of the devil.'

Barry has gone into a world of his own. It seems to be the mention of the Volkswagen Beetle that did it. Then he's swiftly back on the case.

'That,' he says, 'is a matter of debate. When you see how many people die every year because of the motorcar, I think even your Dad would have to admit that it's an evil thing.'

'Well,' says the kid thoughtfully, 'I think my Dad would say that AIDS and cancer and heart disease and diabetes kill people too. And I think he'd say he'd rather snuff it quickly and cleanly in a road accident than hang around dying of some long, slow, terrible wasting disease.'

Barry thinks for a long time. The kid has actually, finally said something he agrees with, and of course, the mention of the Volkswagen Beetle is still much on his mind.

'Maybe I should meet your Dad,' he says.

'No,' says the kid. 'He's a complete dickhead. That's what my Mum says anyway.'

*

There is one woman whom Barry did not love and lose. Her name is Debby, Barry's current, and extremely long-standing, girlfriend. He certainly hasn't lost her, since she comes to his caravan several evenings per week and stays the night, but he's not sure that he really loves her either. He'd like to, because he believes love is the greatest thing, and Debby seems to think very highly of him. She moved to Filey in order to be near him. She got a job in a local building society and shares a flat in town with three of the other girls from work. Barry would like to think that his relationship with her is a good thing and that it has a future, but he has his doubts. Tonight, having dined on several different varieties of Pot Noodles, he asks her, 'Are you sure I'm really what you're looking for?'

'I'm not sure I'm exactly *looking* for anything,' she replies.

'But you know I don't have any money or any prospects.'

'I suppose that's true,' she admits.

'Five years from now, ten years from now, I could still be living in this caravan.'

'Would that be so terrible?'

'I thought you might consider that a terrible way to spend the next ten years.'

'I might,' she said, 'but I have a perfectly pleasant shared flat in town.'

'Yes, but if you wanted a nice house, a nice car, lots of nice children, well, I just might not be your man.'

'But you *are* my man.'

'But I never want to go anywhere or do anything.'

'Well, I admit I wouldn't mind going for a drive once in a while, but Barry, where is all this leading?'

'I was just thinking that if you met another bloke, through work say, someone with money and a career, and if he could offer you more than me, and if you decided he was what you were looking for, well . . . I'd understand.'

'I know you would. That's what's so special about you Barry. You're so wise, so sympatico.'

'Well, I try to be.'

'But wouldn't you miss me if I went off with someone else?'

'Well of course I would,' he says hastily. 'But if you really felt you had to go . . . '

'And wouldn't you miss this?'

And Debby proceeds to perform various moist and intimate acts on Barry's body that he would most certainly miss in their absence, and before long there are torrents of hot semen coursing like molten lava down Debby's moist, yielding, eager throat. Barry would have to admit that his sex life with Debby is fine, in fact it's really rather spectacularly good, but he sometimes wonders if there is more to life than that. From time to time Debby tries hard to assure him there is not.

Next morning Charles Lederer is called into the office of Dr D.K. Hendricks, the director and presiding genius of the Milton Maynard Mercy Seat. The doctor is surprisingly cordial. He smiles a lot. He wants Charles Lederer to know that he isn't angry. He's a little disappointed perhaps, but certainly not angry. He wants Charles Lederer to know he's a friend. Charles Lederer remains unconvinced.

'Why did you do it Charles?' the doctor asks.

No reply is forthcoming.

'Was it a way of getting at me? If so that's perfectly understandable. I appreciate that you will harbour certain unresolved hostile feelings towards your doctor. And who's to say you shouldn't express that hostility?'

Charles Lederer continues his silence.

'Some of the other patients may have suffered severe setbacks as a result of your actions, Charles. You may have destroyed months of diligent, painstaking care and treatment. But that's all right, so long as we all understand why.'

10

At this point he notices that Charles Lederer is carrying a scrapbook, and he's holding it as though it is the crown jewels. Hendricks chooses to ignore it.

'Could it be that you hate me, Charles?' he asks. 'Could it be that you'd like to see me dead? And if so, why? Could it be that I remind you of your father? Or possibly of yourself.'

But Charles Lederer is not listening. He has become deeply engrossed in his scrapbook. He's turning the pages carefully and precisely, his eyes devouring the patchwork of cuttings and photographs inside the book.

'What have you got there, Charles?' Hendricks asks at last.

'This? Oh, I like to think of this as my Bible.'

Dr D.K. Hendricks is always quick to spot the use of religious imagery in his patients' conversation. He doesn't approve of it at all. 'Show me,' he says.

Charles Lederer won't hand over the scrapbook, it's far too precious for that, but he holds it up and opens it so that Hendricks can see one of the pages. It contains a newspaper cutting with the headline 'Torrential Rain Leaves Hundreds Dead In Rio' and there's a photograph of a street in Rio de Janeiro that has been transformed by a mud slide into a wrecked, silted-up disaster zone. Hendricks gives it only a cursory glance. He hopes Lederer isn't developing a morbid fascination with death and disaster.

'Show me another page,' he says.

'No,' says Lederer. 'Not yet. You haven't looked closely enough at the first page. You see, right there on the edge of the picture, up to its axles in mud, there's a Volkswagen Beetle.'

Dr D.K. Hendricks nods, but not in comprehension.

'Or here,' says Charles Lederer, and he turns a page. 'This headline "Simmering Hatred In London's East End". It's a story about racial hatred and violence, about neo-Nazis, and there's a photograph of some Indian vigilantes walking down an East End street, and right on the corner of the street there's a Volkswagen.

'Here's a photograph of some looters in the L.A. riots loading up their Beetle with stolen beer and videos. Here's a picture of the Berlin Wall being erected and there's a Volkswagen right in the middle of it. Here's a photograph showing the aftermath of a volcanic explosion in the Philippines . . . '

'Yes, yes, I get the idea,' Hendricks snaps.

'You see the pattern.'

'I'm not sure I've seen anything that constitutes a pattern,' Hendricks replies.

'Yes, you have,' Charles Lederer insists. 'Isn't it obvious? Wherever there's trouble there's always a Volkswagen. The Volkswagen is therefore quite clearly the car of the devil. In which case we clearly have a duty to destroy it.'

'I see,' says Dr D.K. Hendricks.

'Good. So you're on my side.'

'Of course I'm on your side, Charles. I always have been. The question is whether or not you're on mine. There's something I'd like you to have a look at for me.'

He goes to a filing cabinet and pulls out a ring binder. In it are a series of Rorschach ink blots.

'I've looked at your scrapbook Charles, now take a look at mine.'

He flips open the binder and shows Charles Lederer the first ink blot.

'You *do* understand, Doctor!!' he says joyfully.

'Tell me what you see,' Dr D.K. Hendricks says with suspicion.

'I see what's there,' Lederer says. 'I see a Volkswagen, of course. Very early, maybe a prototype, or even one of the first military versions.'

'And this one?'

Lederer smiles knowingly. If the doctor wants to have fun with his little game then he's quite prepared to play along.

'I see a convertible with its top down, with American specification bumpers.'

'And this?'

Charles Lederer's joy is almost unconfined. There among the ink-blot splatters he sees something strange but not entirely unfamiliar. He sees an exploding Volkswagen Beetle, just like the one he's been seeing in his mind's eye for so long. He tells this to Hendricks who slams the ring binder shut. Lederer is grinning at him in a conspiratorial way that is making him both nervous and angry.

'Do you know what I think, Charles?' he asks.

'Yes,' says Charles Lederer. 'You think much as I do. You think the Volkswagen Beetle is a Satanic abomination that ought to be destroyed. Yes?'

'Not exactly, Charles.'

Lederer looks disappointed and confused.

'What I actually think,' Hendricks continues, 'is that you're wasting my time. I think you're trying to wind me up. I think, to put it colloquially, you're taking the piss. I think you're trying to mock me and all my years of work. I think you're trying to destroy my life, my work, my very being.'

Lederer denies it vehemently. He looks shocked and appalled and sorry that the doctor has turned against him so abruptly. But Dr D.K. Hendricks is not going to be fooled by that.

'You know what else I think?' he says.

'No, doctor.'

'I think you're ready to go back into the community.'

Again Barry is sitting on the stoop of his caravan, and again half a dozen kids are gathered round. It is all going well until one of them asks, 'What's the big deal about Volkswagens anyway?'

Barry is lost for words. 'Well,' he says, 'they're you know, they're sort of absolutely ... it.'

The kids look at him expectantly and he tries, he really

13

tries, to be more articulate, to describe the special appeal and the uniqueness of the Volkswagen Beetle. But his heart and head are too full of feelings and contradictions to allow him to get out anything coherent. He struggles on for a while but it's useless. Fortunately, the Ferrous Kid is there and he is able to help.

'Well,' he begins, 'my Dad says the biggest deal about the Volkswagen Beetle is that in terms of numbers sold, it's the most popular and successful car there's ever been or is ever likely to be. They've manufactured and sold about twenty-two million of them.

'And my Dad says the origins of the Beetle are a pretty good story in themselves. Back in the 1930s Adolf Hitler conceived of a people's car as part of his National Socialism and he employed Dr Ferdinand Porsche to create the car for him. He called it the Kraft durch Freudewagen; the Strength Through Joy car. However, by the time the Second World War started the car still wasn't in production, although the factory made military versions throughout the war years. And at the end of the war it was the British army, mostly in the person of Major Ivan Hirst, who finally got production rolling. In 1949 they gave the factory back to the Germans, and the rest is history.

'My Dad says the Beetle's a design classic. It's not pretty in the ordinary sense but it has a basic simplicity to it that's very appealing. Even people who find it downright ugly will admit that its eccentricity is part of its charm. Visually it strikes a strange balance between the reassuring and the sinister.

'But my Dad says because it's so ubiquitous, so much part of the scenery, that means it's also, in a sense, rather blank. That means it's easy for people to stamp their personality on it. In lots of ways the Beetle is like a kit car; bits can be removed and added quite easily. It's relatively simple to customise and modify it and make it your own.

'My Dad says you should beware of anthropomorphism,

but he says the Volkswagen Beetle does have real character, and in a world where consumer products are increasingly dreary and empty, that counts for a lot. Don't you agree Barry?'

'Yes. I couldn't have put it better myself.'

'My Dad probably could,' says the kid, and Barry doesn't argue.

Sometimes people staying at the caravan site ask Barry what kind of Beetle he has under that car cover.

'It's just a Beetle,' he says dismissively, but that only whets their appetite.

'Does it run?' they ask.

'Oh probably. I don't know for sure any more.'

'You mean you don't drive it?'

'That's it.'

'Want to sell it?'

'I'd rather sell my soul.'

Then, sometimes, real Volkswagen enthusiasts will come by and say, 'Hey that looks like an interesting model. Is it the 1600 with fuel injection?'

'No,' says Barry.

'What is it then?'

'It's sort of a custom model,' he says weakly.

But that only gets them more excited. 'Lemme see it,' they demand.

'No, it's kind of an unfinished project, I'm not ready to show it . . . '

'Go on, just a quick look.'

Once again Barry says no and the Beetle enthusiast pleads for just a little peek, and maybe he grabs a corner of the car cover and attempts to turn it back to reveal the car beneath. At which point Barry gets a wild, intense, murderous look on his face, and, if the enthusiast has any sense, he drops the cover pretty damn quick.

Sometimes people invite Barry to join a Volkswagen

owners' club. Membership, they assure him, will bring with it all sorts of benefits; companionship, travel, sports and outdoor activities, as well as trade discounts and offers of technical assistance. There are clubs of many different persuasions. Some have an historical bent, some go camping, some surfing. Some clubs are for purists, and others are for those who like to attack their Beetles with a power saw, hack off unnecessary items like roofs and wings, and then paint them in hideous colours.

Barry always says he is much happier sitting on the steps of his caravan, with his car kept safely under wraps. But as he sits there considering his conversation with the kid who has the ecologically unsound father, he comes up with what he thinks is a great idea.

He will form a club called the Green Beetles. They will be a group of supremely eco-friendly Volkswagen enthusiasts. They will love and cherish their motorcars. They may clean and polish them once in a while, even sit in them from time to time with their friends and families. The important thing is; *they will never drive them*. They will leave their cars parked next to their house or caravan, never start the engines, never pollute mother earth with their deadly fumes.

And the best part of all from Barry's point of view is the fact that this club, by definition, will never have any meetings, get-togethers or swapmeets. It will have no badges, no subscriptions, no officials, no committees, no membership cards or newsletters. Anybody who owns a Beetle but doesn't drive it can automatically consider himself a member. It appeals enormously to the Zen sage within Barry, even if not to the dormant Zen Road Warrior.

Carlton Bax, a scion of the Bax property and banking dynasty, and its sole heir, has successfully turned himself into one of England's, if not the world's, foremost Volkswagen collectors.

He is a man of middle years but he still likes to think of himself as something of a playboy. Certainly devoting his life to the Volkswagen seems pleasingly boyish and irresponsible, but that doesn't mean it isn't serious.

He wakes early in the bedroom of his London house, a place he always refers to as his 'gentleman's residence'. His girlfriend, Marilyn, daughter of one Charles Lederer, love object of one Barry Osgathorpe, sleeps in the bed beside him. The room is dark. He doesn't know what time it is. He reaches out and turns on the bedside lamp. The lamp is in the shape of a Volkswagen Beetle, is made of blue porcelain, and is surprisingly accurate in its detailing. Light spills out through the windows and windscreen and through holes where the headlights should be. Then he consults the bedside clock, also Beetle-shaped, and sees that it's ten o'clock. He decides to get up, although on many other mornings he might decide to stay where he is. He doesn't bother to wake Marilyn.

He goes into the bathroom, sits on the cold toilet seat, thumbs through a copy of the magazine Volkswagen Universe while he's waiting, a magazine that has recently featured an article about the Bax collection. When he's finished he pulls a flurry of toilet paper from its holder. This holder too is shaped like a Beetle, the rear half anyway; the axle between the rear wheels serving as a core to hold the toilet roll. That over with, he steps into the shower, turns on the water. He draws the shower curtain. It is mostly transparent but it's decorated with a pattern of primary-coloured Beetles that career down it as though it is a busy motorway without lane markings. He starts to soap himself with a brand new block of soap that is, again, Beetle-shaped. He gets through a lot of these, since a single shower will wear away the distinctive contours and styling lines, and that won't do.

After his shower, Carlton Bax goes to his dressing room. As he walks along the connecting corridor he is pleasantly aware of the array of toy and model Beetles that line the walls, secure in their locked and illuminated display cabinets. He barely looks at them but their mere presence gives him a kick. All the great manufacturers are represented here, as well as all the minor and obscure ones. All the examples are in perfect condition, mint and boxed where appropriate, the die-cast and the tinplate, the rarities and the promotionals and the one-offs, the mass produced and the craftsman made. There are Beetles made of plastic and wood and glass and rubber, some fought for at auction, others sought out in obscure and surprising corners of the world, handmade in Nigeria or Egypt or Mexico. The collection spreads throughout the house. Many items are valuable beyond belief. Together they are priceless.

He begins to dress. First he puts on jockey shorts with Beetle motifs. Then he dons a pair of trousers, ordinary enough in themselves, but at least the belt has a brass buckle in the shape of a Beetle. Now he has to choose a T-shirt from several drawerfuls of possibilities, each of them displaying some different manifestation of Volkswagen culture. Some show faithful illustrations of Beetles in all styles and from all historical periods. Some show wild, customised versions. One shows an exploded flat-four engine. Some advertise Volkswagen dealers or specialists; Volksbitz, Bugmania, Wolfsburg World, Air-cooled Heaven, Bugs to Go, Fat Volkz Inc. Others commemorate various Volkswagen events and meetings, various Bug-ins and Bug-jams and Bug-O-Ramas, national charity cruises, show-and-shines and drag week-ends. He decides on a yellow T-shirt with an appliquéd cartoon of a dragster Beetle, massive tyres at each corner, flames exploding from the exhaust pipes, and at the wheel a slavering, red-eyed monster from outer space dressed in full Nazi regalia. There are certain events to which you couldn't wear a T-shirt like that but today Carlton is not going to any such event.

Once dressed, he goes downstairs past the library with its unparalleled collection of Volkswagen books, histories, magazines and technical manuals. And he can't resist sticking his head into the billiards room for the sheer pleasure of seeing the part of the collection that lives there.

Around the walls of the panelled room, Volkswagen memorabilia are displayed like hunting trophies. Here are serried rows of hubcaps and steering wheels laid out to demonstrate changes in design and function. Likewise with speedometers and foot pedals, crankshafts and tail light assemblies, wing mirrors and distributor caps. Above the mantelpiece three plaster Volkswagens fly in a diagonal line, like a trio of ducks. Elsewhere are Beetle tea towels, Beetles that are really decanters containing Jim Beam, special recordings and video tapes of the Beetle in all its forms.

There is a desk in the corner with Beetle stationery, a Beetle ruler, a Beetle sellotape dispenser, a Beetle stapler, a Beetle pencil sharpener and a Beetle rubber. There is a small model of a Beetle set in a cube of clear plastic to act as a paperweight. There are badges of a hundred or more Volkswagen owners clubs from all round the world. Finally there are posters, postcards, stickers, calendars, sales brochures, caps, shoulder bags; the works.

Now it is time for breakfast. He prepares himself a boiled egg. When it's had its three and a half minutes he puts it into a shiny black Beetle egg cup, then adds salt and pepper from Beetle-shaped shakers. He pours coffee from a Beetle-shaped coffee pot, and drinks it out of a mug with a design proclaiming 'Fifty Years of the Beetle'. He eats a biscuit which he takes from his Beetle-shaped cookie jar, and when he's finished he lights a cigarette with his Beetle cigarette lighter, subsequently flicking his ash into a Beetle ashtray.

The phone rings. That too is in the shape of a Beetle. 'Hello?' he shouts into the receiver. He has to shout since the microphone is rather insensitive. 'Hello who is this?' he demands.

The voice on the other end sounds angry, confused, threatening, and yet completely inarticulate.

'If you have something to say, say it,' Carlton Bax shouts, and in the absence of a coherent reply he slams the phone down.

He finishes his cigarette. He feels in his pocket to confirm that his car keys are there, dangling from an enamel Beetle-shaped key fob. Ready now, he leaves his house, trots down the steps from the front door, and goes out to the garage. Actually there are two garages. One is a long, low building at the rear of the house converted from a former stable block. It contains ten or so Beetles, and as such is hardly in itself the home of a major collection, but Carlton has made sure that these few cars are very, very special.

To begin with there is a 1937 Series 30 prototype, conceived so early in the Beetle's development that it doesn't even have a rear window. There's a Rometsch-built taxi, one of the few Beetles ever to be made with four doors. Here is a Hebmuller convertible used by the Munich fire department in the 1950s. There's a military Kubelwagen, as used by Hitler's troops in the Second World War. Here are a couple of immaculate and completely original split-windows. There's a Beetle-based 'stretch-limo', made by welding a couple of extra 'middles' into an ordinary saloon. There's one of the many stunt cars used in the Herbie films; this is one that comes apart in the middle yet still continues to run. Here's a cream and grey, lowered, louvred, dressed-up Cal look Beetle, so slick, so sexy, so shiny, so lacquered as to appear pornographic. Here is a state of the art, electric-blue Baja Beetle with its exposed engine and its stinger exhaust and its big knobbly tyres just waiting to eat up the desert.

But this is just the tip of the iceberg. Carlton Bax lets it be known that he has other garages in secret locations around the country, in Europe and even in America, as well as whole warehouses full of desirable Volkswagen goodies. Nor does he deny the existence of a famous, or infamous, 'locked room' somewhere in his house, a room that is reputed to contain memorabilia of such rarity and value as to be positively dangerous. It contains unnamed, possibly unspeakable, possibly magical, Volkswagen items that a man might lose his reason over, that a man might certainly kill or be killed for. But even while he admits the room's existence he will not reveal its location, and he insists that its contents are strictly for his eyes only.

But today Carlton Bax doesn't go to the garage containing his rare Volkswagens. He goes instead to a garage at the front of the house. There is a trompe l'oeil painting of an oval window Beetle on the garage door. He now unlocks and opens it to reveal . . . a pristine metallic grey Range Rover.

'Volkswagens are all very well to collect,' Carlton Bax thinks to himself, 'but I wouldn't really want to *drive* one.'

A little way out of Southend, at the end of a neat, well-tended suburban street, there is a surprisingly, even suspiciously, clean and flawless Volkswagen emporium. The building is an exhilarating piece of Odeon-style seaside deco, painted a gleaming, snow-blinding white, with curving windows, asymmetrical balconies and sundecks, and curling staircases enclosed in glass-walled towers.

The spotless, marble-tiled showroom houses a row of three superb Volkswagen Beetles. They have been restored, resprayed, and generally tarted up, and the for sale signs on their windscreens reveal prices that defy belief. The workshops out the back, away from the street, are every bit as clean and well-ordered as the showroom. Tools and engine components, accessories and body panels are stacked and stored with military precision; very German. This is not some fly-by-night, rough and ready, underneath the arches kind of operation; and even the customers have a clean, sharp and, of course, deeply fashionable, look to them.

In fact the only thing that looks untidy and out of place in this setting is a podgy, shambling, greasy-haired man, who

21

for all that he doesn't appear to belong, still roams around looking as though he owns the place. And he does. His name is Fat Les. This is his kingdom, and the sign on the outside of the premises says, 'Fat Volkz Inc.' There are no signs saying that he specialises in flat-four engine rebuilds, in complete renovations, in radical paintwork, Resto-Cal customs, etc etc. There is no need for any such sign. If you need Fat Les's services you'll already know all about him.

The years have been kind to Les. Once he ran his Volkswagen business from a garage in a set of railway arches. A few good business decisions, a boom in the Beetle market, the help of a couple of backers, and a monstrous bank loan, have ensured a few changes, and mostly for the better. He doesn't miss the squalor, and he certainly doesn't miss the poverty. He likes his new clean and efficient lifestyle. He likes the business. He likes the hip, cool image. He likes the small team of smart young guys who work for him. It's just that sometimes he can't stand the sight of Volkswagen Beetles.

A more or less typical customer arrives asking to speak to Fat Les. He is young, has a wacky haircut, Bermuda shorts, big trainers and a baseball cap worn back to front. Les steps out of the office. The customer, who introduces himself as Spider, wants to shake Les by the hand and say what an honour it is to meet him. Fat Les goes through the motions of being an incredibly minor celebrity then asks Spider what he can do for him.

'Well,' says Spider, 'I've got a Beetle out there.'

Les looks out through the plate glass of the showroom window and sure enough there's a Beetle parked outside. It looks old and careworn, a bit rusty here and there, sitting a touch softly on its suspension. At the most, it would make a cheap runabout.

'I was thinking of having it done up a bit,' says Spider. 'I was thinking of having it Resto-Cal. I was thinking about

Empis and pearl lacquer, and flared wings, and one piece electric windows and a sun roof.'

'Yeah,' says Les. 'I can do that for you.'

'And then,' Spider continues, 'I was thinking about hotting up the engine, say a BBT 1914, with an Eagle cam, 041 heads, twin 40 Dellortos.'

'Sure,' says Les. 'I can do that.'

'And my girlfriend says it's got to have a nice interior, you know, maybe grey and blue leather, and midnight blue carpets, and a big stereo – detachable. Oh, and shaved door handles and central locking and a damn good alarm system.'

'No sweat,' says Les. 'When do you want me to start?'

'Well, I was hoping you'd give me a quote first.'

Les looks at him with pity and contempt and says nothing.

'I guess this is going to cost me, right?' says Spider.

Les nods.

'I guess it's going to cost me an arm and a leg, right?'

Les considers for a while before saying, 'I think I might have to take your soul in part exchange.'

'Oh well,' says Spider, 'in that case I'll have to think about it.'

Later that same day Les confronts one of his previous customers, and he is not a satisfied customer. He arrives in a pretty spiffy looking Beetle. It has been lowered, given a two-tone paint job in metallic turquoise and peppermint green, given suicide doors, an upgraded engine and heavy duty suspension. It stops abruptly outside the showroom, with a metallic clank. Hip hop music pumps out of the stereo and the driver gets out, a gangly young black man with Lycra cycling shorts and a pair of sunglasses that cost as much as some secondhand cars. His name is Zak. Les remembers a time when a young black guy wouldn't have been seen dead in a Volkswagen Beetle; far, far too uncool. Times change.

Zak strides up to Fat Les and says, 'Les, old pal, I'm not happy.'

Les, who is not a man for the old pals act, replies, 'What is it? Piles?'

Zak would like to laugh, break the ice, establish a rapport with Les, but he can't, and then he sees that Les isn't laughing either.

'It's the car,' he says.

'Get away,' replies Les. 'What seems to be the problem?'

Les is always careful to use words like 'seem'.

'Well, the paintwork for a start,' says Zak.

'Yeah, it's a bit of a bloody eye-sore isn't it, but it's what you asked for.'

'I don't mean the colour. I mean it's starting to bubble.'

'Well, of course it's starting to bubble.'

'But you only did the respray three months ago.'

'Well, it was only cheap respray,' says Les.

'No it wasn't,' says Zak.

'Take it from me, it was a cheap respray. And on a twenty-year-old car. Put a cheap respray on a twenty-year-old car and the chances are it's going to bubble. In fact, even if you'd stripped it back to the bare metal and given it a full rustproofing you'd probably still be standing here saying the same thing, and that would have cost you twice as much money. So basically, I've saved you a wad of cash, right?'

Zak is not quite dumb enough to accept this. He wonders if it would do him any good to get angry, but he suspects not. He has other complaints to air. The quality of the respray is the least of his problems.

'And the performance,' he says. 'I keep getting burned off at the lights by everything; Ladas, 2CVs, Ford Transits, everything.'

'Well,' says Fat Les, 'that's probably because you're driving a Beetle.'

'But I thought that with all the engine modifications I'd be the hottest thing on the road.'

'Did I tell you that?' Les enquires.

'Well no, not in so many words.'

'Not in any words,' Les adds.

'And you know,' the hapless Zak continues, 'it won't handle or go round corners very well, and it doesn't stop the way I'd like it to, and it has a few flat spots and it stalls a lot when it's cold.'

Fat Les looks at him with a certain sympathy, as though he understands and knows what the trouble is.

'Yep,' he says, 'that sounds like a Volkswagen Beetle.'

Zak looks very unhappy indeed.

He says, 'Look, I could get really bloody upset about this, because I think you could be ripping me off, man. I think you might take me for a mug. Like you think I'm ignorant and stupid and don't know anything about cars. And I think you might be doing that because I'm black.'

Fat Les looks at him mournfully.

'No,' he says. 'I treat all my customers the same way.'

After he's gone half a mile or so Carlton Bax hears a sudden muffled bang. It's difficult to tell how far away it is or even which direction it's coming from. But it isn't the sort of bang you become very alarmed about or stop your car for. It certainly doesn't occur to Carlton Bax that it comes from the direction of his own home, and even if it had, he certainly wouldn't have reason to suspect that it had actually come from his own garage. It would never in a million years occur to him that what he had heard was the sound of one of his own precious Volkswagens exploding, which is precisely what it is.

He drives on oblivious. The traffic isn't heavy. He has the radio tuned to a phone-in on female eating disorders. He's feeling buoyant and optimistic. When he hears another, infinitely smaller noise coming from behind his seat in the Range Rover, a kind of metallic rustling, he assumes it can be nothing more serious than an empty drinks can rolling around on the floor. He is completely wrong.

He arrives at a red traffic light and stops. He begins to turn around to see precisely what caused the noise and the moment he does so he becomes aware of a human presence and feels something metallic pressed into his neck. He isn't exactly familiar with the sensation of a gun barrel against his flesh but that is undoubtedly what it feels like. He freezes. He looks in the rear view mirror but can see nothing. Then a voice belonging to someone who was obviously hiding behind the seat, a voice that is so plain and neutral as subsequently to be unidentifiable, says, 'Good morning Mr Bax. Just do what I tell you and you won't get hurt.' Carlton Bax has no desire to get hurt. The lights change and he drives off following directions to some fearful and unknown destination.

And that, essentially, is the beginning of everything. A famous Volkswagen collector disappears, and one of the Beetles in his collection is blown up. That would be strange enough in itself, but there are other forms of strangeness. The explosion in Carlton Bax's garage is only the first of a great many.

In Kilburn, in London, an old man with only half a set of teeth and with soup stains on his navy blue jacket is washing his white, absolutely standard 1972 Beetle. He has owned it for sixteen years and it has only covered 30,000 miles. These days he barely uses it at all, never goes anywhere, but he still enjoys washing it. He's finished now, and the car looks good. He puts his cloths and sponge in his bucket and turns to go back into the house. Suddenly the car explodes behind him, heat scorching his back like a flame-thrower.

In Berwick Upon Tweed a raven-haired housewife and mother of two is about to take her moss green 1976 Beetle to a while-you-wait MOT centre. In a way she hopes the car will fail, because then she can get rid of it and her husband will let her buy a new Fiat Panda. She loads the kids into the back of the car, turns the key in the ignition; and nothing at all happens. The kids now say they need to pee. She gets them out of the car, takes them into the house, and picks up the phone to tell her husband that the car's let her down *again*; at which point the car explodes in a ball of orange and ivory fire.

In Lytham St. Anne's an estate agent is pleasuring a female radiologist on the back seat of her cherry red Beetle convertible. They are hot for each other, but they begin to find the space too confined. They decamp to the beach and move behind a dune. At the very moment she is about to come a deafening bang tells her that her beloved Beetle has been reduced to twisted scrap metal.

In Bath a fifty year old jazz trumpeter is emerging from a club where he was playing. It hasn't been a great night. The audience was sparse and the other musicians were unsympathetic. He just wants to get home. His battered Jeans Beetle is parked in a dark side street near to some derelict warehouses, not the kind of place you'd choose to park your car, but, you know, who's going to steal a twenty-year-old Volkswagen? He turns the corner into the side street and sees a smouldering, burned out shell where his Beetle used to be.

Not far from Wellingborough, a recent engineering graduate is trying out a new set of telephoto lenses on his camera. He parks his 1955 six volt, oval window Beetle in a rural spot and takes a series of photographs of it, getting further away each time and using ever more powerful lenses. He now has on the five hundred millimeter, is employing a tripod, and is some distance away from his car. Nevertheless, as he peers through the camera's viewfinder he feels distinctly too close for comfort when the car explodes in flames. But he is so far away that all he can do is watch it burn.

In Yeovil a thirty year old legal secretary has been trying for weeks to sell her pink and green, J registered Beetle with polkadot interior. Lots of people have been to see it but they were all time wasters and tyre kickers. Nobody has made a serious offer. She is depressed. She needs the money as part of the deposit on the flat she's buying with her boyfriend. She goes to bed wishing she could just be rid of the damned thing, and when she wakes up the next morning the car is no more than a blackened wreck sitting in the road.

Volkswagen Beetles start exploding all over the country. In the home counties and in the Midlands and the West Country, on the South Coast and in the North-West, all across the Pennines and the Mendips and the Cotswolds, Beetles start going up in flames. It seems to make no difference what style or year or condition they are. Whether they're old bangers or customised specials or models of historical importance, they're all just as likely to go up in a big bang. A lonely street corner, a suburban driveway, a supermarket car park; suddenly there's an unattended Volkswagen Beetle and a short time later Volkswagen components are careering through the air, coiled in flame and black smoke. Inevitably this causes stress to a few proud owners and to a few insurance agents, but in the general criminal morass of car theft, joyriding and vandalism it will be some time before anyone realises a pattern is being established here.

Carlton Bax has gone missing. And in his absence, the police are severely hampered in their attempts to investigate the explosion in his garage. One of his Volkswagens has indeed been destroyed, the military Kubelwagen, and it appears to have been a clever and professional job. Just enough explosive was used to destroy the vehicle completely, but the car next to it is more or less intact. However, with the car reduced to scrap metal, it becomes apparent that it was parked on top of a metal trap door. The explosion, it also appears, might have been designed to blow open that trap door as much as to destroy the vehicle.

Blown open it most certainly is, and through the gaping, jagged hole a subterranean chamber is visible. Is this Carlton Bax's famous locked room? Police shine torches into the void to reveal a completely empty space. The chamber has been thoroughly cleaned out, and Carlton Bax is the only one who could tell anybody if that is indeed the locked room of legend, and what, if anything, it contained.

*   *   *

As the shrewd reader will either know or have worked out by now, this is the second novel I have written about Volkswagens and Barry Osgathorpe. The first, called *Street Sleeper*, was originally dedicated to five different people. That was because it was my first book and I had no idea whether I'd ever write another one, much less get it published, so I thought it was as well to dedicate it to quite a few people while I had the chance.

One of those dedications read, 'For Andy who gets run down'. Andy was a friend of mine, an actor and briefly a stand-up comedian. He had been walking along a street in Alnwick, Northumberland, when a passing Ford Capri with bald tyres and a reckless driver had 'mounted the pavement', knocked him down and broken his leg. It was a serious accident. He spent a lot of time laid up, obviously couldn't work as an actor, and eventually got some rather measly compensation from the driver's insurance company.

The leg healed, my book was published and as a sort of celebration, Andy and I, my wife and his girlfriend (who happened to be the daughter of a comparatively well-known television sitcom actor) went out for dinner together. I was feeling fairly pleased with myself for having my first book published and I was no doubt a little smug about it too. Andy at that time was acting in a deeply worthy play about homosexual child abuse, performing to non-existent audiences at a venue in Kennington. I had done my time as a writer of fringe plays and I had rapidly come to the con-

29

clusion that however worthy the subject matter, putting on plays that nobody came to see wasn't something actually worth doing. This was not an opinion I felt any reluctance about expressing.

At a critical point in the evening my wife and I mentioned that we'd recently seen a porn movie in which the hero had fellated himself; an old trick perhaps but one that nevertheless still causes some surprise. Andy's girlfriend offered the opinion that pornography was 'a bad thing', an opinion that on balance I tend to share, but I asked her why. And she said it was a bad thing because it exploited the actors and actresses who appeared in it. I then, in a spirit of intellectual enquiry, asked her to explain the difference between the way actors and actresses were exploited in pornography compared with the way they were exploited in fringe theatre or, for example, in television sitcoms.

Well, this did not go down too well with Andy. He threw a fit. He became violently angry and I was accused of many things, but essentially of being complacent and politically incorrect. We might easily have come to blows, but we didn't, and a part of me stayed peculiarly calm throughout. I managed to walk rather than flounce out of the restaurant. My wife remained behind. I remember that as I left, Andy told me not to be overdramatic, that it would all blow over in a day or two. In many ways I wish it had, but I have never spoken to him since that day.

Several years passed. Then one day I was watching television and a commercial came on that I'd never seen before. A man's car has run out of petrol in the middle of nowhere. He's seen trudging along a deserted road, mile after mile, carrying an empty petrol can, looking for a petrol station. Then suddenly he sees a figure walking along the road, coming towards him from the opposite direction. It's another man, an archetypal Frenchman wearing a beret and also carrying an empty petrol can. He too has obviously been trudging along the road mile after mile. There is obviously no petrol station for miles in either direction.

The Frenchman in the beret was Andy. He was right for the part, having one of those lumpy, humorous, hangdog faces. This was enough of a surprise in itself, but the commercial had a punchline to deliver. As the two men exchanged mournful glances, a car flashed past them and a caption appeared on the screen. 'If only everything in life was as reliable as a Volkswagen.'

When the paperback edition of *Street Sleeper* was published I had the dedication 'For Andy who gets run down' removed.

II

The Unbearable Lightness of Volkswagens

Barry Osgathorpe is having a dream of sexual inadequacy. In this dream he is falling for a devastating seductress who is an amalgam of Helen Mirren and his old maths teacher, a surprisingly buxom old party, called Miss Cornthwaite. The scene is taking place in a large and completely deserted car showroom, and the Mirren/Cornthwaite character is decked out in a length of purple chiffon which seems copious enough but isn't quite sufficient to hide her nakedness.

The seduction is going rather well. Barry has stripped his own clothes off and is down to his underpants. He's about to take those off too but no, the dream woman says she wants the pleasure of removing them herself. Her fingers scamper up and down his torso. She puts her hand into the waistband of the pants and gently lowers them for him. Down they go, down beyond his knees, down to his ankles, and she looks at his genitals and starts to laugh. It's quite kindly at first, as if she's having fun, but soon it becomes mocking, then vicious, and before long it turns into a kind of demonic, hysterical snarl. And now she doesn't look at *all* like Helen Mirren, not even like Miss Cornthwaite, more like a snaggle-toothed, vampiric version of Queen Victoria; and he still doesn't understand what she's finding so damned funny.

So he looks down at his body and sees, with surprisingly little alarm at first, this being that sort of dream, that his penis has been transformed into a small, pink Volkswagen, about the size of a Dinky toy; and not even an interesting, classic kind of Beetle, but some humdrum, ordinary 1970s model with a 1200 engine. And he looks more carefully and sees it's a little rusty and uncared for, and it has no tyres, and oh my God, it appears to be leaking gallons of thick, dirty black oil.

He tells himself to wake up. It's a struggle. His sleeping mind is strangely reluctant to detach itself from these comic horrors, but at last he is awake. He finds himself alone, it being one of the nights when Debby is not staying with him. It's the early hours of the morning but he decides to get up. He steps out of the caravan. The air is cool and the grass is wet beneath his bare feet. He has had an idea. He walks over to the side of the caravan, to the place where his Beetle resides. He slowly unfastens the ropes and buckles that keep the car cover in place. Then he takes a corner of the cover and peels it back, slowly, deliberately, with a certain reverence, until the vehicle beneath is fully revealed.

These days Barry tends to distrust people who give their cars names, but once he was happy enough to call this vehicle Enlightenment. It sits wide and low on its thick wheels and tyres. Every part of it is black. There is no chrome, no badging, no metal handles or window frames. Even the headlamps have black covers. Even the windscreen and windows are made of smoked glass. It looks mean and vicious, positively evil, and that had once been precisely the intention.

Barry tries the driver's door. It has not been open for a while so it sticks at first, but soon he has access to the interior and he eases into the driver's seat. He puts his hands on the wheel, his feet on the pedals, and he remains there without moving for the next six hours.

Barry sits and thinks about the person he was, a different person for sure, a character called Ishmael. Barry has heard that the American Indians say ghosts appear when someone has not been buried right. And that, he suspects, may be the case with Ishmael. He is a spectre, an undead reminder. The stories Barry tells about him to the children gathered around the steps of the caravan, are tales of adventure and estrangement, but they are also ghost stories.

That ghosts are pitiable, uneasy spirits, he would not deny, but he knows they can also be monsters. Ishmael's search for enlightenment was no mere intellectual enquiry. It was a quest steeped in violence and anger and the smell of leaded petrol. It was not merely the bad guys who got hurt. Some innocent bystanders also suffered, became his victims. But perhaps the real victim was himself.

Halfway through the morning Sam Probert, the owner of the caravan site, comes along, sees Barry, and assumes he has just got into the car and is about to drive off.

'Going somewhere nice?' he asks Barry cheerfully.

'No,' says Barry, 'I'm already there.' But he knows he's lying.

A man answers the phone when Marilyn calls her mother. She does not recognise the voice, though she certainly recognises the type: young, muscular, surly, impecunious.

'I want to speak to my mother,' Marilyn says sternly.

'Oh, right you are, love. Hang on.'

There is a good deal of rustling and mumbling, and the noise of things, very possibly empty gin bottles, being knocked over, before Marilyn's mother makes it to the phone.

'Yes, cupcake?' she enquires.

'Something strange is going on,' says Marilyn.

'How exciting.'

'No mother. Carlton's disappeared.'

'Carlton?'

'My boyfriend. You remember?'

'Oh yes, of course I remember, a very generous young man. He was always giving me presents. It's a shame he's gone because you were rather fond of him, weren't you? You can't trust them, can you?'

'It's not like that, Mother. He hasn't just gone off. He's genuinely disappeared. He left home a week ago and he hasn't been seen since.'

'Oh dear,' says her mother.

'And this is the really strange part, there was an explosion in his garage and one of his cars was destroyed.'

'An explosion? Oh dear.'

'Yes, I know it sounds weird. And the police have been round and they're completely useless. They seem to think the explosion was caused by an electrical fault or some such nonsense and that Carlton's run off with a floozy.'

'Well, that *is* a possibility, isn't it?' says her mother.

'Not if you knew Carlton.'

'I see. What kind of car was it that got blown up?'

'Oh Mother, I've told you all this. I wish you'd listen sometimes. You know he collects Volkswagens.'

'Oh dear,' says Marilyn's mother.

'Why do you keep saying, "Oh dear"?'

There is a poignant hesitation before Mrs Lederer asks, 'When did you last see your father?'

'More recently than you, I'm sure. But what does that have to do with anything?'

'When?' her mother insists.

'I drove down to the hospital about a month ago. Why?'

'And how was he?'

Marilyn tries to think of a gentle, sympathetic way of putting this, but settles for, 'He was barking mad, as usual.'

'Yes, I thought so when I last saw him too. So you'll be surprised to hear that he's been returned to the community.'

'Which community?' Marilyn asks, a hint of panic in her voice.

'You know, *the* community, our community, the world at large.'

'Oh dear,' says Marilyn. 'Oh dear me.'

That night Marilyn goes along to the television studio as

35

usual and tries to perform her regular duties as a late night weather presenter. This is not exactly the glittering kind of media stardom that she once had in mind for herself, since her weather bulletins are broadcast well after midnight on a satellite channel, but at least it's something. She has a small but significant reputation for being vivacious, irreverent, slightly zany. She bounces onto the screen, all primary colours and messed up hair, stands in front of a computer generated image of England and speaks in the rootless, studied, inauthentic, South London accent she reserves for her television appearances.

'Well, it's going to be a wet one!' she blurts cheerily. 'Over here in South-East England there'll be scattered showers, heavy in places. Moving north there'll be intermittent drizzle in all parts. In Wales there'll be a wet start and it'll be wetter later. In the North-West it'll be bucketing down, and in Scotland it'll be a real cats and dogs number. Everywhere there'll be cloudbursts, downpours and deluges. Let's face it, whatever you're doing tomorrow, you're going to get peed on good and proper. Oops did I really say that?'

So far she has been rushing through her words but now she stops, puts on a serious expression and eyeballs the camera.

'Look,' she says, 'I've got to end this programme on a personal note, right? Some of you probably know that my Dad's been locked up in a loony bin these past few years. I mean, you ought to, it's been in all the bloody tabloids. Anyway, he's out now, and me and my Mum don't know where he is. And we're a bit choked, right?

'So I just want to say, if you're out there Dad, watching this, there's one or two things I want you to know. Basically, I still love ya Dad. I know we've had our ups and downs, but it'd be really ace to see you again Dad. Don't become a stranger. Come home Dad. And if you can't come home, at least stay out of the rain.'

In the end it is rather a good piece of television. She uses the camera well and towards the end her voice catches in her throat very effectively. Afterwards the floor manager says, to nobody in particular, 'If her Dad's really out there watching weather forecasts like this, at half past two in the morning, he must be even more bonkers than when he was banged up.'

It is raining. To Charles Lederer who is standing with his thumb out at a traffic roundabout somewhere in the West Midlands it feels as though it has been raining forever. His Panama hat has turned to pulp on his head. His blazer and flannels have been made limp and ragged by the rain. His carpet slippers have absorbed so much water they feel like heavy sponges weighing down his legs.

The world looks grey and industrial. He has been in motion from the moment he left the Milton Maynard Mercy Seat. He has a wife out there somewhere, and a daughter too, but he thinks neither would welcome him. He has been hitchhiking, briefly entering other people's strange, private, mobile worlds. He has been seeing England through glass, through tinted windscreens and streaked side windows. It is not quite the England he used to know. Perhaps something critical has changed during his incarceration. The landscape he sees now looks inhuman, a savage place of ring roads and by-passes and orbital routes, of traffic snarl-ups and crawler lanes solid with eighteen wheeler trucks. Where once he had seen (or had he just imagined?) rolling hills and village greens, there were now parks; industrial parks, retail parks, car parks, theme parks. The ground itself seems to be in some constant state of tumult and mutation. Processes of demolition and rebuilding, of growth and decay, of creation and dereliction, all seem to be occurring at the same time, all cancelling each other out. He could not tell you where he has been and certainly he cannot say where he's going, a fact that is the cause of some irritation to the people who offer him lifts. He sees the best and worst of people while hitchhiking. Some drivers see an old man in need and are overwhelmingly generous. Others see an old tramp whom they fear will mess up their upholstery. Some drivers buy him coffee and sandwiches, slip a couple of pounds into his hand as they drop him off. Others just shout abuse out of the window as they drive past him; mostly young men with honking voices who call him a wanker because he hasn't got his own car. Or they slow down as though to give him a lift then, as he hurries hopefully towards the car, drive off at speed. Or they swerve their cars towards him as though trying to run him down. It is a depressing state of affairs.

The rain continues to soak into him. It is starting to get dark, and the traffic is looking ominously thin. There is nothing in sight, no houses, no barns, no petrol stations where he might shelter. A vast truck hauling a container load of petrol, so lumbering yet so fast moving, negotiates the roundabout and fetches up a tidal wave that breaks across Charles Lederer's chest. Inexplicably, he smiles a little. Perhaps he has the very slightest consolation in knowing he cannot possibly get any wetter.

It occurs to him that he might have to spend the night here. It is rural enough but there's no hope of comfort or shelter, nowhere you could imagine sleeping. Not that he's been getting or needing much sleep lately. He has learned that people don't like you to accept a lift from them and then immediately nod off. The staff of service station restaurants certainly don't like you falling asleep at their tables. What little sleep he's had has arrived unbidden, and he has dozed off at the roadside or in a hedge. But sleep has always been fitful, disturbed by the hard ground and the roar of passing traffic.

He thinks he might be about to nod off again now when a pair of low, blurred headlights appear through the rain. Charles Lederer sticks out his thumb, more out of habit than in hope, and the car miraculously stops. It is a Volkswagen Beetle, old and careworn, a bit rusty here and there, belonging to Spider, the boy whose soul Fat Les threatened to take in part exchange. He has not followed through with the plan to have his car completely tarted up by Les. Instead he got him to fit a cheap set of moon disc hubcaps. Very smart they look too, and the best part of it is he can still go around saying his Beetle was worked on by Fat Les. He throws open the passenger door for Charles Lederer.

'Get in, mate,' he shouts. 'Quick.'

Charles Lederer hesitates. He moves towards the car's open door then stops.

'No, I'd probably better not,' he mutters to himself.

'What?' shouts Spider.

'You're probably not going my way,' Charles Lederer says speaking louder and more clearly.

'In this rain, what does it matter?'

Charles Lederer hovers on the threshold, obviously torn, wanting to get in, and yet it's as though he's suffering from some terrible anxiety, some phobia.

'What the hell's the problem?' Spider shouts.

'Well, this is a Volkswagen, right?'

'Right.'

'I've had some bad experiences with Volkswagens.'

'So have I!' says Spider. 'Now get in before you catch your death.'

Charles Lederer grits his teeth and forces himself to get in the car. Spider says 'Well done' and the car pulls away into the cold grey curtains of rain.

Charles Lederer has been troubled by the problem of what to say to the drivers who give him lifts. A lot of them just want to talk *at* you and that's fine by him. Others want to discuss issues, to talk about money or work or cars or politics, all things that once exercised Charles Lederer quite passionately, but today they arouse nothing in him at all. Consequently he finds he is not much of a conversationalist in these matters. But the most objectionable drivers are the ones who insist on questioning him about his life and times. He doesn't want to tell them all his secrets and yet he doesn't want to lie. So he just tells them he's been in a mental home for a few years, and that generally shuts them up very efficiently.

He has none of these problems with Spider. The stereo system in the Volkswagen is too loud to permit conversation, but he doesn't complain. He is quite happy with his lot. The interior of the car is dry, and warm enough for steam to start to rise from his wet clothes. They drive for an hour or so before Spider abruptly turns off the music and says, 'Fancy a burger, old timer?' Charles Lederer thinks it's best to say yes.

They drive until they come to a highly accurate though utterly ersatz replica of a nineteen fifties American diner. There is a sweep of cheap stucco, a lot of glass, some multi-coloured neon. It is profoundly not Charles Lederer's kind of place but he runs alongside Spider as they dash across the rain strewn forecourt of movie America, into the diner.

They find a booth. There is a juke box console on the table, and salt and pepper shakers in the shape of the Empire State and Chrysler buildings. Charles Lederer finds the menu a mysterious and lurid document, so when he hears his companion ordering a chilli dog he orders one too. It's easiest that way. They don't exchange more than a few words all the time they sit there, but it is not an uneasy silence. They recognise they have nothing in common and are grateful for it.

After the food has arrived and been eaten Spider seems in no hurry to leave. That's fine with Charles Lederer too. They both stare out of the windows at the streaked, black view, and as they innocently watch the rain, the scene suddenly, abruptly dislocates, explodes into yellow and white, like a bleached negative or a smashed fried egg. Spider's Volks-wagen explodes, is savagely ripped apart, flayed into shrapnel. The remains of the car sit twisted and angular, writhing in a ball of scorching orange flame that no amount of rain can extinguish.

Spider's face hangs open in horror and disbelief. Charles Lederer's face is beatific, as if he has just seen a miracle.

It is nine o'clock in the evening and Fat Les locks up the workshops and showroom of Fat Volkz Inc, and starts the journey home. His everyday vehicle is a big, battered white Ford Transit, the kind of thing that can burn off quite a few Beetles at the traffic lights. But these days Les can't be bothered to burn off anybody. Who needs it? Who needs that kind of aggression and competitiveness, that whole small-penis stuff? But that doesn't prevent others trying to provoke him. Les is a calm, leisurely, laidback driver these days, and that means he is constantly being cut up, overtaken on blind corners and hooted at for being too slow off the mark.

He isn't feeling particularly ill-disposed towards the world tonight, but it's been a long day and he's tired and he'd like to get home smoothly and without hassle. The journey home is a slow, uninspiring, urban and suburban drive, with a lot of lights and stop and give way signs, and he really doesn't need the kind of clown who's currently playing silly buggers in the car behind behind him. The fact that the car's a fairly good-looking yellow Beetle certainly doesn't make Les any more sympathetic.

Each time Fat Les comes to a set of lights or a stop sign the driver of the Beetle pulls right up to his rear bumper and then, when Les can go, sounds the horn to tell Les to get a move on, that he's not driving briskly enough. This happens several times, and despite Les's willingness to let himself be overtaken, the yellow Beetle never quite manages to get past. When they arrive at the fourth set of red traffic lights Les has had enough. When the lights change to green he doesn't move. The driver of the Beetle sounds his horn again. Les, quite coolly, raises the engine's revs on the Transit. He puts the van in reverse, rapidly lets in the clutch and the Transit leaps backwards at some speed. It collides with the front end of the Beetle, completely demolishing it.

There is no damage whatsoever to the Transit, and even if there was, it wouldn't look especially out of place on the battered old rear end. There are no witnesses and Les reckons that even if the driver reports him to the police, Les will simply say the car ran into the back of him. Who'd believe that a van driver would deliberately reverse into someone behind him at a traffic light?

Les can't see how the driver of the Beetle is reacting. He or she doesn't even get out of the car. Les drives away. He feels peculiarly pleased with himself. He savours the fact that destroying Beetles can be every bit as much fun as restoring and recreating them.

Next morning when Fat Les arrives to open up Fat Volkz Inc, there appears to be yet another customer waiting for him. It's a woman. She doesn't look like the usual type of punter but Les knows that Volkswagen enthusiasts come in all shapes and sizes. She's tall, not old, and has cropped red hair. Her body is athletic, perhaps toned up by a little body building. She's dressed in a long, trailing raincoat over an expensive charcoal two piece, and she wears a pair of very high-heeled alligator skin court shoes. She says, 'Good morning, I'm Detective Inspector Cheryl Bronte and I understand you know a thing or two about Volkswagens.'

'Who told you that?' Les asks, never too keen to help the police with their enquiries.

'Everybody tells me that.'

'Must be true then.'

She smiles at him, but it is a smile for her own benefit, not for his.

'Adolf Hitler's favourite car, right?' she asks.

42

'In a way,' says Les.

'Is that what *you* like about them?'

'No,' says Les. 'I like the fact I can make a living out of them. Okay?'

'Okay. I'm looking for a friend of yours. Somebody called Carlton Bax.'

'Who's that?'

'Come on Les, he's a customer of yours. You did some restoration for him,' and she consults a notebook, 'three months ago.'

'If you say so.'

'Yes I do. It was a Kubelwagen. I take it you don't restore one of those every day.'

'Oh, him,' says Les. 'Was his name Carlton Bax? I always forget names. But yeah, okay, so I remember him. He was all right. More money than sense, but all right.'

'Have you seen him lately?'

'No. Has he gone missing?'

'How did you know?'

Les looks suitably and indeed genuinely surprised. Of course he has no idea that Carlton Bax has disappeared. Even if it had been reported in the papers, which it still hasn't, Les, being no great reader, still wouldn't have known about it.

'I *didn't* know,' he protests. 'I mean it was the way you said it. How do you mean, disappeared?'

'One day he's here, the next day he's not,' says Cheryl Bronte. 'That sort of disappeared.'

'Kidnapped?' Les enquires.

'Do you think so?'

'I don't bloody know, do I?'

'We're not ruling it out,' says Cheryl Bronte. 'We're not ruling out anything.'

'Well, I hope you find him,' says Les.

'You can't tell me where he is, then.'

'Of course not,' says Les. 'Don't be silly.'

43

She gives Les a stare that says silliness is no part of her make up.

'Do you know anything about exploding Volkswagens?' she asks.

'Eh?' says Les.

'You haven't heard of any Beetles around here being blown up, fire-bombed, that kind of game?'

'This is Southend,' says Les.

'Mmm,' says Cheryl Bronte meaningfully, but Les doesn't know what she means. 'And obviously it's the kind of thing you'd hear about, being in the trade.'

'Yes,' Les admits.

'Because you see it's curious isn't it? There are Volkswagen Beetles blowing up all over the country, but you haven't heard about it.'

'What?' says Les.

'It's a coincidence, isn't it? Or maybe the opposite.'

'I don't know what you're talking about,' says Les, thoroughly confused.

'Well, here's a number you can ring if and when you hear anything,' Cheryl Bronte says, and she hands Fat Les a card bearing a phone number. 'If I don't hear from you, well, one way or another I'm sure I'll see you again.'

Les says thank you for the card. It's a stupid thing to say, but he's just so glad the conversation is coming to an end. Cheryl Bronte walks away, clacking on her alligator skin heels, and Les is left wondering whether members of the police force normally go around handing out business cards.

Barry has devised a logo for the Green Beetles. It shows, in profile, a Volkswagen Beetle which has had its wheels removed, and has grown large angel-style wings which sprout from the rear of the car's roof. The initials G. B. flank the design.

He has painted his own rendition of this logo, in white-wash, on the bonnet of Enlightenment. He has done his best, been painstakingly careful, and tried hard to get the drawing of the Beetle as accurate as possible. But Barry is no artist and he knows it. He doesn't need anybody to tell him that the painting is crude and messy, but that is precisely what the little tyke with the environmentally unfriendly father, the so-called Ferrous Kid, is telling him right now.

'How come it's got no wheels?' the kid asks.

'Because it doesn't need them,' says Barry.

'Beg to differ Barry. My Dad says everybody needs wheels.'

'It doesn't need wheels because it's not going anywhere.'

'I see,' says the kid, impressed by the unassailable logic of this, but he is soon thinking on his feet again. 'What's the point of a car without wheels?'

'Well, I don't want to get pretentious about this,' says Barry, 'but it seems to me that in today's world everybody is rushing but nobody's going anywhere. Everybody's in such a hurry that they waste their time. Everybody wants to travel but they can't decide on a destination.'

'Maybe they're just travelling hopefully,' says the kid.

'But what are they hoping *for*?'

The kid only has to think for a moment before saying, 'I suppose they're hoping for fun, material wealth and good sex.'

'How old are you?' Barry asks again.

Ignoring him, the kid continues, 'Surely it's worth a bit of a journey in order to find those things.'

'Well, yes and no,' says Barry. 'The thing you're journeying to find is probably where you already are.'

'I think my Dad would say you should get out a bit more.'

'He very probably would.'

'He'd probably say you should get in your car, put your foot down, feel the throb of the engine, the thrill of move-ment, the rush of adrenalin on the open road. He'd say you'd feel very different about all this green business if you did that. And I agree with him.'

'Do you really?'

'Yeah. So how about it?' says the kid. 'The car's sitting there doing nothing. I can get hold of some petrol if that's the problem. How about it? Why don't we go for a bit of joyriding?'

'Why don't you get your Dad to take you joyriding if it's so important?'

'Nah,' says the kid. 'He's a miserable bugger. My Mum says he never takes her anywhere.'

This gives the kid a moment of reflection, and as he reflects he stares again at Barry's ham-fisted logo. One or two thick drips of whitewash are starting to bleed down the car's bonnet.

'So why the wings?' he asks Barry.

'Because it's the only way to fly,' Barry replies.

A shiny blue and white Volkswagen camper van, complete with elevating roof, cooker, sink, fridge, awning and chemical toilet, is threading its way through a narrow, dappled, English country lane. At the wheel is Davey, formerly one of Ishmael's younger, more impressionable disciples. Until last month he worked for an agency that recruits accountancy personnel. It was a steady job but it failed to satisfy the inner man. So he handed in his notice, took his holiday pay, polished up his Volkswagen camper and then took to the roads of England, just the way Ishmael once did.

It's been pretty good so far. He's stayed at some attractive and well-appointed camp sites, been invited to one or two interesting barbecues, and chatted quite amicably with his fellow campers and holidaymakers. However, if he was being absolutely honest, he would have to admit it's been a little tame.

The truth is, Davey has an ambition that he hopes to fulfil on this trip. He knows it might sound a bit silly, but what he'd really like to do is fall in with a group of New Age travellers. He doesn't want to trespass or damage property or leave behind him a trail of unsanitary toilet arrangements, but he wouldn't mind at all briefly becoming part of a New Age convoy. He imagines he'd feel rather bucked to be among some exotic people with Mohican haircuts and rings through their noses. He'd share their food and drink, play with their dogs and entertain their barefoot children, discuss numerology and auras. He would walk with them in some ancient places. But mostly what he'd like to do is take some Ecstasy and dance in a field till dawn, while a barrage of techno dance music overtakes his senses and gives him a sense of total unity and love.

It's easier said than done. As he drives along he very seldom sees the battered old vans, ambulances, army lorries and retired buses that he knows would signal the presence of a hippie convoy. Mostly what he sees are spanking new caravans, reps' cars, hot hatchbacks. But he still has hopes of finding what he's looking for.

He is well into the second week of his trip before he sees, in a lay-by not far from Scotch Corner, a little tangle of appropriate-looking vehicles. His heart lifts up. There's an old gypsy-style caravan, a flatbed truck with a sort of log cabin built on the back, and a double decker bus painted with scenes from the Tarot. At the centre of the lay-by there is a wobbly looking teepee and a handful of tents. A fire churns out white smoke, vast speakers pump out dance music, dogs and children roam free. Ragged but supremely hip-looking men and women sit around being themselves.

Davey pulls into the lay-by and brings his camper to a halt right in the middle of the encampment. The inhabitants ignore him completely. He steps out and smiles broadly at everybody.

'Hey,' he calls. 'Anybody know when and where the next rave is?'

He addresses the remark to the whole company and gets no response. Perhaps, he thinks, he is being too general. He approaches a man whose head is shaved at the sides, with his hair tied up in a top knot. He has rings through various parts of his body and any number of tattoos.

'I say,' says Davey, changing tack, 'any idea where I can get some E?'

The man laughs wetly through his nose but can't be bothered to offer an insulting reply. He waves Davey away, wearily, but he isn't to be dismissed quite that easily.

'Hey,' he says, turning back to the whole group, 'I can see you guys are all really chilled out. Mind if I join you for a while?'

This is enough to stir at least one of the travellers into action. A woman gets up from her place by the fire. Davey notices that her hands and feet are caked with black dirt. Her skinny body is wrapped in tatters of big, ill-fitting clothes, but her face, he thinks, is rather sensitive, soft, serene, saintly. He could definitely imagine sharing some space with her. She comes up to him and says, 'Fuck off and die you middle class dweeb.'

Davey can take a hint, but that doesn't mean he isn't deeply hurt. He climbs into his van and drives away. It seems to him that the travellers looked at his vehicle, his clothes and his haircut, and immediately dismissed him. They thought he didn't look enough the part. This, in his opinion, is not what New Age travellers should be all about. They should take a looser, more accepting attitude towards their fellows.

But he knows this is a difficult area. Only a few minutes later, a couple of miles along the road, he decides to stop for lunch at one of those large pubs you find marooned beside dual carriageways, with a roomy beer garden and a large piece of historic, agricultural machinery arranged outside the front entrance. He parks, gets out of his van and walks towards the pub, and he sees a group of vicious-looking skinheads.

He does not feel at all accepting of them. There are only half a dozen or so of them, though he doesn't dare look at them long enough to do any counting. At first he thinks they might be football supporters. Certainly they look like a peer group, a gang. But he knows it isn't the football season, and the more he thinks about it, the more it appears to him that their shared interests are probably not very sporting.

They have extremely short hair and very big boots, but those things in themselves might not be so very decisive. No, it's the tattoos that really give them away; the spider's webs around their necks, the union jacks, the swastikas. These are, unless he's very much mistaken, neo-Nazis. He submits to a small shudder.

They stand in an invisible, though palpable, cloud of anger, hostility and violent obscenity. They are hyperactive, like a barrel load of monkeys. At the moment they are fighting among themselves, but it seems only a matter of time before they find some more proper object. No doubt a Jew or a black or a homosexual or a woman would be ideal, but failing that it seems perfectly likely that they might set about a man in a camper van who could all too easily be mistaken for a middle class dweeb. Davey thinks about scurrying back to the van but suspects that might only draw attention to himself. They would see his fear, and like a pack of dogs they'd know he'd identified himself as a victim. He stands on the forecourt of the pub, equidistant between his van, the pub entrance and the gang of skinheads, and he feels utterly paralysed.

At which point a man emerges from the pub. He is a middle aged man in a rather elegant black suit. The suit is sombre and sober enough but he's wearing it with highly polished, studded cowboy boots, and he has strange items of adornment; a gold hoop earring, a belt buckle in the shape of a dog's skull, a number of big, flashy rings on his fingers. His hair is cropped and silver. His face is large but solid and a short deep scar runs mournfully down from the left corner of his mouth. He walks purposefully but coolly towards the gang. At first Davey thinks it might be the landlord of the pub asking them to leave. That would be enormously brave of him, but it soon becomes obvious that a more subtle and convoluted transaction is taking place.

The besuited man talks to the skinheads quietly, slowly, and they immediately fall silent and listen attentively enough. He is apparently a man of few words. After barely a minute he has said all he has to say. He returns to the pub and as he does so the skinheads walk across the car park, over to a shabby white Transit van, their means of transport. They scuffle and throw punches at each other as they pile into the back.

Davey watches as they accelerate away in a screech of gravel and rubber. He's glad they've gone. He saunters into the pub. It is spacious. There are beams and artexed walls, and a booming colour TV is showing a film about hyenas. Davey feels quite reassured. He enjoys a very leisurely ploughman's lunch and a half of low alcohol lager. He consults his guide to local campgrounds and decides to head for a four star site situated twenty or so miles away. He will have to double back on himself and drive past the lay-by containing the hostile New Age travellers. He thinks he will give them a cheery wave as he passes to show there are no hard feelings.

He leaves the pub and sets off, but as he approaches the lay-by, he realises something is terribly wrong. The camp fire may have been a bit unruly before, but now a big roll of black smoke hangs over the place, and as he gets closer he can see that the entire site is in disarray. The vehicles have been attacked, smashed up, overturned. The teepee and the huddle of tents has been flattened, and there are now no signs of children or dogs. Davey slows the van and he can see some of the travellers. They are sitting or lying around, looking as though, well, as though they've just been beaten up by a gang of neo-Nazi skinheads. Several are clutching bloody rags to their faces and heads.

Davey thinks of stopping to offer assistance. After the way they rejected him it would be extremely noble, positively Biblical, to help them out. However, the memory of being called a middle class dweeb is still smarting, and he thinks 'Sod it', floors the accelerator and drives on.

* * *

Here is Elvis Presley at the wheel of a dune buggy making the movie *Easy Come, Easy Go*. Now, at heart Elvis will always be a Cadillac man. Even at his funeral he will travel in a white Cadillac hearse with one silver Cadillac limousine in front and sixteen white Cadillac limousines behind. One of the first things he ever did when he became rich and successful was to buy his Momma a pink Cadillac. It probably looked a little loud and out of place on the streets of Memphis, but Hell, the boy has never been one for understatement and his heart was undoubtedly in the right place. Maybe the real problem is that Elvis has trouble expressing affection. When he wants to show people that he loves them he gives them something expensive, like a Lincoln convertible or a pick up truck. On one occasion he spent 950 thousand dollars buying trucks for each and every one of his entourage before the Colonel finally put his foot down.

Elvis loves all kinds of machinery, be it cars or motorcycles or tractors or golf carts. He drives Ferraris and a Stutz Blackhawk and all kinds of Mercedes and any number of muscle cars. But this dune buggy is something different again. Yes, it's noisy and small, it's cheap, it's certainly hard to drive compared with an American automatic, and it's based on one of those Volkswagen Bug things. He saw plenty of those

51

things when he was stationed in Germany and he wasn't too impressed. As a matter of fact, when he was in Germany he drove a white BMW which the press nicknamed the Elvis-wagen. And when he was courting Priscilla, he regularly sent a chauffeur-driven Mercedes to pick her up from her home in Wiesbaden and drive her all the way to his place in Bad Nauheim.

The Volkswagen, then, is just about as un-Elvis a car as you could imagine, and yet as he uses it to drive round the *Easy Come, Easy Go* movie set, as he ferries girls and friends around the lot, he gradually starts to like it. It's kinda fun. It's young and it's hip and it's funky. It's more California than Vegas, and at this point in his career he doesn't think that's such a bad thing. He decides he'll get one for his automobile collection.

At any given moment the best of Elvis's cars stand on the drive of Graceland, ready and waiting, clean and polished, full of gas, and raring to go. Of course, even the best cars, some would say especially the best cars, can be a little temperamental; but Elvis has no time for other people's or objects' temperaments. He has to be able to get into any of his cars, start the engine first time, floor the accelerator and drive away. And if one of those suckers won't start, he gets angry as hell. Not that he can't deal with that anger. He has a pretty good way of dealing with it. He simply gets out of the offending car, draws his gun and *shoots* it. He shoots lots of things, like televisions and stereos and radios, but shooting automobiles is most fun. Of course, it doesn't make the car any easier to start, but it definitely makes him feel a whole lot better.

He emerges from Graceland, dressed in his karate robes, his hair and sunglasses firmly in place. He walks along the line of cars put there for his consideration, wondering which one he'll favour today, and he decides it'll be the good old Volkswagen dune buggy. He climbs in, and it settles a little on its suspension. He turns the key in the ignition and it won't start. He gets out, swearing under his breath about Kraut technology, takes a thirty-eight from the shoulder holster that he wears under his karate gear and pumps a couple of shells into the engine block. Then he moves on to his next choice, a Ferrari Dino which starts immaculately first time, and he drives away.

Next day the King is a little surprised to see the dune buggy still parked on the drive. Once he's shot a car it generally isn't much use for anything. He sends for his mechanic and tells him to get rid of the car, how it let him down yesterday.

'Oh, but I took care of it,' the mechanic explains. 'It was just the starter motor. They can be temperamental. I fitted a new one, Mr Presley.'

Elvis laughs at him, one of those dirty, mocking, good ol' boy, Southern laughs.

'It ain't the starter motor that's the problem,' Elvis says. 'Problem is, I fired a couple of slugs into the critter.'

'Yeah, I know that sir, but it's no problem,' says the mechanic. 'These cars have bullet-proof engines. That's the way Adolf Hitler wanted 'em.'

'Adolf Hitler drove a Volkswagen?' Elvis asks.

'He sort of invented it, sir.'

Elvis scratches his armpit inside the white robes.

'You know,' he says, 'I thought there was something kinda funny about these things.'

The engine block from that dune buggy, complete with two bullet scars, is, according to rumour, one of the more minor treasures to be found in Carlton Bax's famous locked room.

III

The Perfumed Volkswagen

It is a quiet afternoon at Fat Volkz Inc, quiet enough that Les can leave work, get in his Transit van, drive along the Essex coast, find a quiet spot and spend a long time staring out to sea. He realises this is probably a sign of creeping middle age. The beach was once a place for playing football, chasing girls and kicking sand in people's faces – not that he ever did any of these things with much success – but now it has become a place to be alone, a place of peace, tranquillity and spiritual solace. He finds that pretty bloody strange. In the good old days he wouldn't have known spiritual solace if it had come up and kneed him in the kidneys, but he's wise enough to accept it now that it's here.

Les walks along the beach for a mile or so. The weather is blustery and wet. He feels his face reddening in the wind but he doesn't mind that. He stops walking, sits down on a patch of shingle, and looks out to sea. Small fishing boats and windsurfers scud across the scratched surface of the water. Les feels meditative, content, hypnotised.

He sits like that for a long while, his head clear of thoughts or of any sense of time, so that when he finally looks up he has no idea how long the stranger has been standing beside him. Les's first impression is that this could well be another police presence. The man is bulky, heavy, stern. He has authority and toughness, and a complete lack of good humour. But when Les looks more closely there are one or two little touches that seem a shade too rococo for the police, the cowboy boots, the belt buckle in the shape of a dog's skull, the fancy jewellery. None of this looks like plain clothes. But most alarming of all is the scar that runs down from the left corner of his mouth. Something about him scares the hell out of Les.

'Volkswagens,' the stranger says. 'They're great items, aren't they?'

'If you like that sort of thing,' Les replies.

'Well, I'm sure you do. Aren't you Fat Les the Veedub King?'

Les nods, not enthusiastically.

The stranger says, 'So how do you explain these exploding Beetles?'

'I don't,' says Les. 'I don't have to.'

'But what kind of maniac do you imagine would do a thing like that?' the stranger asks.

'Just your run of the mill kind of maniac, I guess.'

'If I got my hands on the person doing it. Well . . . you can imagine.'

Les thinks perhaps it is best not to.

'Adolf Hitler's favourite car, you know,' says the stranger.

'So I hear, but that's not why I got into them,' Les replies.

'Adolf Hitler is much misunderstood,' the stranger says. 'He knew a lot about the human spirit. He conceived the Beetle. He built the autobahns. He had unfailing dress sense.'

'Oh please,' says Les.

'You don't think there's something eye-catching about jack-boots, Nazi uniforms, death's head insignia?'

Les can't quite understand why this conversation has such marked similarities to the one he had earlier with Cheryl Bronte. As far as that goes, he can't for the life of him understand why he's having this conversation at all.

'I've never been a snappy dresser,' Fat Les says.

'No,' says the stranger, looking Les over and adjusting the lines of his own suit. 'I can see that.'

Les gets to his feet. 'Well, I'd best be getting on.'

'No,' says the stranger. 'Not until we've discussed something.'

Les wonders if he could make a run for it and get to his van. Something tells him this guy isn't going to be very easy to shake off. He decides he'd better listen to the 'discussion'.

'Go on then,' says Les.

'My name's Phelan.'

Les wonders if he ought to be impressed.

'A good friend of mine, well I say a good friend, I tend to think of her more as a sex slave actually, well, she had a bit of a prang in her Volkswagen. Some bastard in a Ford Transit reversed into her. Made a real mess of the car. It's going to take a skilled craftsman to get it back to normal.'

'I bet,' says Les.

'Is that perhaps the kind of job you could do?'

'Yes,' says Les.

'And could you do it for me cheap?'

'Good work never comes cheap,' says Les.

'I suppose not. Nevertheless, I think I'd like you to do the repair work for me, Les. I'd like you to do a good job at a reasonable price. In fact I'd like you to do it for free. That'll be all right won't it Les?'

'I don't know about that,' says Les.

'Oh, I think you do.'

He grasps Les rather insinuatingly by the shoulder and says. 'I'll tell her to drop the car in. Don't let me down, Les.'

'Okay,' says Les a little hoarsely. His mouth feels unusually dry.

'I won't be around for a little while Les. But don't worry, I'll be thinking about you. We'll have another talk just as soon as I get back. I could have all sorts of work to put your way.'

Marilyn's mother has been drinking. There is nothing

unusual about that. Marilyn's mother is famous for her drinking. She's famous for being extrovert, for being the life and soul of any and every party. It is a rainy summer night. She walks down the street, she wiggles, she teeters, she giggles at some joke known only to herself. She feels just fine. She knows she drinks too much. She knows it is no good for her body, but she thinks it could all be a lot worse. She could be addicted to much more dangerous things, like tranquillisers or sleeping pills or heroin for heaven's sake. Whereas in the current arrangement she's only addicted to drink and sex.

She thinks her husband must be to blame for this. He never had enough time for her. He would say he had to spend all night sittings in the House, and his weekends were always taken up with constituency matters. She was left alone. He didn't want her there, didn't even want her to play the good MP's wife. She was sure he had affairs. She imagined a mistress installed in a studio flat around the corner from the House. She imagined him bedding various female members of the Party faithful. She began to take her revenge.

She began by seducing one or two of Charles's closer friends. The fact that she was married to their crony seemed to be a large part of her attraction for them. They were enthusiastic, sometimes grateful, always discreet. But discretion somehow wasn't what she wanted. She wanted to be wild and scandalous. Rather than enthusiastic, grateful Tories, she decided to plump for dodgy strangers; gardeners, builders, postmen, barmen. When she is particularly drunk and feeling particularly needy she has even been known to offer herself to cab drivers. They always accept. She sits in the cab, on the edge of her seat, loosens her clothing, tells them she is lonely, that her husband is away, that she needs some sympathetic company. Sometimes she invites them into the house at the end of the journey, but more often they drive to some secluded place and do it quickly and fiercely in the back of the cab.

She loves it, this rapid association, this desperate coming together, the sense of transgression, of wickedness, a stranger touching her with dirty hands, his cock suddenly in her. Then it's all over, and she's left feeling used, soiled, wonderful. But she is not totally indiscriminate. She never goes for unlicensed mini cab drivers; only for drivers of black cabs, men with the Knowledge.

Lately she has come to the conclusion that perhaps poor Charles wasn't really having affairs at all. She has decided he was probably a genuinely dedicated politician who worked too hard for his own and his family's good. His mental breakdown and subsequent lengthy incarceration seem to have proved this, but now it is too late. She did not do right by Charles and she knows it. However, life must go on. She has tried hard to forgive herself, and in the main she has succeeded.

She has always felt sorry for Charles, but she was never sorry enough to want to visit him very often in the Mercy Seat, she usually left that to Marilyn. Now that he's out on the loose somewhere, she prefers not to think about him at all. She knows it will only depress her and she hates to be depressed.

The cool, wet air fails to sober her up. It's hard to get a cab. A few splash past but they're all occupied. She decides to shelter for a moment and stands under the canopy of a hotel entrance. She continues to watch the street for taxis. Suddenly a young black man comes out of the lobby. She's not sure what it is about him, but somehow he looks like a taxi driver. In fact it is Zak, Fat Les's unsatisfied customer, and he works in the hotel as a bar steward. He needs to do all the work he can in order to pay off his car loan and he has just finished a double shift.

She says to him, 'Excuse me, are you a black cab driver?' and he thinks to himself, 'Well I'm black and I'm a driver. Two out of three can't be bad.'

'Where do you want to go?' he asks.

She says Crockenfield, a good twenty miles away. The cab fare there would cost a fortune, and Zak is in need of a fortune.

'It'll cost,' he says.

'Money's no object,' she replies.

He tells her to follow him, his car's round the back of the hotel. She walks beside him, takes his arm. She notices his biceps are hard and thick. She thinks this is going to be fun.

They come to a row of parked cars and she can see there isn't a black cab amongst them. She realises she must have made a mistake, though she suspects it isn't such a terrible one. Oh well, she thinks, even if he doesn't have a black cab she'll go along with it, just so long as it's a reasonably smart new mini cab in good condition. If it's some scruffy, tatty old thing she'll turn on her heel and depart. Then she sees that her driver is heading straight for a Volkswagen Beetle. Her immediate reaction is to be offended. Who does he think she is? Does she really look like the sort of woman who accepts rides in strange Volkswagens? But then she looks at the car more closely. Volkswagens have been much on her mind of late, one way or another, and now that she sees it more clearly, it isn't quite as objectionable as she first imagined. It is a pretty spiffy looking Beetle. It has been lowered and painted in metallic turquoise and peppermint green. Oh well, she thinks, this might be a night to remember after all.

She gets into the car. The interior is roomier than she would have imagined and it smells rather sweetly of incense and musk. They have only gone a mile or so when she begins to unbutton her cerise silk blouse and says, 'It's not such a bad body, is it?'

Zak is enough of a gentleman to say, when he's recovered from the shock, 'No, it's very nice.'

'Why don't you take a better look,' she says, and she lifts one of her breasts out of her bra for him to see.

'It's a bit tricky while I'm driving.'

'I understand that you have to keep your eyes on the road,' she says, 'but you could always use your sense of touch.'

She takes his left hand and places it on her left breast. They both become aware of her nipple getting hard and pointed.

'What exactly have you got in mind?' Zak asks, and then he takes his hand away because he has to change gear. He does not put it back immediately.

'Well,' she replies, 'I was thinking we could find some dark alley and you could park the car and fuck me like a beast.'

'You want me to do that?'

'Now that you mention it, I think I do.'

'Why?'

It seems an absurd question but she doesn't object to a little shyness in a lover.

'You're a very sexy man,' she says.

'How can you say that when you don't even know me?'

'I don't want to know you. I just want to fuck you.'

'Why?' he asks again.

'Oh, for God's sake, I don't know; because you've got a nice face.'

She sort of means it. He does have a nice face, although that wouldn't be strictly necessary for the kind of transaction she has in mind.

'I know why it is,' he says. 'It's because I'm black, isn't it?'

She is wise enough not to answer. She would have been happy enough to have sex with a white cab driver if one had presented himself, but there's no denying that this young man's black skin would add a certain frisson. However, she can tell this is not what he wants to hear.

'I get pretty sick of it actually,' he says. 'I get pretty sick of that whole racial, sexual thing, you know, that black men are supposed to be studs with big cocks and that white middle class women go to bed with them as a way of debauching and degrading themselves. I find that all pretty sick and objectionable, as a matter of fact.'

She is surprised by the vehemence of his response, but she has no objection to vehemence.

'It wasn't your blackness that made me decide to have sex with you,' she says.

'No?' he sneers. 'What was it then?'

'If you must know, it was your car.'

'Really?' he asks.

'Yes really.'

'You're not winding me up?'

'No.'

'Well in that case . . . '

A few minutes later Zak's Volkswagen Beetle is parked in an alleyway behind a freezer centre in Streatham, and Marilyn's mother is being quite extraordinarily friendly to him. Zak is a big man and the car is too cramped to allow the full repertoire of sexual movements, and he has to be content with fellatio. He is soon very content indeed.

Debby has always had the good sense not to try introducing Barry to her friends at the building society. They're a good and lively bunch and she likes them very much, but she wouldn't want to inflict Barry on them. She often goes out with them after work on the evenings when she isn't seeing Barry. In the early days they used to encourage her to bring him along but now they know better. There are occasional campaigns to fix her up with a new, more socialised man, but Debby says, with absolute accuracy, that after Barry most men in the world seem a little ordinary.

She has been thinking about what Barry said to her about their possible futures. He had it quite wrong when he thought she might be looking for a settled, materialistic future. She isn't looking for a nice house and a nice car, and she certainly isn't looking for a man to provide them for her, and children do not figure at all in her scheme of things. However, since Barry pressed her into thinking about her hopes and needs, it has been brought home to her that she wouldn't at all mind widening her horizons a little, the building society and the caravan site making for a rather limiting ambit. However, she would be delighted to share that wider horizon with Barry. She doesn't want to become Marco Polo but she would quite like to get out and about a bit more. A foreign holiday would do nicely for starters, and she'd even be prepared to pay for him.

When Barry took the cover off his Volkswagen she felt quite optimistic. She felt that perhaps they were changing and growing as a couple, that Barry too was feeling a renewed need to be footloose and fancy free, but it hasn't turned out that way. All he ever does is sit there at the wheel of the damned car, going nowhere. It isn't enough for her.

Since he brought it up, she realises she's been more than fair to Barry. There are, she knows, many girlfriends who'd be egging him on to get a job. They'd be asking him to take them out wining, dining and dancing. They'd be criticising him for having no interests, no ambitions, no prospects. But she isn't like that. She stands by her man. She's there for him. She takes care of his sexual needs which, while not particularly outrageous, are certainly specific and demanding. Not every girl in the world would do that for him. She still wants him to be happy, she would just like to be a bit happier herself.

She begins in what she thinks is quite a subtle way. She buys a new road atlas and waves it around conspicuously when she's with Barry. She leaves it lying around open to reveal route planners, mileage charts, maps of town centres. She traces journeys. She makes little pointed comments such as, 'Anglesey, now there's a place I've never been to.' She's trying to fire Barry's imagination. When all this fails she is reduced to saying, 'Why don't you just have a look at these bloody maps, Barry? We could go somewhere. It wouldn't kill you. I'd even be prepared to do the driving.'

Barry takes the atlas, holds it, weighs it in his hands, looks at it as though it is an artefact from another time and culture, possibly even from another planet. Then he says, 'Wasn't it E.F. Schumacher who wrote that a man who uses an imaginary map thinking it a true one, is likely to be worse off than someone with no map at all?'

'But this is a real map,' Debby insists.

'Ah, but what do we mean by real?'

At this point, despite all her considerable love and respect for Barry, she asserts the reality of the atlas by pulling it away from him and beating him over the head with it for a while.

Barry is rather taken aback by this. He says, 'Later I'll forgive you for that, but right now I'm very hurt.'

'Good,' she says, 'I'm glad.'

'You're glad that you hurt me?'

'Yes,' she says, 'it's called being cruel to be kind.'

He looks at her sadly, pathetically, like a lost puppy. So she hits him again, this time to be cruel. It turns out not to be one of their happiest nights together and Barry ends up having to sleep in the back seat of Enlightenment. In some peculiar way he realises that is perhaps what he wanted all along.

Davey has developed a rather ambivalent attitude towards hitchhikers. He has picked up several of them on this trip, and while he doesn't exactly resent having given them lifts, they have all proved to be very disappointing company. He thought they might be good company and good, chatty conversationalists. In his supremely optimistic moments he has even fantasised about picking up some amazing, young, bony New Age type female who would initiate him into the mysteries of her world. She would surely be prepared to tell

63

him how to go about taking Ecstasy and dancing in a field. It looks like it is not to be.

The incident with the neo-Nazi skinheads remains painfully with him. It appears he was on the edge of something utterly foul. No doubt skinheads would enjoy beating up New Agers in any circumstances but it seems now that the man at the pub, he of the dark suit, silver hair and scar, somehow motivated and organised the lot in the car park. Davey knows he isn't in any way culpable, and he knows he couldn't have intervened, but it still disturbs and occasionally depresses him.

What's more, he hasn't come across any other New Age travellers. It is beginning to dawn on him that he could spend this whole summer just missing them, driving around the campsites of England like any other boring holidaymaker. Before he set off he liked to think he would have an instinct for finding them, but that has proved to be far from the case. And all this rain hasn't been helping. No doubt travellers stay put when it rains, and these recent downpours have been so bad that the elevating roof of his camper has sprung a leak in a couple of places.

He is driving along the coast road between Great Yarmouth and Cromer. It isn't raining at the moment but that looks like a very temporary state of affairs. The road is empty and the sky sags down, and he pulls into a lay-by to stare out at the slate coloured sea. He sits there for some time before he becomes aware of a figure standing at the other end of the lay-by. It is an old man, his face streaked with dirt, his clothes covered in mud. He has no luggage and he is standing bolt upright, but his eyes are closed and Davey realises that the man is asleep on his feet.

It is, of course, Charles Lederer, though Davey doesn't recognise him. He has no reason to. They only encountered each other briefly and it was a long time ago.

Davey looks at him with a certain distaste. At heart he would prefer not to have such a filthy, disgusting character in his nice clean Volkswagen van, but his failure to play the good Samaritan to the New Age travellers after they'd been beaten up by the skinheads makes him a lot more sympathetic. He sounds his horn. Lederer's eyes pop open and he is abruptly awake. He looks around him lost and frightened. Slowly he settles and sees that Davey is beckoning him, inviting him to come over to the van. Charles Lederer has even less reason to recognise Davey than Davey has to recognise him, so he ambles slowly over towards the van.

Davey winds down his window and says, 'You need a lift?'

'Well, I'm not absolutely certain,' says Lederer, 'but I think so, yes.' His voice is exhausted and comes from very far away.

'Where are you going?' Davey asks.

'Where are *you* going?'

This isn't the easiest question to answer so Davey says, 'Just along the coast a little ways.'

'Then that's where I'll be going too.'

It seems to Davey that this is a little presumptuous of the old man, but even as Lederer speaks, he looks in danger of falling asleep again. He looks ill and paper thin and Davey's heart goes out to him.

'When did you last sleep in a bed?' Davey asks.

After a long pause, 'I can't remember.'

'And when did you last eat?'

'Oh, comparatively recently, certainly in the last few days.'

Davey sees his duty. He opens up the big, sliding side door of the van and tells Charles Lederer to get in and take a seat. Clambering in is a difficult job for his stiff, tired limbs but he makes it. Davey opens a tin of oxtail soup and heats it on the van's Calor gas stove. He gets bread rolls from the storage compartment under one of the seats and gives them and the soup to Charles Lederer. For a man who has been so long without food he seems peculiarly uneager. Perhaps

65

he is suspicious, or perhaps he just has impeccable table manners.

'This is terribly kind of you,' says Lederer. 'Very Christian.'

'I don't know about that,' says Davey.

'You're not a Christian?' Lederer asks.

'I don't know what I am. I think I may be part of a brand new breed, sort of pagan, pantheist, humanist, hedonist.'

'Hedonist?' Lederer repeats.

'Yes, but that's the hardest part.'

The moment Charles Lederer finishes his soup he slumps in the seat, his head cocks onto his shoulder and he falls asleep again. Davey watches and is moved. He's glad to be there when he's needed. He looks closely at his guest and sees that the slippers he's wearing are split right open. His blazer has lost its buttons and his trousers are held up by safety pins and some rope. Gradually however, Davey also becomes aware that a malevolent odour is seeping out of Lederer's unwashed body and clothes. He doesn't want the smell in his van but neither does he want to wake the old man from what is obviously much-needed sleep. It is not a peaceful or untroubled sleep, however. From time to time Charles Lederer twitches, jerks his legs, moans something indistinct but urgent-sounding.

Davey doesn't move from the lay-by, lets Lederer sleep for several hours, into the late afternoon, but then he decides it's time he was moving on and finding a caravan site for the night. His guidebook says there's a well-equipped place about fifteen miles along the coast. He gently shakes the old man awake. Again he sees that lost, startled expression.

'Look,' says Davey, 'I'm going to make a suggestion.'

Lederer looks extremely apprehensive.

Davey continues, 'Why don't you come along to the camp-site with me. They've got showers and sinks. You could get cleaned up, have a shave, and you could get rid of those stinking old clothes and I'll give you some of my old jeans and shirts and trainers. And I'll give you a proper hot meal, and after that, well, after that you can go on your way.'

Lederer looks distrustful. He says, 'And what do I give you?'

'Nothing. You don't have anything, do you?'

'So why are you offering to do this? What will you be getting out of it?'

'A good feeling,' says Davey.

Charles Lederer weighs that up for a long time before he says, 'Well, thank you very much. That would be most acceptable.'

At first they don't talk much as they drive. Davey has thrown the windows wide open to disperse his passenger's smell. Now that he's awake, Lederer is vibrantly restless. He refuses to wear a seatbelt and bounces up and down erratically in his seat like an eager child.

'I used to tell them,' he says at last, 'in the House, I used to tell them that public transport wasn't the answer.'

'Yes?' says Davey, not listening.

'I used to say that public transport would be all very well if it wasn't full of the public.' He laughs rather uncontrollably at his own joke. 'People want to shut themselves up in little tin boxes, and I say good for them. Best place for them. This is a very pleasant vehicle.'

'Yes, I like it,' says Davey.

Suddenly Charles Lederer throws himself back in his seat. Davey fears he might have been stung by a wasp, or even had a heart attack.

'Stop this vehicle at once!' Lederer shouts.

Instinctively Davey slams on the brakes and the van slews to a halt.

'I've just seen. I've just realised,' says Lederer. 'You've been very kind, very generous, but now I realise this vehicle, it's a Volkswagen isn't it!!'

'Well yes,' says Davey.

With that Charles Lederer lets out a scream, flings open

67

the passenger door and sprints away from the van, over a barbed wire fence and into a field of cows. He moves at top speed, his limbs flapping as he goes. Davey is surprised he can move so fast and watches as he recedes without ever looking back.

Davey waits for a long time and at last realises there's nothing to be done. The old man has gone for good. He closes the passenger door and drives on to his intended campsite. That evening he falls into conversation with a group of German tourists who assure him that Germany is one of the world's great liberal democracies. That night it pours with rain again.

Barry Osgathorpe is sitting at the wheel of Enlightenment when a voice outside the car shouts, 'What a wicked-looking Beetle!' Barry thinks, 'Not again' but turns his head to find that the person offering the opinion on his car is not the usual sort who offers such opinions. This is a middle-aged man in an immaculate black suit, with silver hair and a scar at the corner of his mouth. The man is somehow so impressive, so authoritative-looking and sounding that Barry can only say, 'Well, thanks very much.'

'Do you mind if I pop in beside you?'

And before Barry can say yes or no the man is sitting next to him in the car, and making himself very comfortable.

'I think it's the blackness of this vehicle that's so impressive,' the man says. 'It's the smoothness, the sense of a whole. It has a power, an elemental, archetypal quality, a sense of sculptural integrity.'

Barry stares at the man, checks his facial expression for irony or mockery, but he can find no trace of either.

'Well, yes,' says Barry, 'that's pretty much the way I see it too.'

'Of course you do,' the man says, then adds, 'God, I really love Volkswagen Beetles.'

He says it not as though he is expressing some happy enthusiasm, but rather as though he is confessing to a deep, dark obsession.

'The name's Phelan,' he says, and he extends a hand to be shaken. Barry takes it and says, 'Call me Barry.'

'I'm just like you, Barry,' he says. 'I love my own Beetle so much that I could just sit in it all day long, experiencing that sense of pleasure, that feeling of strength through joy, Kraft durch Freude.'

Barry nods. He is almost tempted to ask the man what kind of Beetle he owns, but he resists.

'Only a genius could have created a machine like the Beetle,' the man continues. 'But of course you know all this.'

'Yes,' says Barry.

'Good. Since you know the history I won't be doomed to repeat it.'

The man laughs lifelessly and Barry says, 'I'm not intending to repeat anybody's history, least of all my own.'

'Very good,' says the stranger. 'You want new experiences. You're ready for the next step. You're ready to move on. Maybe I can be of service.'

Barry fears he may be about to try selling him his services as a removal expert, or as an insurance broker, or possibly as some kind of pimp. None of these will be at all welcome so he says, 'I don't think that seems very likely.'

'Of course it doesn't seem *likely*. Nor did it ever seem likely that a car conceived in pre-war Nazi Germany would go on to conquer the world. But it did, didn't it?'

Barry is not sure that the Beetle actually conquered the world, and even if it did, he's not sure that world conquest is per se such a very good thing. He prefers to believe that the Beetle was a well-made, slightly unusual, not too expensive, reasonably soulful car that gave pleasure and service to a very great number of people, even if it also caused pollution, congestion and death to a certain number of others. Nevertheless, he doesn't argue with the man, not that the stranger is really waiting for any response from Barry.

'I'm a pretty good judge of character,' the man says. 'I can see you're not some boring, run of the mill Beetle enthusiast. I can see that you have some spirit, some unconventional attitudes.'

Not even Barry can deny that.

'You're one of us,' the stranger says.

'I don't know who you are,' Barry says.

'Don't you? I think perhaps you do.'

Barry insists that his ignorance is authentic, and the stranger takes this as another cue to hold forth.

'Look Barry,' he says, 'you and I know it's hell out there. There are too many people competing for too few resources.'

Barry has to agree.

'But it's more complicated than that. It isn't just a question of reducing numbers, or of slicing the pie more evenly as some fools might suggest. The problem is that the wrong people are in control.'

'You can say that again,' Barry agrees.

'You're like me Barry. You look at all these people and what do you see? Do you see your equals? Do you see creatures made in God's image? I don't think so Barry. I think you see a lot of useless clutter. Don't you think a lot of that clutter could be tidied away?'

'I've never thought about it,' Barry says.

'Oh, I think you have,' Phelan says insinuatingly. 'Haven't you ever thought to yourself that the world would be a much better place if only there were more people like you in it?'

'I suppose so.'

'I'm here to tell you Barry, that there are more people like you in the world than you might think.

'Take a drive round the M25 Barry. What traits are displayed by your fellow man? Aggression, selfishness, bad temper, competitiveness, madness brought on by stress. That's not what the world ought be like, is it?'

'No,' Barry admits.

'When Adolf Hitler conceived the idea of the autobahn that's not what he had in mind at all. He saw long straight fast motorways uncluttered by riff raff and deviants.'

'What?' says Barry.

'You're a good citizen, aren't you Barry? You're law abiding, moral, politically middle of the road, not sexually or socially deviant. You're male and you're white.'

'Well, to an extent,' Barry stutters.

'Why deny it Barry? Why be ashamed? You don't want the world left in the hands of extremists and perverts, do you? Of course you don't. In your heart of hearts you're just like me, just like us. You know that Adolf Hitler was right.'

'About motorways?'

'About everything. He designed the Beetle didn't he?'

'Well, he had a certain amount of help from Ferdinand Porsche, not to say the British Army.'

'Of course he did. We all need a little help, Barry. I need yours. You need mine.'

Barry is about to deny this vehemently, but there's no stopping the stranger now. He continues, 'I have a dream Barry, a vision if you like, and you could be part of it.'

'What sort of vision?' Barry asks, and immediately wishes he hadn't.

'Well,' says the stranger, 'I see us as a band of supermen, roaming this great country of ours in chariots of fire, by which of course I mean Volkswagen Beetles. We would be dominant. We would be loved, feared, worshipped. We would be as Gods, Barry. Or should I call you Ishmael?'

'No, don't call me Ishmael!' Barry insists. 'How do you even know about Ishmael?'

'I know all about you Barry. What do you say? Do you want to be a superman?'

Barry prides himself on being slow to anger, but a strange

71

milkshake of emotions is frothing inside him. Its ingredients include pain, annoyance, anger, disgust. He looks the stranger right between the eyes and says, 'You're one of those bloody neo-Nazis, aren't you?'

Phelan smiles condescendingly as if to indicate that Barry's response is pathetic and childish. 'There's nothing neo about me,' he says.

'Get out of my Beetle,' Barry says, white and trembling with anger.

The man shrugs and gets out immediately and quite willingly. He closes the door gently behind him. He moves round to the driver's side of the car. He starts to walk away, but when he's twenty yards away from Barry he turns and says, 'You can take the Nazi out of the Volkswagen, but can you take the Volkswagen out of the Nazi?'

After he's gone, it takes Barry quite a while to come to the conclusion that this is an almost entirely meaningless remark.

He kneels in the dark beside the big iron bed. His ankles, wrists and throat are ringed with studded leather. A lattice-work of steel chains connects these points of restraint. Their metallic rattle stirs with his every movement. The links touch his body as coldly as a mistress.

His body is tied in a sheath of black and red leather, a construction of straps and buckles, thongs and studs that encloses and holds him, yet leaves him more vulnerable, more truly naked, than ever. Genitals and buttocks are left bare. Access is guaranteed. There will be no resistance. His body, where it shows, is marked with small cuts, bruises, 'love bites'. Around his biceps are swastika armbands.

The room is stiflingly hot and smells of rubber, metal, hot oil, sweat. It is swathed in patchy candlelight. The candles flicker in twisted, wrought iron holders, and wax decays and carves itself into white, brittle stalagmites. All the walls are draped thick with flags. Some bear German eagles, some death's heads, some crisscrossed with swastikas. The flags creep over the ceiling and hang over the bed like a red and black canopy. The rest of the room is decorated with swords, guns, axes, chalices, examples of Nazi uniform. There is an oak table into which SS flashes have been carved, then a series of exhibits have been laid out on its surface; rubber truncheons, riding crops, canes, cords, gas masks, dildos made of wood and metal and ivory.

Suddenly he knows she has entered the room. He knows even before he hears her footsteps, loud and precise, militaristic and decadent. He doesn't turn round, he doesn't need to. He knows the games, the rules, the costume. He knows she will be dressed immaculately in Hitlerian kitsch, fancy dress that is sexier and more exotic than any real uniform; some baroque combination of knee boots and breeches, bare breasts, braiding, a service dagger.

She is approaching. When she is near enough she prods his buttocks with the shiny tip of her right boot. She moves it into more intimate space, pushes in between his thighs, forcing his legs open.

'Well, Phelan,' she says, 'what shall we do with you today?'

It is a rhetorical question. She pulls a knotted silk cord that dangles at the side of the bed, and one of the 'walls' of flags draws back to reveal a small anteroom. It is the size of, say, a domestic garage, and it contains, spotlit and on a raised dais, a silkily black Volkswagen cabriolet. More properly it should be called a Kraft durch Freudewagen, a Strength through Joy car, since this car dates from the model's very earliest days. In fact, this is a vehicle once owned and driven by a Gestapo officer called Hans Krauss, a personal friend of Adolf Hitler, who received the car in exchange for certain special services rendered to the Führer.

Phelan is pulled to his feet and led across the room by the chain at his neck. He stands briefly beside the car, like a driver about to plunge into a dark, bottomless ocean. She pushes him down onto the front passenger seat, onto the very spot where he knows a murderous Gestapo officer once planted his taut, black-uniformed buttocks. The thought brings him an orgasm rather sooner than he would have liked.

Nevertheless, he has to say, 'Thank you Miss Renata. Thank you so much.'

A yellow Volkswagen with a demolished front end is delivered by tow truck to Fat Volkz Inc. The driver of the truck manoeuvres and unhitches the Volkswagen so that it stands forlorn and skewed on a patch of gravel adjacent to the workshops. The owner of the car has been sitting in the cab of the truck, but now she descends. She is no longer dressed in Nazi gear, although her black leather jacket, her leggings and her black high heels still look mean and sexy enough for most people.

Les surveys the damage to the Volkswagen. It is a terrible, squashed, tangled mess. He feels quite proud of himself for having caused it. On the other hand, he knows it's going to take a hell of a lot of work to get it back into shape.

'Hello Les,' says the woman.

Les is quite used to having strangers address him by his first name. He says hello in return.

'Why did you do it, Les?' she asks.

'Do what?'

'Reverse into me?'

'I don't know what you're talking about.'

'Oh. Come on Les.'

The way she talks suggests a friendliness, a familiarity that he doesn't understand. He's pretty sure he's never met her before. He'd certainly have remembered her if she'd been one of his previous customers.

'Do I know you?' he asks.

74

'I'm Renata Caswell,' she says.

He considers the name for a moment, and it does sound ever so vaguely familiar, but he can't place it and he remains none the wiser.

'You seen anything of your friend Ishmael?' she asks.

Ishmael. The very name hurts him. He remembers a time when his life was entangled with that of Ishmael. They drove too fast. They drank lager. They fire-bombed stuck up twats in Range Rovers. It all seems a long time ago, but not quite long enough.

'I was the journalist who finally exposed Ishmael,' she tells Les. 'I'm the one who stopped him turning into a complete little Hitler.'

It all comes flooding back like a bad Indian meal. There was a time when Ishmael looked like becoming some sort of cult leader. It was Renata who found out that he'd once appeared in a coprophiliac porn movie and that, mercifully, ended his ambitions. Fat Les hadn't absolutely seen why you couldn't be both a cult leader and a bit part player in a coprophiliac porn movie. After all, to the true believer all things are holy, even coprophiliac porn movies. But he still knows that he was a damned fool ever to have got involved with the little jerk Ishmael, and it still makes him both angry and embarrassed.

'No, I haven't seen him,' says Les.

'Pity,' says Renata.

'I don't think so.'

Les walks round to the other side of the Volkswagen and pretends to be examining the chassis for twisting or hidden damage.

'This is a real mess,' he says. 'Look, why don't I give you a good price for it and take it in part exchange on a restored one?'

'That's not the deal,' says Renata. 'That's not what he wants.'

'Who's he? Your boyfriend?'

75

'He's not my boyfriend.'

'But you're his sex slave, right?' says Les with a snigger.

'Did he say that?'

'Yeah he did.'

'He's full of little ironies, isn't he?'

Les has no idea what she means.

'Have the police been bothering you?' she asks abruptly.

'The police don't bother me,' says Les.

'But they've been around, haven't they? Asking you about Volkswagens that go bang in the night.'

'Yeah,' he says a little angrily. He really doesn't want another conversation about exploding Volkswagens, nor about kidnapped Volkswagen collectors.

'Are you still a journalist?' he asks.

'I'm just a lady of leisure,' she replies.

'Must be nice to have a rich boyfriend.'

'It's okay, but he's not my boyfriend.'

Les leans against the busted Beetle. This is a job he doesn't want at all. It feels as though he's paying a very high price for a simple, if illegal and destructive, bit of reversing.

'It's a pity he can't afford to buy you a decent car,' says Les.

'He can,' she says dismissively. 'But he chooses not to. He loves Volkswagen Beetles. I think he's crazy. I think they're crummy, overrated, overpriced.' She watched Les's face closely to see if he reacts. He doesn't.

She continues, 'If the police happen to think you've been blowing up Volkswagens, well so what, I wouldn't worry too much. But if Phelan thinks you've been blowing them up, then you're in serious shit, Les.'

'And what about this Carlton Bax geezer?' says Les. 'Am I supposed to have kidnapped him too? Am I supposed to shit myself if Phelan thinks I kidnapped him?'

'Oh, that's okay, Les. He *knows* you didn't kidnap him.'

*

76

Another day. Barry is still sitting at the wheel of Enlighten-ment. He is in a meditative state, focussed but alert. He is gradually aware of another approaching presence, a woman in a long raincoat worn over a charcoal grey suit. He has no idea that she's a policewoman, but he can tell that she thinks rather highly of herself. Putting in appearances at a caravan site is clearly some way beneath her dignity. She tries to sweep effortlessly towards Barry and his car, but the local topography of paths and lawns, picnic tables, barbecues and children's paddling pools works against her.

When she gets to the car, she tilts her head down at Barry and says, 'Good morning. I'm Detective Inspector Cheryl Bronte. Is this your car?'

'No, I'm just keeping it warm for a friend,' he says with uncharacteristic sarcasm.

She ignores this insolence.

'You wouldn't want to lose it would you? You wouldn't want it to explode, for instance, would you?'

'Well of course not. Although, of course, if it did, well, you know, it's only a material object isn't it? It wouldn't be the end of the world, unless, of course, I happened to be inside it at the time, but you know, how likely *is* it to explode?'

His reply doesn't seem to make her happy at all. 'I see the tax has expired,' she says casually.

'Oh yes, years ago.'

'I suppose you do have insurance and a current MOT.'

Barry laughs. 'Of course not.'

'But you do have a licence.'

'Somewhere, I'm sure.'

'I have every right to get very nasty about this,' says Detective Inspector Cheryl Bronte. 'Driving a car without insurance or an MOT is a serious business.'

'I know,' he says. 'But I'm not driving a car. Surely you must have noticed. I'm not driving at all.'

'So what the bloody hell *are* you doing?'

'Saving the world in my own small way.'

Cheryl Bronte walks round the car. There is no doubt that the tyres, exhaust and lights are in various states of illegality. What really catches and holds her attention, however, is the Green Beetle logo. She looks at it closely, as though its messily executed design might offer up some latent, secret meanings.

'Are you a neo-Nazi?' she asks Barry.

'No,' says Barry, offended.

'Are you into uniforms, jackboots, shaven heads, that sort of thing?'

'Well of course not.'

'Or maybe Nazi regalia, flags, whips, death's heads, swastikas, the ark of the covenant.'

'Not me,' says Barry.

'Then good for you, Barry. If there's one thing worse than a Nazi in my book, it's a neo-Nazi. So what does this insignia of yours mean? What does GB stand for? Are you trying to invoke the greatness of Great Britain to come to the aid of some threadbare, sicko Nationalism of yours?'

Barry tries, and he's aware that he's not making a great fist of it, to explain the Green Beetles and their logo, and about using inactivity in the service of a better world. Cheryl Bronte listens very carefully, but Barry isn't sure she understands a word of it.

'That's the problem with symbols isn't it?' she says when he's barely halfway through his intended explanation. 'They can mean just about anything you want them to mean. A union jack flying above Buckingham Palace has a rather different resonance from a union jack tattooed on some yobbo's forehead. When Kipling uses the swastika it is a holy symbol. When it appears on the side of a Volkswagen it means something rather different, wouldn't you say?'

'I suppose so,' says Barry.

'But you say your symbol is just another bit of half-brained conservationism.'

'Well . . .'

'A man sitting alone in a Volkswagen that's going nowhere. What do you think that might symbolise?'

'I don't know. Not everything has to be symbolic, does it?'

'Or how about an exploding Volkswagen,' Cheryl Bronte enquires. 'Is that a symbol?'

'What *is* all this about exploding Volkswagens?' says Barry.

Cheryl Bronte suddenly looks mighty serious. She says, 'Every night we lose a few more: a couple in Coventry, a handful in Middlesex, one or two in Whitley Bay. It's making the police look very stupid.'

Barry is finding all this very confusing and he can't see why any of it is at all relevant to him.

'There could be some bunch of neo-Nazis behind it, couldn't there?' she continues. 'Or it could be some conservationists, couldn't it? If cars are evil why not blow them up? Neo-Nazis, eco-freaks, they're all much the same to me.'

Barry is about to protest bitterly about this slur on the Green lobby, but decides against it.

'But, of course,' says Cheryl Bronte, 'you don't know anything about exploding Volkswagens, do you?'

'No.'

'And you don't know anything about the kidnapping of Carlton Bax, do you Barry?'

'No, I don't. I've never heard of Carlton Bax.' Then suddenly something dawns on him. 'How do you know my name?'

'From the files,' she says irritatedly.

'What files?'

'Come on Barry, Ishmael, whatever you call yourself these days, you kidnapped the daughter of an English MP, you barricaded yourself in his house, you called a news conference. Okay, so you got away with it, but you have to expect there'll be a file.'

There it comes again, that old blast of stale air and shameful memories. The alter ego who was Ishmael stalks the stage again. Barry feels dreadful.

'I suppose so,' he admits. 'Does that mean you think I'm going around blowing up cars and kidnapping people?'

She looks at him briskly and thoroughly, as if one good look is all it takes to see right into his centre, right through him.

'Actually no,' says Cheryl Bronte. 'But we *do* know from the files that you have an intuitive, maybe even mystical, connection with the Volkswagen Beetle. There aren't many people like you about. What we want to do is get you back on the road, fuel you up and let you go. Something tells me that you're going to lead me right where I want to go.'

'Where do you want to go?'

'Where I can get my hands on the villains who are causing these explosions and holding Carlton Bax hostage.'

'Are you sure they're the same people?'

'Not absolutely, but I'm making an intuitive connection of my own there.'

Barry ponders for a while. Cheryl Bronte thinks he's considering her offer but actually he's wondering whether he has any chance of making her understand where he's at these days. He tries. He says, 'The only journey worth making is an inward one. The way ahead will only bring you back to the point from which you started. All routes lead to the same destination, to a place you have never left.'

Cheryl Bronte thinks of threatening to book him for wasting police time but contents herself with saying that she'll see him again. Barry says that will be nice. She walks away with as much dignity and elegance as she can manage and Barry remains at the wheel of Enlightenment and tries to get some sleep.

*   *   *

Street Sleeper was also dedicated to my then wife, my now

80

ex-wife. When we got divorced I felt no need to remove the dedication. We had more going for us than a shared enthusiasm for Volkswagens, but that was not the least of what we had in common.

We had no car when we were first married, and I couldn't even drive, but we bought a Volkswagen and I learned. In retrospect I don't really know why we bought a Beetle. We needed a cheap car but we decided we wanted something soulful, and we thought about buying a Mini or even a Morris Minor, but the Beetle got the vote. I wouldn't do it now. These days I'd buy something cheap and soulless, an old but reliable Volvo or a newish and very cheap Lada or Skoda. But I was young, naive and newly married.

The car we bought, from a slightly too distant acquaintance of my father, turned out to be a lemon. The starter motor only worked intermittently, we once broke a clutch cable in the middle lane of a crawling traffic jam on the M1, and the engine eventually blew up. We seemed to spend a lot of time parked on the hard shoulders of motorways waiting in the rain for the AA van to arrive; but even that failed to turn me against Volkswagens.

We eventually got rid of the car but by then I was 'into' Beetles, indeed I had started writing *Street Sleeper*. We went to a number of Volkswagen meetings and events and we had a very good time, and by then we were a little more affluent and we decided to buy a Volkswagen Karmann Ghia. This is basically a Beetle in a fancy Italian suit. It consists of a more or less standard Beetle chassis, but wrapped around it is a superb, elegant, streamlined body. It looks like a real sportscar, but the Beetle engine ensures it is not. It was a car that I'd admired and idly lusted after since I was a boy, and I still tend to think it's one of the best-looking cars ever made. My wife loved them too. We searched long and hard for a good secondhand Karmann Ghia, and eventually we picked a good one. And that's how things were when *Street Sleeper* was published.

The author biography on the first edition says, 'Geoff Nicholson is married, lives in Kent and drives a Type 1 Karmann Ghia.' All this has now changed.

In working out the divorce 'settlement' my wife got custody of the Karmann Ghia. I was sorry to say good-bye to it, but it seemed fair enough, and one or two people had always offered the opinion that a Karmann Ghia was something of a lady's car.

Getting divorced was a surprisingly quick and unbureaucratic process. My wife and I were hardly the best of friends during this process but we were civil, and we met once in a while for a drink. It even occurred to me that we might have dinner together on the day our decree became absolute, as a sign of our maturity or urbanity or some such nonsense.

However, on that day my wife, to be precise my ex-wife by a matter of some hours, went to visit her grandmother who was in an old people's home in Kent. The grandmother, for whom I had a lot of affection, suffered from a whole collection of illnesses, the most visible of which was Parkinson's disease. She was unable to fend for herself physically, but when she first went into the home she was perfectly compos mentis. On that day when my wife went to see her, the old lady was confused and distressed beyond recognition. She looked drugged, miserable and helpless. My wife had a fierce and frustrating argument with members of staff about the fact that this home of theirs was responsible for her grandmother's rapid and pathetic decline. It was not an argument she could possibly win. She stormed out in tears, got into her Karmann Ghia and drove away. At the first set of traffic lights she had to make a right turn across a dual carriageway of fast-moving vehicles. She was upset, her mind was elsewhere, her timing was bad, and she misjudged the speed of the oncoming traffic. As she made the turn across the carriageway a car ploughed into the front and side of the Karmann Ghia, demolishing it and making it an insurance write-off. The car was woefully under-insured.

That this should happen on the day our divorce was final-ised is, I suppose, a surprising though hardly devastating coincidence. Certainly it might be thought appropriate that my wife rid herself of the car and of me on the same day, although if you presented that as fiction I think it might seem a little too glib and facile. Besides, given the state of our marriage, she was by then far fonder of the Karmann Ghia than she was of me.

The next weekend she went out and bought a perfect, immaculately restored Volkswagen Karmann Ghia from a specialist dealer a little way out of Southend.

IV

Whose Volkswagen Is It Anyway?

Debby's car pulls up beside Enlightenment. She gets out looking brisk and business-like, and homes in on Barry who is still sitting at the wheel of his car. She throws open the passenger door and gets inside. Barry is about to offer a few words of greeting and endearment but she has no time for that. He sees that she's holding, nay brandishing, two manila envelopes. Her sense of purpose is awe-inspiring, but as yet he can't begin to guess what that purpose is.

Very determinedly she says, 'I've been doing some thinking, Barry, and here's what's going to happen. I'm going to give you the first of these envelopes. You're going to open it and then I'm going to ask you a question. You'll give a simple yes or no answer, and that answer will determine whether or not I give you the second envelope. Do you understand?'

'Er, yes.'

It seems pointless to say anything else, so he takes the first envelope. It feels as though it contains a small booklet, and he opens it up to discover that the booklet is a passport, and not just any old passport, but *his* passport, at least a passport in his name with his photograph inside. He is both surprised and affronted. How could she go behind his back like that? Okay, so she may have owned a photograph of him, but she must have filled in a passport application form without consulting him, must have even forged his signature. He thinks he has every right to feel angry and abused, but

84

something in Debby's face tells him it would be inappropriate and pointless to tell her this.

'Now for the question,' she says. 'Will you leave this caravan and come travelling with me?'

'What?' says Barry. 'When? Where to? What will we do for money?'

'A one word answer,' says Debby. 'Yes or no.'

In normal circumstances he would be very happy to answer with a good many prevarications and hesitations, but he can tell that Debby in her current mood wouldn't wear that. With great reluctance, the reluctance being because he doesn't want to have to answer, he has to answer, 'No.'

'In that case,' says Debby, 'you get to open the second envelope.'

She hands him the second manila envelope and while he's still struggling to open it, she's got out of Enlightenment, got into her own car and driven away. He takes out a single, small sheet of paper, but by the time he's read the message written on it, it's more or less superfluous. It says,

Goodbye Barry. I'm off.
If you want me back you could always get in your car and find me.

One night she's there again. It's late. Fat Les is working alone in the garage on a Baja style Beetle, fitting Desert Dueller tyres to a set of aluminium wheels, and sanding down the body kit ready for spraying, when he hears the clack of high heels approaching, and he stops what he's doing, looks up and sees Detective Inspector Cheryl Bronte standing in his space. The harsh overhead light is unflattering. It makes her look older and more lined, but it also makes her look harder and more formidable.

'Hello Les,' she says.

'Yes?' he says.

'That's an ugly looking thing you're working on there,' she says nodding at the Beetle.

'Well, it's all in the eye of the beholder, isn't it?' Les replies.

'I've never like Beetles much,' she says. 'I don't know why. I guess I've always found them too small, too slow, too noisy, maybe just a little too strange for my tastes.'

'Am I supposed to be interested in this?' Les asks.

'I thought you were interested in Beetles, that's all,' she says and she wanders around the workshop. She is keen to appear casual, curious, unsystematic. She wants to make it clear that she is not doing anything so unsubtle as looking for clues. She picks up and considers some spare parts that are lying around on shelves and benches; a set of braided, stainless steel ignition leads, coloured window seals, some chrome push rod tubes. She appears to find them fascinating.

'You see Les,' she says, 'I have a theory about you.'

'Well, I'm flattered,' he says sarcastically.

She doesn't react. She says, 'My theory is that you're the one blowing up Volkswagens.'

'Is that a theory?' Les asks. 'It sounds more like an unsubstantiated allegation to me.'

'You're full of surprises, aren't you, Les?'

Les doesn't rise to that one.

She continues, 'I think it might all be about mid-life crisis, the male menopause, waning sexual powers, that kind of thing.'

'Oh really?'

'About the fact that you're socially retarded, about being stuck in a perpetual adolescence. I mean, think about it, the Beetle is a car of the young, and let's face it Les, young, you're not.'

'I never was.'

'My theory, my assertion, is that you see all these kids coming through this place, all with money and ideas, having their cars tarted up, going out partying, raving, getting high, getting laid, and it makes you feel very jealous. Why wouldn't it? Anybody might feel the same. Anybody might get angry and resentful. The difference is, you want to destroy. You want to destroy Volkswagens.'

'Why would I want to destroy the thing I make my living out of?'

'Men always destroy the thing they love.'

'I don't love 'em. I just make a living out of them.'

'That's what you say. Volkswagens are nothing special to you. You're not obsessed by them, you're not hung up on them.'

'Too bloody true.'

'You don't fool me Les.'

'You don't fool me, either,' Les barks, finally losing his rag. 'Okay, you've told me your bloody theory, now arrest me or leave me alone.'

'It's not just a theory,' she says softly.

'This is fucking silly,' says Les. 'You don't know anything about me, and what you think you know is completely wrong.'

'You wish,' she says.

'You're crazy,' says Les. 'What possible evidence have you got against me?'

'You don't seriously think I need evidence do you? I just know. Call it instinct, call it a gut feeling. Sometimes I think it's more like a sixth sense, a kind of precognition.'

Les is looking and feeling like a cornered rat. How can he prove his innocence to someone who has established his guilt through extrasensory means?

'Besides,' says Cheryl Bronte, 'you're a fat bastard and I don't like the look of you. I'm coming for you Les. I know where you live. I'll see you again.'

Marilyn does not want to believe that her father is the kind of man who would kidnap her current boyfriend and then blow up one of his cars. But she realises that the fact she doesn't want to believe it is neither here nor there. She'd rather believe that her father is safe, sober and well-balanced, but he is clearly none of the above.

If her father was going to kidnap anyone surely it ought to be Barry bloody Osgathorpe. He was the one who drove her father insane. There would be some logic, some sense in taking revenge on him. But why Carlton? Just because he collects Volkswagens? It seems reasonable enough that her father should hate Volkswagens after all that he's been through, but that hardly justifies kidnapping Carlton. And how would her father know that Carlton was a collector? How would he know that Carlton even existed? How would he know he was her boyfriend? Well actually it has been in one or two gossip columns, if her father was allowed to read gossip columns in the asylum, but still . . .

He's out there right now, somewhere, who knows where, and what the hell is he doing? Sleeping in ditches, in shop doorways? And how is he managing to live? By begging? By stealing? She tries to picture it, but mercifully she can come up with nothing.

Ever since Carlton disappeared she has been staying in his house rather than her own place. The fact that his house is a rambling gentleman's residence while hers is a studio flat has nothing to do with it, she insists. She feels safe here. There is a high wall around the garden, closed circuit cameras that pick out wanted or unwanted guests, a wrought iron security gate that can only be opened from within the house; not that any of that was enough to save Carlton.

She meanders slowly from one room to another, looking at the diversity and profusion of his Volkswagen collection. It all feels special to her. It's all so terribly Carlton. And yet without him it seems so inert, like a deserted museum, a burial chamber. But she needs to be there in case Carlton returns, or in case someone delivers a ransom note, or in case the police suddenly solve the crime (which seems totally unlikely), or in case the worst happens, the worst still being mercifully undefined. She doesn't understand the police. She has been interviewed twice by this Cheryl Bronte woman, but the interviews haven't been much more than general, perfunctory little chats. The woman seems barely interested, doesn't even seem wholly convinced that Carlton has actually been kidnapped. Marilyn doesn't see why they can't launch a vast nationwide media campaign, get every person in the land to go searching through basements and sheds and disused buildings, looking for her Carlton. Failing that, they could always put out a wanted poster for her father, not that she's told the police that she suspects her father might be behind it all, that would be giving too much away.

She continues broadcasting her weather reports from the television studio. They seem considerably more poignant now that she thinks her father is out there exposed to the elements. Sometimes she finds it hard to be vivacious. And then one day in the newsroom she overhears a reporter arguing with a producer.

The reporter says, 'I don't see how we can justify sitting on this one. If nothing else, if we reported it we might save a life or two, at least prevent some property damage.'

'The gag is coming from a very high source,' says the producer.

'Anti-terrorist?'

'Yep.'

'Well they're a bunch of drama queens. Look, these cars are being blown up all over England – at least fifty to date. And we're supposed to pretend it's not happening?'

'We're not pretending anything. We're just not reporting it. We're helping the authorities in their battle with terrorism, that's all.'

'Oh please.'

'Look, if we report that somebody's going around blowing up these things, then every would-be terrorist, vandal and general nutter is going to start copycatting. At the very least

89

you're going to spread panic. Every arsehole who owns a Volkswagen Beetle is going to think his car's about to go bang.'

Marilyn listens and weeps. Oh God, it all fits. It must all be true. Until now she might just have believed that her father wasn't behind it all, but now . . . She takes the reporter aside, makes him tell her everything he knows. She listens carefully, takes it all in. What she has to do next is perfectly clear to her.

That night she bounces onto the television screen looking slightly more manic than usual. Behind her the computer map of England has gone hallucinatory, blurring into acidic yellows and fuzzed electric blue.

She looks at the map and says, 'In the south of England there have been intermittent explosions of Volkswagen Beetles. And there have been similar outbreaks in the Midlands and the North-East. Showers of broken glass and twisted metal have been affecting the South Coast, and the pattern seems to be spreading and becoming prolonged. Things are pretty unsettled and the outlook isn't very bright.'

She stops for a moment, fights back the tears, struggles to find the right words.

'Dad,' she says, 'if you're out there, if you're watching, please don't blow up any more Volkswagens. What do you say?'

The floor manager was quite right. The audience for Marilyn's nocturnal weather forecasts is not large. But one person who is still insomniac enough to be watching is Fat Les. He knows Marilyn and her father from way back and he doesn't for a moment think her words are going to have any effect on crazy Charles Lederer, but they do have a profound effect on him. He immediately knows what he has to do. He has to go and re-establish contact with Barry Osgathorpe, maybe even with Ishmael.

*

90

Barry is asleep at the wheel when Fat Les arrives. The caravan site is quiet. The weather is fine, a relief after all the rain they've been having. Les has chosen a special vehicle for this trip, one of the cars he has for sale at Fat Volks Inc, a burnt ochre Beetle roadster conversion, with a milk chocolate-coloured velour interior and tonneau cover, American eagle centerlines, Monza exhaust and a louvred engine lid. It looks slick and sexy. It does not match Fat Les's personality in any way.

Les has been driving for several hours, growing ever more tense and impatient. This is an important mission he's on. The site has taken some finding. Once there, he does a noisy circuit around the caravans, barbecue areas and children's playground while looking for Barry. But it's obvious who he's come to see, and a group of little kids point the way without even being asked. The noise of Les's car fails to rouse Barry, so Les has a moment or two to examine Enlightenment. He kills the engine of the roadster, gets out, peers closely. It was Fat Les who rebuilt and customised Barry's wicked-looking vehicle and it appears that his handywork has held up pretty well, although he doesn't understand why there's a bad rendition of a Beetle and the initials GB painted on it.

When he's finished having a good look at the car he reaches in through the open car window and shakes Barry awake. Barry stirs disorientatedly from a deep sleep, and when he opens his eyes and sees Fat Les's plump, sweaty features no more than two feet away from him, his first thought is that he must still be dreaming. It is not a very pleasant dream. The face of Fat Les is one that he thought he would never see again.

'You've got to help me,' Les says while Barry is still rubbing his eyes.

'What?'

'The heat's closing in,' Les continues. 'They're out to get me. They want to lock me up and throw away the key.'

Barry, only gradually becoming convinced that he is actually awake, shoves open the car door and climbs out. He walks up and down, trying to shake himself into alertness.

'Who's out to get you?' he asks.

'The pigs,' says Les, as though that's perfectly obvious.

Barry blinks and scratches himself. He's not quite ready for this level of intensity and paranoia.

'Long time no see,' he says as a stalling tactic. 'How've you been, Les?'

'Okay till now.'

'Why are they after you? Why are they going to lock you up?'

'Because of the exploding Volkswagens.'

'Oh, that old thing.'

'You know about this?' Les demands.

'No, not really,' says Barry. 'People assume I ought to, but actually I don't. And really I don't want to.'

'That's all right for you.'

'Yes it is.'

'But not for me. They think I'm the one doing it.'

'Are you the one doing it?'

'No!' Les insists.

'Then why do they think you are?' Barry asks.

'Because they're pigs.'

Barry isn't finding this a particularly fascinating conversation. He'd rather be asleep than talking with Fat Les, but he attempts to be sympathetic.

'Look at it this way Les, the fewer cars there are in the world, the more chance we have of saving the planet.'

'I just want to save my own skin,' says Les.

'Well that's a little short-sighted of you, isn't it?'

Les isn't enjoying the conversation very much either. He remembers that Barry always had a penchant for the naive and gnomic utterance but this is ridiculous.

'Look,' says Les fiercely, 'it's not me doing it.'

'I never said it was,' Barry replies reassuringly.

'But I reckon I know who is.'

'Then you should tell the police.'

'No. We've got to find him first.'

'We?'

'You and me Barry. The old firm. We used to be a great team. We used to be able to do wonders. We can find bloody Charles Lederer and turn him in.'

'Charles Lederer?'

'Yeah. It's Marilyn's old man who's doing the blowing up.'

The very name of Marilyn Lederer still holds an overwhelming allure and fascination for Barry. She's the real thing. Debby was a perfectly serviceable everyday kind of girlfriend but as an object of fantasy and desire she couldn't possibly compete with the distant and unattainable Marilyn. Just thinking about her now he comes over all misty-eyed, which is a source of considerable irritation to Fat Les.

Les says, 'If Marilyn thinks her old man's doing the bombing then that's good enough for me.'

'Does she think that?'

'Yeah.'

'You've spoken to her?'

'No, but I've seen her on the telly.'

'Television?'

Les explains that she is a late night weathergirl on a satellite channel. Barry thinks he might faint. The very idea that images of his dream girl are being beamed through the ether is almost too much to bear. But that's of no interest to Fat Les.

'You see,' he says, 'if we can find her old man and beat a confession out of him and hand him over to Cheryl Bronte, then I'm in the clear, right? But we're going to have to be smart. We'll have to use all our wits to work out where he is, then hunt him down and trap him like a dog.'

'No,' says Barry quietly.

'Come on Barry, I'm prepared to beg if I have to.'

'That would be undignified,' says Barry. 'And it wouldn't work.'

'You want me falsely accused? Arrested? You want me thrown in jail?'

'No, not particularly,' says Barry. 'But, you know, I really don't give a lot of thought to what happens to people like you, Les.'

Actually, Barry is thinking about how he can get to see some of Marilyn's television broadcasts. He thinks he might buy a satellite dish, a television, and, of course, a video recorder so he can tape her performances and watch them over and over again in the privacy of his own caravan.

'You're being a real shit, Barry,' says Les.

'I never claimed to be anything else,' replies Barry.

For a moment it looks as though Fat Les is about to hit him, but Barry looks so weak, so ineffectual, there'd be no joy in it. Les spits a lump of phlegm onto the bonnet of Enlightenment. It lodges just below the Green Beetles logo. Barry does not react.

'You see,' Barry says solemnly, 'a journey of a million miles begins with a single step.'

Fat Les looks blank. Then Barry takes three steps towards Enlightenment, gets inside and returns to his pose of meditative calm in the driver's seat. Les is disgusted. He goes back to his roadster, guns the engine wildly and scrapes a rear wing against a gatepost as he powers angrily away.

It is quite an occasion for Barry Osgathorpe. For once he is not to be found either in his caravan or at the wheel of Enlightenment. It is one o'clock in the morning and he is in the clubhouse of the caravan site. This is a place he normally stays well away from. It is a large, unhomely barn of a place, with plastic tables and stacking chairs and a small stage in one corner where country and western acts perform every Friday and Saturday evening.

Now the place is empty, but Barry is still, in a sense, there to be entertained. The clubhouse has satellite television, and Barry has obtained special permission from Sam Probert, the owner of the site, to be there alone after hours and to watch the weather forecast. Of course Sam Probert thinks Barry is raving mad, but he is not the first to have thought that.

Barry sits on the edge of his seat, watching the big wall-mounted TV screen, waiting for the end of the current pro-. gramme. Suddenly there's a tap at one of the clubhouse's uncurtained windows. Barry leaps up in surprise and is then alarmed that some disturbance might prevent him from seeing Marilyn's appearance. But he looks over at the window and sees the face of the little boy who calls himself the Ferrous Kid.

'Let me in,' the Kid mouths through the window.

Irritated, flustered, and keeping one eye on the television screen, Barry goes to the door and lets the Kid in.

'What are you doing?' the Kid asks.

'Watching television.'

'I thought this place closed at midnight.'

'Usually it does. There's a programme I have to see.'

'Don't tell me, some sort of environmental special, right?'

'Well, the environment certainly comes into it,' says Barry. 'Why don't you shut up and watch?'

The Kid does as he's told. The pair of them sit there, staring up at the television set, experiencing their different types of anticipation. Then all at once Marilyn fills the screen and her voice is saying. 'Tomorrow will be sunny in eastern areas but cloud and showers over exposed western districts will spread across the country during the day. Cloud will thicken in the north . . . '

But Barry is not at all interested in the words, he's just absorbing the image, the iconography. She is lovely, shimmering and perfect. He's tried denying it. He's tried wishing it away, but the fact remains he's still as totally obsessed with her as ever. He loves her more than he can possibly express. At the very end of the forecast she says goodbye and winks at the camera. It feels as though it's meant specially for him.

When the commercials start Barry says to the Kid, 'What do you think?'

'I don't know,' the Kid replies. 'You can never rely on these weather forecasts.'

'I don't mean the weather,' Barry says. 'I mean what do you think of *her*?'

It's only then that the Kid understands. He realises she must be the one who has figured so largely in some of Barry's traveller's tales. Actually, he finds her a bit ordinary. He had been expecting something more, but he decides to be encouraging for Barry's sake.

'She's great,' he says. 'She really revs my engine.'

'Mine too,' says Barry, completely forgetting about the ecological dangers of a really revved engine.

Marilyn sits off camera. A make-up girl fusses around her face, even though there has been almost no time for it to become disarrayed. Marilyn thinks her performance tonight was a little lack-lustre. In fact it's been lack-lustre for a while. How could it be otherwise? Her boyfriend has disappeared and her renegade father is blowing up Volkswagen Beetles. But the show must go on, and she has stopped inserting daughterly messages in her weather forecasts. It was a pragmatic decision. It did no good. She has spoken again to the reporter who wanted to break the exploding Beetle story and he has told her that it's still going on and that the gag is still in place. Perhaps her father has never even seen her broadcasts. Now more than ever she craves prime time.

She feels impotent. She feels desperate, desperate enough to try one last, high-risk gambit. She doesn't know exactly how she expects it to work. She can't even be sure it will help at all, but she has made up her mind. She's going to see Barry Osgathorpe.

She drives all night. The motorways are dark and littered with roadworks. She runs through all her Suzanne Vega cassettes in the course of the drive. She arrives in Filey a little before dawn, but it is light by the time she locates the site and Barry's caravan.

She doesn't bother to knock. She simply tries the door and finds it open. She enters quietly, not wanting to wake him yet. He lies there in a cocoon of tangled, frayed, grey sheets. She looks at him closely. Yes, she can still sort of see why she once agreed to sleep with him. Her tastes have moved on a little since then, but it won't be entirely disagreeable to do it again. She sits on the edge of the bed and strokes his head, just gently enough to bring him out of sleep. His eyes open, he looks at her and he doesn't even seem surprised to see her.

'You came,' he said. 'I had a feeling you would.'

'Did you?'

'Yes. Life usually brings a man those things he most truly needs.'

'Well, good,' she says.

'I used to think I didn't need a weathergirl to know which way the wind blows, but now I see it differently.'

Even given Barry's penchant for eccentric behaviour, Marilyn is taken aback by this reception. Surely he has a duty to be surprised.

'No doubt you need me too,' he continues, 'otherwise you wouldn't be here.'

'Well yes, there's something you can do for me. You can find my father.'

'It'll mean going back on the road, won't it?'

'Of course.'

'I wouldn't do that for just anyone.'

'I'm not just anyone.'

'Yes, I'd do it for you.'

'There's even a reward,' she says.

'Yes?'

A moment later she is in bed with him, and minutes after that, torrents of hot semen are coursing like molten lava down Marilyn's moist, yielding, eager throat. Barry is impressed. He thinks she must quite like him. And later that same day Enlightenment has fresh tyres, a new battery and is full of petrol. The whitewashed Green Beetles logo has been carefully sponged away. Barry is wearing a familiar blue leather motorcycle suit and he looks every other inch a Road Warrior. He sits in the driver's seat, starts the engine. A fog of choking, dirty blue exhaust fumes expands behind the car. Barry doesn't give a shit. He guns the engine some more. A group of children comes running and congregates around the car. 'Where are you going Barry?' the Ferrous Kid asks, and Barry replies, 'Call me Ishmael.' He floors the accelerator, lets in the clutch, and he's on the road again.

* * *

Here is Charles Manson living at the Spahn Movie Ranch; a permanent, though rundown, movie set in the style of a cowboy town. It consists of one main street, with the façades of a jail, a café, a funeral parlour. Occasionally the set is used by makers of TV commercials or moderately ambitious porn movies. The only things that look out of place here, and not at all cowboy town, are half a dozen or so stolen Volkswagen dune buggies parked a little way off the main drag.

Manson has moved his whole extended family out here, and they receive a lot of company; mostly outlaw biker types who belong to chapters with catchy names like Satan's Slaves or the Straight Satans. Manson is free with his food and dope, and the girls in the family will do just about anything he tells them; 'anything' meaning, in general, that they're extremely willing to have sex with unhygienic guys they've never set eyes on before.

Out here at the edge of the desert, Manson has decided that things are going to get fairly Apocalyptic before too long. Helter Skelter is on its way. There'll be an armed uprising by the blacks, who will slaughter millions of white folks, take over America, and then not too much later, realise they've been damned fools, recognise that Charles Manson is both God and the Devil incarnate, and invite him to become their leader.

In order to lie low during those years of conflict and turmoil, Manson has arranged a hideout in Death Valley, at the Barker Ranch, but he needs a means of getting there when all Hell breaks loose. Until now he has always favoured old school buses à la Ken Kesey as family transport, but he knows that not any old vehicle will make it through the rough desert terrain to the hideout. He needs something special, namely a fleet of Volkswagen dune buggies.

There are all sorts of practical reasons for choosing Volkswagens. They're rugged and reliable, and they're small enough to get through tight gorges and caverns where police vehicles can't follow. With special outsize gas tanks they'll have a range of a thousand miles or so, and if the going gets really tough, they're light enough that two or three people can pick them up and carry them. Manson imagines a whole fleet of them, some loaded up with food, some with dangerous drugs, some with ammo. He sees them charging through the desert in V formation, himself at the front like Rommel, churning up the earth, a cloud of thick dust obliterating the world behind them.

But there's more. Manson, not usually much of a reader, has been studying his Bible, and it's all in there, all this stuff about the significance of the dune buggy, right there in the

Book of Revelation. The dune buggies are going to have breastplates of fire, in other words they're going to be horses of the Apocalypse, you dig? And the Beetles, who've recorded the song 'Helter Skelter' for their *White Album*, will be the horsemen. And there'll be a fifth Beetle, no not George Martin, but Manson himself. And of course in England a Volkswagen Bug is called a Beetle, so you see it all makes sense, right, motherfucker?

Manson starts to live out more of his fantasies. He sets up a production line behind the Spahn Ranch, which he calls the Devil's Dune Buggy Shop. Volkswagens are stolen from town, taken to the ranch, stripped down, converted into vehicles of the Apocalypse. Some of them can be bartered for drugs and weapons, and he hopes they'll be useful in some of his other fantasies, like kidnapping busloads of schoolgirls, raiding a military arsenal, murdering a few rich pigs.

Pride of the fleet is Manson's own Command Vehicle. It is one Hell of a dune buggy. It looks both futuristic and ancient. There is a 'magic sword' sheathed in the steering column, locks of human hair tied round the roll bar, a sleeping platform, armour plate, a machine gun mounting, a fur canopy. It has been recently resprayed, then desert sand thrown onto the paint while still wet, to form a kind of camouflage.

When the whole shooting match is over, this Command Vehicle will be displayed at a car show in Pomona, California, and get a lot of admiring attention from the custom Volkswagen fraternity.

It is July 15, 1969 and Officer Breckenridge of the Los Angeles Sheriff Office is making a routine helicopter patrol flight over the desert, looking for . . . well, for anything that doesn't look quite right. And he passes over the Spahn Movie Ranch and sees three Volkswagen floorpans lying below in the desert. It looks to him as though somebody down there is seriously

100

into car theft and stripping down. He makes a note to take a closer look at ground level before too long.

But a few stripped Volkswagen chassis out in the desert, well it hardly looks like the crime of the century. It will be a month before he organises a police raid, quite a hectic month for the Manson family, a month in which the Hinman-Tate-LaBianca murders will take place. Manson and his family will indulge in murder, in the slashing and shooting and strangling of seven Los Angeles 'piggies'. There will be pierced lungs, lacerated necks, the death of an unborn child. Words will be scrawled on walls in the blood of the dead. It will all be the devil's business. People will talk of Satanic murder, as though there might be such a thing as Godly murder.

And here in the aftermath, when every newspaper and magazine and television channel has covered the murders, is one Mrs McCann thinking about her missing daughter whom she knows was a member of the Manson family. To Manson, the daughter was known as Malibu Brenda and she was with him all the way from the beginning to the end of the madness. Mostly Mrs McCann prefers not to think about all the things her daughter must have done while in that man's clutches. That it involved weird drugs and weirder sex she has no doubt; and she knows that violence, Satanism and murder were also on the menu, but there are limits to how much chapter and verse she can take. However, when Manson makes the cover of *Life* magazine, even she finds it hard not be interested.

Her relationship with Brenda had always been a difficult one, but she always tried to understand, to be, you know, permissive. She didn't even mind too much when Brenda relieved her of her ocelot coat; after all, she might need it for those cold desert nights.

But suddenly, here's Mrs McCann perusing *Life* magazine and there are pictures of Manson and the family and of the

101

Manson Command Vehicle, and she sees with horror that the vehicle's canopy is made from the very fur coat that her daughter stole from her. She is speechless. Her heart suddenly hardens. There are some things, many things, you might forgive a daughter, but turning your best ocelot fur coat into a canopy for a dune buggy of the Apolcalypse is surely not one of them.

That same fur canopy is another of the relics that is supposedly to be found in Carlton Bax's locked room.

V

Gravity's Volkswagen

On the shores of Loch Ness a junior road safety officer parks his maroon, 1971, Beetle, gets out, locks up and ambles down to the water's edge. For a long time he scrutinises the ripples puckering the loch's surface and concludes that he does not believe in monsters. He decides to return to his Volkswagen and feels in his trouser pocket for the keys. They are not to be found. Maybe he's dropped them, or maybe he's left them in the ignition and locked himself out of the car. He doesn't want to admit this second option so starts searching the ground at his feet, thereby missing the sight of his car exploding; although he certainly hears it, and a flying wing mirror narrowly misses his left ear.

At a DIY warehouse on the ring road outside Norwich, a fifty-five year old ex-merchant seaman, now an Inspector of Taxes, parks his gold and black Beetle and enters the store to buy tiles, grouting, a new set of screwdrivers, five litres of brilliant white vinyl emulsion and a pair of dimmer switches. He likes to browse, and also has a debate with himself about whether to have plain white dimmers or to go for the brass versions. Consequently he's in the store a good forty minutes, and when he comes out there's very little left to see of his exploded Beetle.

In Tideswell, in Derbyshire, a young couple – he's a rep for a kitchen equipment company, she's an aerobics instructor – are being shown round by the owner of a detached, three-bedroomed, stone-built property. He admires the original

103

sash windows and the spacious breakfasting kitchen. She is less sure about the whisper-peach bathroom suite. He asks how big the garage is. The owner says it's plenty big enough for his grey, 1976 Volkswagen Beetle. A moment later he has neither Beetle nor garage.

A traffic warden born in Bombay some forty-five years ago, who knows six languages including conversational Maltese, spots a rusty, cream-coloured Beetle parked on a double yellow line outside a chemist's in St Albans. He assumes the owner, probably young, probably not well off, possibly collecting a prescription, won't be parked for long, so he decides not to issue a parking ticket and he continues on his round. When he gets to the street corner he thinks again, wonders if the car's still there, and decides that if it is he'll go back and give it a ticket after all. When he turns to look, he sees the Beetle burning brightly as a bonfire.

In Central London, Mal and Becky have decided to take the plunge and go to a fetish party in a subterranean nightclub in a dark street not far from Tottenham Court Road. They're lucky enough to find a spot nearby where they can park their white, 1970, Karmann-bodied Beetle convertible, and they enjoy an evening at the club which, although undeniably unique, is perhaps a little less wild than they were expecting. It's two in the morning when they return to their car. It is, of course, a black, smouldering hulk. They wonder if any taxi drivers will stop at this time of night to pick up two people dressed head to foot in black rubber bondage gear.

And so Barry Osgathorpe, now styling himself as Ishmael, begins a new journey into Vastness. The first few hundred miles are a peculiar blend of the nostalgic and the alien. There is something strange about the car and the roads, the feel of driving, the idea of movement, and yet there is something utterly familiar. The sensations are not brand new

104

and yet it has been so long since he experienced them that they arrive fresh and revitalised.

But gradually he gets accustomed to the sensations and they become increasingly pleasurable. The adrenalin starts to flow and he feels the old excitement. He feels the G forces, the acceleration, the electrical impulses moving rapidly through the spinal cord, the increase in muscle tone. He feels alert and in control. Sometimes he even feels like his old self.

He tries to apply understanding and self-discipline as he drives, and on occasions this leads to a very welcome sense of ease and tranquillity. Sometimes the driving is like a form of meditation. There is Mindfulness and detachment, an absence of desire, an end to craving.

Some things have definitely changed in the years since Ishmael was last on the road. There seems to be more of everything: more vehicles, more roadworks, more service areas, more speed restrictions. The traffic patterns have changed. The cars all look so sporty, so futuristic, so Japanese; and they all run on unleaded petrol. (Barry can't actually use unleaded fuel in Enlightenment since it would damage the valves of his old Volkswagen engine, but that's not the point.)

In the lobbies of the motorway services where there used to be kids playing violent and destructive video games, there are now machines that will print business cards for you. Barry supposes this is progress of a sort, though he wonders what kind of businessman gets halfway down the motorway and suddenly decides he needs a new set of business cards.

On the motorways he doesn't see too many Beetles. That's understandable. They may have been designed for Hitler's autobahns but they aren't quite up to the cut and thrust, the sudden accelerations and brakings of modern English motorway driving. But off the motorways, in the heart of England, he's pleased to see there are still plenty of them, more than ever it seems, in all their forms and in all conditions.

He looks hard at people as they drive their cars, and

whereas, if he believed Phelan, he might expect to find faces taut with mania or tension or aggression, in fact he sees ordinary people going about their ordinary business. They are insulated from the outside world. They are perhaps a little inert, a little weary from the strain of concentration but in the main he sees – and this would once have been a most unwelcome surprise – people just like him. In fact there are times when he feels a powerful sense of unity with his fellow human beings. He likes that.

As he travels he sees a few acts of driving insanity, some dangerous breaking of the speed limits, some vicious cutting up, the occasional act of suicidal overtaking, but chiefly he is struck by the enormous good sense of it all. For all the dangers and risks, the frustrations and competing needs of driving, the cars continue to move, the traffic continues to flow. People do, sooner or later, get where they want to go. Sometimes Barry admires and envies other drivers since they have specific destinations and itineraries whereas he has very little idea at all where he's going. Not that he minds. He's on a quest, not a motoring holiday. He has a goal, of course, to find Charles Lederer; but that is something quite different from simply having a destination.

He scans the faces of the hitchhikers waiting on motorway sliproads. He surveys the customers eating in the cafés and fast food outlets and motorway cafeterias. He stands in car parks and shopping malls and city streets and he looks around him knowing that one day he will turn and face Charles Lederer. He knows it is a strange search, a strange process by which the two of them will be delivered to each other, two random particles whose paths must eventually cross, but somehow he knows it will happen.

He no longer expects life to be easy or logical, yet it is still odd to think that whereas he once travelled along these roads looking for eternal verities, he is now simply looking for a strange, disturbed old man who blows up Volkswagens. Well, why not? Times change. The world moves on. You have to go with the traffic flow.

At first he listens to a lot of radio, to the phone-ins and the traffic news and the shipping forecasts, the chart shows and the consumer advice programmes, but after a while he gets bored. It all starts to sound like static, like interference or white noise. He decides to keep the radio turned off and to listen to his own internal sound.

He sees the dead bugs on the windscreen and wonders how a true Zen follower could ever be a motorist. If you believe in reincarnation then every time you drive along the motorway you have no choice but to slaughter hundreds of your ancestors. He tries not to let this bother him. He drives on. He obeys the laws. He sees the signs. He negotiates accident black spots and bottle necks and blind corners. He deals with contraflow systems and sleeping policemen. He pays and displays, he waits here when red light shows, he gives way to oncoming traffic in the middle of the road.

Occasionally he talks to people; to waitresses in caffs, to cashiers in petrol stations, to fellow travellers, but he tries to keep these conversations brief and not to the point. He now knows the value of brevity and superficiality. Where once he might have talked about inner wisdom and the Way, he now prefers to talk about the weather or the price of petrol. This is not because he has abandoned his search for truth and wisdom, but rather because he now knows that these apparently banal conversations contain just as much wisdom as any discussion about God or the meaning of life. He knows that the world can be seen in a grain of sand, so why shouldn't it also be found in a traffic cone or in a couple of litres of overpriced four star? He never asks people to share their personal philosophies with him. And neither does he ever ask anyone if they've seen Charles Lederer. He's on a search but it's not *that* kind of search.

He goes on, crossing and recrossing the country, driving on motorways and A roads and B roads, on urban clearways and country roads and single tracks with passing places, visiting cities and villages, passing through new towns and conurbations and seaside resorts. Sometimes at night he finds a quiet, lonely spot and sleeps in the back of Enlightenment, but Marilyn sent him on his way with a healthy chunk of money, and there are nights that he spends in a motorway Travel Lodge or hotel.

Sometimes he feels lonely. There are times when he wouldn't mind having a little company: and given the choice, he would, of course, always choose Marilyn as his companion. Sometimes he sends her a postcard. She has given him her address and it sounds very fancy indeed. She says she's staying at a friend's place and he's pleased that she has such generous friends. The simple act of writing to her helps stave off the loneliness.

There are also times when he feels a little guilty about using up fossil fuels and polluting the atmosphere in his search, but somehow he can cope with the guilt. The quest is everything. He knows, with an unshakeable certainty, that he will find Marilyn's father. And once he's found him it will all happen. Marilyn will be happy, and then she will surely take him to her heart. She will be grateful and she will love him because of what he has done for her. They will then be happy together; perfected, elevated and enlightened. And if it requires a little bit of air pollution, a touch of global warming, to bring about that end, then so be it.

Barry puts the pedal to the metal and motors on.

Carlton Bax sits in darkness. He is being kept in the dark, in isolation, in captivity. He is blindfolded by bands of hot, thick, woollen cloth, and his hands are tied behind him. His legs are free so that he can stand and he can walk, but there is nowhere for him to go. He has paced the room, measured it out, and it is less than four paces in either direction. There is no chair, no bed. It is an airless place, a basement or cellar he thinks, a place without windows or fresh air, and increasingly it smells of himself, of his bodily waste. At first he thought he would never be able to sleep here because of the cold, the discomfort and his own anxiety, but it is amazing what changes exhaustion can bring.

He tries to listen for clues, something that will tell him where he is; voices perhaps or music or birds, but all he can hear is a distant and unidentifiable rumbling. Food arrives at irregular intervals and at that time someone unties his hands, though the blindfold always remains in place. He feeds himself and uses the slop bucket if necessary and then he's retied and left alone again. The man who brings the food, who unties his hands, never says a word, and yet Carlton feels that he knows his jailer. It is always the same person, a man, someone young but heavy and slow-moving, someone whose breath sometimes smells of cigarettes and sometimes of onions. Occasionally Carlton will try to make conversation but there is never any reply. This is not the one who does the talking. The one who *does* speak, who asks the questions, is someone quite different, someone older, surer of himself, someone far more confident and frightening.

Carlton Bax hasn't been beaten, not really. He certainly hasn't been hurt. He was kicked and punched a little at the beginning, but it felt like a warning not a methodology. And then the interrogation began. A man's voice – dry and strong and very patient – kept asking, still asks, the same things over and over again. And Carlton Bax makes the same replies over and over again.

'Where is it?'
'Where's what?'
'You know what I mean.'
'No I don't.'
'The Volkswagen. Where's the Volkswagen?'
'Which Volkswagen? I own dozens of Volkswagens.'
'You know which Volkswagen.'

'No I don't.'

'I think you do.'

'No I don't.'

'I think you'll tell us sooner or later.'

'I won't. I can't. I don't know what you're talking about.'

And so it goes on, so it repeats itself. A series of meetings, of interviews, interrogations, always the same, the same steady voice with the same questions, Carlton Bax's own voice becoming increasingly plaintive, saying nothing, admitting nothing. Carlton doesn't see where this can go, nor where it will end.

Will they soon begin to beat him in earnest? Will there be torture with cigarettes and ice and electricity? Will they cut off a finger, or a testicle? Will they kill him when they finally decide he isn't going to tell them what they think he knows? And who are 'they'? Are they just criminals? Opportunist kidnappers? Or is there some wider brief, and is his kidnapping part of some greater, grander movement?

Surely, he thinks, there must be people out there looking for him by now; police, his family, Marilyn. He wonders how she is, whether she misses him as much as he'd like her to. He thinks of his gentleman's residence and his magnificent collection of Volkswagen memorabilia, and it all becomes too much to bear. Tears form in his eyes but the black blindfold won't let them fall. It absorbs them completely.

He tries to imagine a future, a time when all this will be over. He walks round the room, slowly but as if with a purpose, and he walks straight into the slop bucket. It falls over. Piss and shit mark the floor of the room like streams and islands; but he cannot see this. He stands motionless now and listens, and he realises that the strange rumbling he can hear, muffled and up above the head, is the sound of heavy traffic.

*

The phone rings. Marilyn answers. 'Hello,' she says eagerly, urgently, hope and desperation twined around her voice. At first nobody speaks at the other end. Could it be? She says, 'Carlton?'

'No. It's me. Ishmael.'

'Oh. Hello Barry. Have you found my father yet?'

'I'm afraid not.'

'Are you getting warm?'

'Well, I could be.'

'Where are you?'

'I'm on the road.'

'Don't be tiresome, Barry.'

'I'm out there. I'm white-lining, I'm on the hard-shoulder, on the speed limit. I'm following my inner directives.'

'And this is going to help you find my father?'

'Let me put it this way, Marilyn; the path of indirections leads to the same destination as the hasty shortcut.'

'Are you on something, Barry?'

'I'm on the road.'

'Of course you are. I know that. Why did I bother to ask?'

'It's all right Marilyn. I'm following a course of random moves.'

'Oh great.'

'It is. You see we're all heading for the same place. All of us. It's just a question of finding where the paths cross. Once I've done that I'll be right where your father is.'

'Is this really going to work, Barry?'

'Yes. It has to. I know that if I don't find your father then you'll think less of me. I couldn't bear to have you think less of me.'

'Stay in touch, Barry,' she says, the hope having largely been erased from her voice, the desperation taking over.

'Call me Ishmael,' he says. 'Please.'

Marilyn soon discovers something of the nature of his random moves. He starts sending her postcards. They reveal a strange and erratic progress. She receives picture postcards

111

of Canterbury, St Ives, Fleetwood, the M52 at Huddersfield. However, the photograph on the front never matches the postmark on the back. A postcard of the Salcombe foot ferry arrives from Staffordshire. A postcard of the Birmingham University Students' Union building is sent from Alnwick. Barry's messages are brief but suitably opaque. 'All roads are one,' he writes, 'with the possible exception of the M18.' He writes, 'Greetings from the crawler lane.' He writes, 'There are serious delays on the motorway to sapience.' Marilyn is getting fed up.

What's worse is that Barry is looking increasingly like her best bet. The police are offering her no joy, no hope, no consolation. Carlton's family assume he is off on some madcap, playboy escapade and will return unharmed. If he'd really been kidnapped there'd be a ransom note, a set of demands. She has mentioned her plight to some of her colleagues at the television company and, to her dismay, nobody thinks there's a story in it. And as if that wasn't enough her producer has been on her back saying she's underperforming. She isn't sparky enough for him any more. What's happened to the old zany extrovert self, he wants to know. As if it isn't obvious.

It is late. Alone in Carlton's gentleman's residence now, Marilyn feels so lonely, so helpless and bereft. As on every other recent evening she is drinking Brandy Alexanders and watching videos of the Herbie movies. It feels like a downward slide.

Then a bell rings. She isn't expecting anyone, and yet she feels that anyone who would be ringing Carlton's bell at this time of night must surely have some connection with him, however vague, and might just possibly offer some clues. A little unsteadily she goes into the hall and looks at the video monitor which gives her a picture of her visitor. She sees a woman standing outside the gate. She is alone. She wears a leather jacket and leggings and a big studded belt. Marilyn doesn't know her at first and yet there's something definitely familiar about her. Marilyn throws the switch that opens the gate and the visitor walk in. Marilyn greets her at the front door.

'Hello, I'm Renata Caswell,' she says.

'My God, so you are.'

'You remember? I'm the one who exposed your friend Ishmael for the dangerous little charlatan he was.'

'I remember it all,' says Marilyn.

'Can I come in?'

'Why?'

'I want to talk to you about Carlton.'

Those are the magic words, the open sesame. If she can't have Carlton, if she can't know that he's safe, then she'll have to make do with talking about him. It will only be a small pleasure but it will be as great as any she's got. Marilyn invites Renata in. They go into the kitchen, a room only lightly marked by Carlton Bax's mania for Beetles. Apart from the Beetle salt and pepper pots, the Beetle mugs, the beetle cookie jar and the Beetle tea towels, it looks like a fairly normal kitchen. Renata can barely hide her disappointment.

'What do you want to say about Carlton?' Marilyn asks.

'I'd like to ask you a few questions about him, that's all.'

Marilyn is desperate to talk about him but she still has the dignity to ask, 'Why?'

'Oh,' says Renata breezily, 'I think I might like to write a piece about him.'

Marilyn looks daggers at her and she drops her breeziness.

'Okay,' she says, 'I know he's gone missing. Maybe I could help. Maybe I could stir public sympathy, stir some public outrage about the fact that the police are doing so little. It just might help to find him.'

'How do you even know that Carlton's missing? It hasn't been in any of the papers.'

'I have my sources.'

'I bet you do. And I bet you have to protect them.'

'Of course.'

113

Nevertheless, Marilyn talks to her about Carlton. She talks about his kindness, how inherited wealth hasn't spoiled him, about certain conflicts he experienced when he refused to toe the line and become another cog in the Bax family empire. She mentions his education and his first unsuccessful marriage. She denies that he was ever a playboy or gambler or self-destructive drinker. Renata jots down a few shorthand notes but she doesn't seem quite as interested as she ought to be if she's really planning to write a campaigning article. All this amounts to little more than background. Surely Renata could have got all this from a cuttings library.

'And what about the Volkswagen collection?' Renata asks.

It's asked politely enough but somehow Marilyn knows that Renata Caswell is more interested in the Volkswagens than in the man; a problem Marilyn has seen before. And when she asks to be shown round the collection, Marilyn fears Renata will be writing another article, the latest in a series, that depicts Carlton as some sort of poor little rich boy, ageing but immature, childishly eccentric, with more money than sense.

'There have been an awful lot of boring articles about the collection,' Marilyn says, but she still agrees to show it to Renata.

The tour begins. Marilyn points out items that she has learned are of interest to visitors: a KdF saver's card; a model of a Beetle made out of cigarette packets by a German prisoner of war who had worked on Dr Porsche's prototypes before the war; a number of pre-war Volkswagen badges designed by Franz Xavier Reimspiess showing the familiar interlocking Volkswagen logo but here it is surrounded by the DAF cogwheel design.

Renata seems intensely and genuinely interested, and Marilyn has witnessed this before too. Carlton was always showing his collection to visiting enthusiasts, and although Marilyn understands this enthusiasm intellectually, she can't exactly share it, and it seems strange to find any such enthusiasm in a woman like Renata.

'Is there a catalogue?' Renata asks, innocently enough.

'A what?'

'I mean there must be a filing system or an archive or a computer disc maybe that lists anything and everything in the collection.'

'How would I know?' says Marilyn. 'It's Carlton's collection, not mine.'

'But surely, a collection of this size . . . '

'I said I don't know.'

'Well, that's a shame,' says Renata, and although Marilyn can't see that it's such a shame, it's about now she realises that Renata Caswell must know a great deal more than she's telling.

'Are you saying that Carlton's disappearance is because of the collection?'

Renata has to ruminate carefully before she says, 'That's what my sources seem to suggest.'

'But I don't understand. How could that be?'

Renata takes a deep breath before saying, 'Well, what if Carlton had some piece of unique Volkswagen memorabilia, something impossibly rare, something utterly priceless that some rival collector would want very badly indeed. And what if that other collector tried to buy it, and what if he begged and pleaded and cajoled, maybe even threatened; but Carlton wouldn't part with it. Well, if he wanted it badly enough he might think the only way to get it was to steal it. But that wouldn't work. Carlton wasn't stupid. If he knew someone wanted to steal something he'd keep it doubly safe, maybe off premises, maybe in some kind of vault, in some sort of locked room. Yes?

'And what if the rival collector was aware of all this. Well, the next step might be to try to locate this locked room and break into it. But locating it wouldn't be easy. You'd need Carlton to tell you where it was, and that's the last thing

115

he'd want to tell you. So someone might pick him up, knock him around a little, tell him he'll be released just as soon as he spills the beans. And if he didn't spill them, then this could go on for a very long time, and this rival collector could get very angry and very dangerous indeed.'

'Is all this true?' Marilyn demands.

'It's what my sources suggest.'

'Do you believe them?'

'I think so.'

'And where does my father fit into all this?'

'Your *father*?'

Something tells Marilyn that she should keep at least some information to herself, so she says no more about her father and nothing at all about Barry. Instead she asks, 'But how could this be? How could anyone want a piece of Volkswagen memorabilia so very badly? What sort of item could possibly be that important or that desirable?'

'That's what I'm trying to find out,' says Renata. 'It's a dirty job, but I could be just the girl to do it.'

Barry pulls into an open air car park in the centre of Petersfield, in Hampshire. It's a Saturday morning and the place is busy with the cars of people doing their weekend shopping. Enlightenment looks a little out of place among the hatchbacks and the Range Rovers, but Ishmael is used to having a car that looks out of place. Indeed he is used to feeling out of place himself. Dressing in a blue leather motorcycle suit doesn't exactly help him to feel accommodated. People have a tendency to stare, to giggle, to talk behind his back. He knows that's par for the course when you're on a Zen quest.

He looks around him. It's all so English, so prosperous, so comforting. He sniffs the air, tries to feel the vibes. Is this the sort of place that he might find Charles Lederer? He is still pondering this when he sees a Volkswagen Beetle making extremely rapid and somewhat erratic progress across the car park. The car is a red Super Beetle, with fat wheels, extended wheel arches and a rather ungainly and unfashionable duck's tail spoiler. It is eye-catching but a bit naff. The car is heading straight for him, appears to be on a collision course, when at the last moment it slows, swerves and screeches to a halt in the parking space beside Enlightenment.

Barry looks towards the car to see what kind of maniac would drive like that, and is a little surprised to find that the driver is barely visible above the top of the dashboard. Barry remains curious as the driver's door pops open and a small, extremely youthful figure emerges. It is the boy from the campsite who calls himself the Ferrous Kid.

'Hi dude,' he says.

'My God,' Barry blurts. 'But you're only nine and a half years old.'

'So?'

'So what in God's name are you doing driving a car?'

'It's not a car, it's a Volkswagen,' says the kid, making a conscious allusion to a well-known Volkswagen ad.

'How come you even know how to drive?'

'My Dad taught me. My Dad has many failings, but in fact he's not bad at teaching people to drive.'

'But it's illegal for you to drive.'

'Hey Ishmael old pal, don't we obey a higher set of laws than that?'

'We? Who's we?'

'You and me Ishmael, we're two of a kind, aren't we?'

'No,' says Barry firmly. 'I'm not a nine and a half year old kid who drives illegally. And as far as that goes, whose car is it anyway?'

'I'm not sure. I mean. I stole it.'

'I think I probably knew that. Why did you steal it?'

'I'm a joy rider,' the kid says confessionally. 'And that's what joy riders do. But you know, I'm not an idiot. I don't go racing in the street, I don't play dodgems with police cars,

117

and I certainly don't run down innocent bystanders. As far as that goes, I don't run down *guilty* bystanders either. I'm a very responsible joy rider.'

Barry isn't sure that this is entirely good news. The notion of stealing cars responsibly is one that he has some trouble with, but he can see no real future in debating the matter.

'But what are you doing here?' he asks.

'I came to see you.'

'Why?'

'I thought you might need help.'

'I don't.'

'Are you sure? I have a good instinct for finding people. I mean, I found you. I could be your right hand man.'

'Wrong. At best you could be my right hand nine and a half year old in a stolen car, which is something I don't need at all.'

The kid looks crestfallen, positively wounded.

'Okay,' he says a touch sulkily, 'if I can't be your right hand man, maybe I could be your disciple.'

Barry shakes his head and looks at the kid severely.

'Listen,' he says, 'I don't need a disciple, and you shouldn't want to become one. Be yourself. Take nobody's word for it. Question everything. Take nothing for granted. Don't trust anyone under twenty-five. Don't follow leaders. Be your own man.'

The kid looks close to tears. 'But I'm only nine and a half years old,' he says.

Barry cannot deny that. He puts a hand on the kid's shoulder and says, 'That's why you should go home to your parents.'

'Back to that poxy campsite? That's not my home. My home is the road.'

Barry is impressed by the kid's passion, though he doesn't see how that can make a difference to anything. The kid can see he's not getting through.

'Okay,' he says. 'I'll stop stealing cars. I'll stop driving under age. Just let me sit next to you as you complete your quest.'

Barry is not made of stone. He has some sympathy for the boy, but he's absolutely certain that driving round England with a nine and a half year old runaway would get him into all sorts of trouble.

He says, 'I tell you what I'll do. We'll find a phone box, call the campsite, tell your parents you're okay, then I'll take you for a quick ride in Enlightenment before dropping you off at the nearest station and packing you off home.'

The kid looks at Barry with contempt. He feels betrayed. He says, 'Sod that for a game of soldiers.' Then, before Barry can say or do anything the kid climbs in behind the wheel of the stolen red Volkswagen and burns away out of the car park. Barry does not pursue him. Neither of them is quite sure whether this is a victory or a defeat.

Here are eight neo-Nazi skinheads in a white Transit van, a van not unlike the one Fat Les uses as his daily transport, although that shouldn't be taken to indicate any shared ideology. The van bowls along the road, erratically, travelling too fast, the engine being gunned mercilessly, the gears being mashed, the tyres leaving skids of rubber at moments of manic acceleration and braking. But considering that the driver, known to his friends as Butcher, has half a dozen cans of extra strong lager inside him, the van's progress perhaps isn't that erratic at all, at least not until they hit a corner. Then Butcher really goes for it. He puts his foot down, swings the wheel hard round to achieve the maximum centrifugal force, whereupon the seven other skinheads in the back go flying. So does their beer, so do their fists and after they've all knocked into each other and called each other cunts and threatened to kill each other, they have a good laugh about it.

These are boys looking for trouble, though some of them

are rather old boys. Fighting is certainly one kind of trouble they like, along with a little shoplifting, car theft, burglary and mindless criminal damage, but scaring people is the kind of trouble they do best, and they *are* genuinely scary. Some are lean as whippets, other are more like bulldogs bred specially for their coldness and viciousness. Their facial expressions indicate fury and dumb insolence. Their necks and temples throb with wild blood. They definitely look the part. But this question of appearance and image is a tricky one and sometimes Butcher worries about it. These days it seems to him, although he wouldn't put it quite this way, that the semiotics of the skinhead look have become all confused. These days there are homosexuals who have skinhead cuts. Christ, there are even dykes who do! He doesn't like it at all. It gets him angry. It makes him want to hit something.

He is also aware that this is not exactly a golden age for skinheads, and he often feels like a man out of his time. He wishes he'd been born a bit earlier, in the days when a skinhead could wear a Crombie and a cravat and carry an umbrella and not be thought a ponce; in the days when you could go down to the local fleapit and see *A Clockwork Orange*; when the police confiscated your boot laces if you went to the seaside on a bank holiday. He thinks it might have been especially ace to live in a time when Desmond Dekker and Max Romeo and the Upsetters and Judge Dread were regularly top of the pops, not that he's ever really worked out why it is that skinheads are supposed to hate black people and yet love reggae.

Up ahead, standing in a lay-by with his thumb out, is some pathetic looking old geezer. 'Hey,' Butcher says to the others, 'this'll be a laugh.' He stops the van and flings open the door for the hitchhiker. 'Get in squire.' Even the most desperate and trusting of hitchhikers might be reluctant to get into a van containing eight drunken skinheads, but Charles Lederer simply says, 'This isn't a Volkswagen, is it?' They assure him it isn't and he gets in.

120

Half an hour later, without stopping, they throw him out of the back of the van. He has been laughed at, mocked, abused, threatened and sprayed with beer. He has been slapped and kicked though not given a serious beating. His weakness, his inability to fight back, has saved him from that. But the skinheads have committed one unusual act of violence to his appearance; they have shaved his head. For all their practice, it hasn't been done very skilfully. There are nicks and cuts on his scalp and there are a few tufts of grey hair that they have missed, but nevertheless, the point has been made.

Butcher drives on feeling somehow more whole after this shared act of comic aggression. Charles Lederer lies at the side of the road, his fingertips exploring his newly bared scalp. He does not look like a real skinhead any more than he looks like a certain kind of homosexual. If anything he looks like a victim of Nazi atrocities, which in a sense he is. But as he lies there on the ground with the lorries rolling by, he wonders if perhaps the time has come to cease being a victim.

The skinheads arrive at a Little Eater family restaurant some way off the A6. At first they don't go inside. It is one of those places with a children's playground, with a climbing frame and a slide in the shape of a baby elephant. The skinheads soon scare off the children playing there and begin having their own robust fun all over the playground. They improvise a game of football with some empty beer cans, but it soon degenerates into rugby, into kick boxing, into all-in wrestling. A harmless Sikh family walk by and are jeered and sworn at. A couple of skinheads climb to the top of the slide and urinate so that a long, narrow waterfall of piss sweeps down it and cascades from the elephant's trunk.

They are too occupied to notice the wicked-looking black

Beetle parked beside the restaurant, and at first Barry, who is inside about to tuck into a ranch style all-American breakfast, doesn't really notice the skinheads either. But eventually he becomes aware of their raised voices and he looks at them through the window, and like everybody else in the Little Eater, he hopes they don't come inside.

These hopes are not realised. They enter the restaurant. They don't wait to be seated. Amid much effing and blinding they descend and sprawl across four tables, light up cigarettes in a non-smoking area and look around them, proud of their capacity to cause offence.

Some customers, the ones who have either finished their breakfasts or not yet ordered, decide to leave immediately. The ones who remain try to pretend that the skinheads are invisible, that there's nothing untoward happening. Barry falls somewhere between these two camps. He can't leave because he's only just started his breakfast, but neither can he make the imaginative leap that would allow him to pretend that the skinheads aren't there.

They meanwhile, after much difficulty, argument, high jinks and obscenity, manage to place an order with the waitress. Essentially they have ordered two of everything, with double orders of chips and extra grease. Now they discover the delights of the squeezable ketchup bottles and squirt each other with long red streams of tomato sauce. They also manage to squirt a family at the next table. The father, as meekly as possible, says, 'Steady on now lads,' is sworn at savagely and immediately escorts his family from the premises. The place is emptying fast, the more so when the skinheads begin mooning and giving Nazi salutes. It is no time at all before the only customers still in the Little Eater are the skinheads and Barry. Barry tries to stay calm. He orders another pot of coffee from the waitress and it arrives soon enough, there being rather few other diners to be served.

It would be impossible to ignore the storms of anarchy and

aggression bursting out on the other side of the restaurant, so Barry doesn't try. He begins to watch the skinheads closely. It is not done out of idle curiosity. It's an active, intrusive sort of watching and soon enough they become aware of Barry's gaze. And then they start looking back, and then they get up from their tables and move over to Barry's. They surround him. They're very quiet now, the lull before all manner of storms.

'What are you looking at?' one of them asks.

'You,' Barry replies accurately enough.

'Why? You fancy us or what?'

'Yeah, he looks like a puff doesn't he?'

'Looks a bit Jewish too.'

'And maybe he's got a touch of the tar brush about him.'

One of them now stands close beside Barry, turns his back, shoves out his backside and farts wetly in the direction of Barry's face.

Barry ignores this and says, 'I'm staring at you because you're spoiling my ranch style all-American breakfast.'

Even they see the funny side of that. They laugh like drains, or at least they pretend to. They enjoy Barry's quip so much that two of them are moved to spit onto his plate where half his breakfast remains uneaten.

'And I'm thinking,' Barry continues without missing a beat, 'you know, given enough time and enough love, I'm sure you people could be turned into decent, warm, likeable human beings. The problem is, I don't *have* that amount of time. So why don't you just go away and leave us all in peace?'

'Who's us all? There's only you here. You're on your own, pal.'

'Ultimately we're all on our own,' says Barry.

'You know,' says Butcher, 'this guy's really starting to fuck me off.'

'The feeling's mutual,' says Barry, and in one movement he picks up the pot of coffee and hurls it so that a hot, black wave of coffee flies through the air at eye level and breaks

123

across the faces of the nearest three skinheads. Barry is already up and running out of the Little Eater, out across the car park towards Enlightenment. The skinheads race after him and he only wins the race by a short head, but that's enough. Now he's in his car, locking the door, starting the engine. The skinheads are furious, delirious with rage. They beat on the windows, kick his doors, but he drives through them at speed, clipping at least one of them with his right front wing. They decide to give chase. They pile into their white van, seething, howling, spitting. Butcher takes the wheel. He shoves the key into the ignition, turns it savagely, floors the accelerator, and absolutely nothing happens. He keeps trying, becoming apoplectic with frustration. He beats his fist against the wheel, against the dashboard, against the roof. Finally he headbutts the windscreen. It hurts like Hell but he doesn't mind that. There is still no starting the van's engine. Barry and Enlightenment are now half a mile down the road.

'Christ!' says Butcher. 'If only everything in life was as reliable as a fuckin' Volkswagen.'

* * *

After I wrote *Street Sleeper* people got the impression that I was 'interested' in Volkswagens. Sometimes I would protest about this and say that I was only interested in Volkswagens in the way that, say, Herman Melville was 'interested' in white whales. But most of the time I let it go. I found that a great many people had had a Volkswagen in their lives at one time or another, they'd owned one or driven one or learned to drive in one or had a boyfriend or girlfriend who'd owned one, and they were all very keen to tell me their Volkswagen stories. I was happy enough to listen, although at the time I had no idea that I'd ever be writing a sequel to

124

Street Sleeper. Some were fairly ordinary motoring stories about breakdowns or difficult journeys or seductions or driving tests, but the following was in quite a different league.

A man called Hilton Cunliffe was in Holland in 1945 with the British Army, driving out the Germans, gradually destroying the sites from which the sub-sonic V1 and supersonic V2 flying bombs were being launched against Britain. Hilton was a traffic marshall and somehow he'd got his hands on a captured Schwimmwagen, the amphibious, military version of the Beetle. His job was simply to drive it back to HQ, but the vehicle wasn't very healthy and it was a long slow journey. The road was rutted and very narrow, barely more than a single track, and a certain amount of other traffic was also using it, so that once in a while a faster-moving army truck headed in the same direction would come up behind him and be unable to get past. When that happened he'd pull the Schwimmwagen over to the side of the road and let the truck go by. This happened many times in the course of the journey, and after a while the pulling over became more or less automatic. As soon as he heard the sound of a truck behind him, he'd pull over without so much as looking round. This happened innumerable times.

So once again he heard what he thought was the sound of another approaching truck, and more or less without thinking, he pulled over; just in time to see a V1 flying bomb 'overtake' him and explode thirty yards up the road.

The above is a true story, at least it's as true as I can make it. The story wasn't told to me directly but came via my friend Steve who worked in road safety in Sheffield. Incidentally, Steve is one of the other dedicatees for *Street Sleeper* and so far we haven't fallen out. When I decided that I wanted to include Hilton Cunliffe's story in this book I asked Steve if he could check the exact details of it; the year, the place in Holland, the name of Hilton Cunliffe's regiment and so forth. Steve tried, but it was too late, Hilton had died in

125

the years between my hearing the story and wanting to retell it.

In 1934 when Ferdinand Porsche signed the contract to develop the German people's car, the Type 60 as it was then known, his design business operated from office premises and he had no workshops. Therefore the prototypes had to be built in the garage of his own home in Stuttgart. The pictures show this to have been a fairly grand place and the garage was no doubt roomier than most. He built both a saloon and a cabriolet version of the Type 60, but in order to distinguish between the two models he called the saloon the V1 and the cabriolet the V2.

This seems somehow significant, though I'm not entirely sure how. The V1 in Porsche's designation stood for Versuch – experimental. The V in Hitler's V1s and V2s stood for Vergeltungswaffe – retaliatory weapon. It's also worth noting that the V1 was known in England as the Doodlebug.

Of course, if it had been a V2 rocket coming up the road behind Hilton Cunliffe, it would have been flying faster than the speed of sound, he would never have heard it, never have pulled over and never known what hit him.

VI

Paint Your Volkswagen

The first skinhead says, 'What if we went down Brick Lane and did over a few Indian Restaurants?'

'It's definitely a possibility,' says Phelan.

'Or,' says another, 'what if we went to a Jewish cemetery and, you know, knocked over a few grave stones and painted 'em with swastikas?'

'Why not?' says Phelan approvingly. 'Crude perhaps, but undeniably resonant.'

They are in a scout hut adjacent to some overgrown allotments somewhere within striking distance of the M25. Phelan is having what he calls a Mission Session. He is instructing, persuading, motivating, setting goals. His audience consists of eight skinheads, the same ones who attacked Barry at the Little Eater and who previously destroyed the New Age travellers' campsite. He tells his charges that they are only one cell of a growing movement, but he flatters them into thinking they are his crack squad, his storm troopers. The room is brightly lit and bare. There is no stage, no podium, no backdrop of Nazi flags. Phelan believes there will be a time for oratory, for the big rally and the triumph of the will. That time is coming soon but it has not arrived yet. For now he chooses to remain low-key, makes one or two allusions to the effect that the Western world is in thrall to a cabal of 'international bankers', but generally remains informal, intimate, a style that is interestingly at odds with the exuberance of the skinheads, and yet he feels wonderfully safe and in control when he talks to them. He feels they are *his* skinheads.

'What about doing over a rap club?' one skinhead says. 'I hate rap music. I hate niggers, of course, but I hate rap music even when whites play it.'

'Well,' says Phelan, 'mightn't it be more interesting to attack a club that was, say, frequented by black drug dealers? That would be morally ambiguous. That would give the liberal press something to think about.'

His audience are not the type to give much consideration to the thoughts of the liberal press, but Phelan sounds as convincing as ever.

'And maybe we could burn some crosses,' one of the skinheads shouts.

The others like this and for a while they become uncontrollably wild and exuberant. After this has died down one says, 'I hear there are these things called gay centres. Fuck knows what they are, but I wouldn't mind smashing one of 'em up.'

Phelan smiles approvingly. He enjoys these little chats. What he likes best is the noble savagery, the instinctive correctness of these young men. He is a thinker. He has theory and ideology behind him. He knows why he wants an end to immigration, to political softness, to social and sexual divergence. The skinheads don't, and yet they've come to the same conclusions as him. They have a natural, unthinking energy that he knows he is too studied to possess. But he can admire it, and he can most definitely use it.

'What about massage parlours?' one of the skinheads shouts. 'I mean, all that sensual massage and hand relief that goes on, that can't be right, can it?'

'No, I don't think it can,' Phelan agrees.

'And what about building societies?' another yells. 'I 'ate fuckin' building societies. And banks. I wouldn't mind doing over a few of them.'

'Ah, usury,' says Phelan, but this rather goes over their heads.

128

Butcher, the gang's driver, has been unusually silent throughout the meeting. He has been looking at his boots, chewing his already chewed-up nails. Phelan doesn't like it when one of his boys has moods. It makes him uneasy. It makes him feel less in control.

'Why so silent, Butcher?' he asks. 'Something wrong?'

Butcher remains surly, and says nothing.

'Come on, Butcher. You can tell me.'

'All right then. I think all these big ideas of yours are crap.'

'And why exactly do you think that, Butcher?'

'Because beating up nignogs and doing over graveyards is all very well, but it's no bloody good if you haven't got reliable transport.'

'I'm not sure that I follow,' says Phelan.

'Look, I'm bloody sick and tired of driving around in that crappy old white van. It keeps letting us down. I want a decent fuckin' set of wheels.'

The others have never given this a moment's thought but they immediately see that Butcher is right.

'And what do you think constitutes a decent set of wheels?' Phelan asks, suddenly the school master.

'A tasty old Jag,' someone says.

'Nah, a Ford Capri.'

'Nah, a BMW,' says another

'Bollocks,' says Butcher with feeling. 'It's got to be a Volks-wagen Beetle.'

'And why's that?' Phelan asks, hoping he knows the answer.

'Because it's a Nazi car, isn't it?' says Butcher. 'Because it's the car Adolf Hitler dreamed up.'

'You know Butcher,' says Phelan, 'sometimes your instinctive grasp of theory leaves me breathless with admiration.'

It is some time before Butcher is certain that Phelan isn't taking the piss.

*

129

The yellow Beetle belonging to Renata Caswell, the one that Fat Les deliberately backed into, stands proudly on the forecourt of Fat Volkz Inc. To say that it now looks as good as new would be a pathetic understatement. It looks better than it ever has, better than when it was first in the showroom. It looks magnificent, resplendent, luminous. This is not so very surprising. This, after all, is what Fat Les does with Volkswagens.

Renata stands admiring her car. Next to her is Phelan and beside him is Butcher. They too are taking great pleasure in looking at Les's handywork. Les, not a man burdened by extravagant modesty, receives their admiration as no more than his due.

'It's seriously nice,' says Renata.

'It's more than that,' says Phelan. 'It's a work of art. And it's even nicer when it's on the house, eh Les?'

Les grunts.

'And like I said,' Phelan continues, 'this could be the start of something very big. Isn't that right, Butcher?'

'Yeah,' says Butcher.

'Butcher and I have plans,' Phelan says. 'More than that, we have hopes, dreams. You can help make those dreams come true, Les.'

'Can I?'

'Yes. You see Butcher needs transport, and so do a few of his mates. So I'd like to place an order with you for eight more Beetles.'

'Eight,' Les repeats.

'Yes. You see Butcher and his pals like to think of themselves as tough guys. You can't see them all piling in and out of the back of Volkswagens every time they do a job, so I'd like them to have one each.'

'I see,' says Les.

'Probably you don't, actually. Today I'm ordering eight, but that's only a start. A time will come when I'll want dozens, scores, thousands. You'll be able to cope with that, won't you Les?'

Les wonders if the guy is joking, or if he's just raving mad. Les looks at Renata, then at Butcher, to see if they're in on the joke, but they both look perfectly serious.

'I have a lot of friends,' Phelan says. 'There are a lot of people who think the way I do. One day there'll be millions of them, and they'll all want Beetles. What do you say Les? Do you want to play Ferdinand Porsche to my Adolf Hitler?'

Les does not particularly want to play anyone but himself, problematic though that sometimes is. Nevertheless, business is business, and he can see there could be some nice margins on supplying a fleet of restored Beetles.

'But we don't want any old Beetles,' Phelan says. 'These eight have got to be very special. That's where Butcher comes in. Butcher knows what he wants. Tell him Butcher.'

Butcher is not good at verbal communication but this is clearly a special occasion and he's trying very hard indeed.

'Yeah, I know what I want. I seen one like it once. It was all black, dead black, all of it, windows, wheels, the lot. And it was dead low and wide, and it looked absolutely wicked. It was being driven by some prat at the time, but it was a great set of wheels and that's what I want.'

'You want Enlightenment,' says Fat Les.

'We all want that,' says Phelan. 'But in the meantime we'll settle for eight wicked-looking black Beetles. Okay?'

It is morning. Barry wakes up. He has spent the night sleeping in Enlightenment. The back seat is formidably uncomfortable but he feels that a little physical discomfort, a little mortification of the flesh, must be good for the inner man, even if it leaves the outer man careworn and with back ache. It was dark when he parked here and after he's sat up and cleared away a patch of condensation from the rear window, he finds that this spot was not quite as lonely or as bucolic as he had thought and hoped. The place is rural enough, being on the edge of a forest, however, in the light of day he sees he is rather close to what looks like a gypsy encampment. There's a group of old vans and buses, the odd ambulance and some derelict-looking but inhabited caravans. Then suddenly the music starts. Barry is not entirely sure what this kind of music calls itself, but it is relentlessly rhythmic, hard-edged, and mechanical, and it is very loud. He thinks it would no doubt be great to dance to if you were out of your head on drugs, but as music to wake up to it's a bit excessive.

Barry is not the complaining sort. He isn't fool enough to go and ask them to turn it down. He knows that the greatest joy of being on the road is that if you don't like your neighbours you can always move on. A certain sort of Zen traveller would argue that ultimately all places are one, but Barry doesn't quite see things that way. He tries to shake the sleep from him, tries to pull himself together and scrambles into the front seat of Enlightenment. He is about to start the engine and drive off to a quieter spot when he sees a man coming towards the car carrying a large tin mug. The man looks formidable. His head is shaved at the sides and he has a long, black top knot tied up with what looks like electrical insulating tape. His age is hard to guess, although he perhaps looks old enough to know better. He has rings through his ears and nostrils, and since he is bare chested Barry sees that he has rings through his nipples too. There are tattoos all over his arms and hands and neck; some quite finely done, of dragons and Celtic symbols, others are crudely drawn names and initials.

Barry watches as this character approaches Enlightenment, unsure what he could want. However, despite his fearsome appearance, he looks friendly enough. He comes right up to the Volkswagen and taps on the window. Barry winds it down and the man proffers the tin mug which Barry now sees contains hot, strong tea.

'For me?' says Barry, although he has to shout to be heard over the music.

'Yeah, of course,' says the man.

'Well, thanks very much.'

Barry takes the mug. The tea inside is scaldingly hot and he has to move the mug from hand to hand so as not to burn his fingers. He is no great fan of hot, strong tea but he takes a drink and tries his best to smile appreciatively, at which point the man sticks a hand of friendship in through the open window and Barry shakes it as best he can while juggling the tin mug.

'The name's Cliff, Planetary Cliff,' says the man. The voice, far from being savage or fearsome, has an educated, well-modulated, home counties ring to it. 'That's my bus over there, the double decker with the scenes from the tarot painted on it, the one that the music's coming from. It's like *Summer Holiday* only New Age, and this is a newer bus, for one man operation, with closing doors.'

'I see,' says Barry.

'And you are?'

Barry says, 'Call me Ishmael.'

'All right, I will.'

He then falls silent so Barry sips the tea again.

'There's plenty more where that came from,' says Planetary Cliff. 'In fact we've just made breakfast. You want to come and have some?'

Barry is never at his best this early in the morning and he doesn't particularly want to have breakfast with this stranger, but he knows the importance of not spurning hospitality, so he accepts.

'That's very kind of you,' he says.

'It's what we're here for,' says Cliff. 'We know how to look after our own.'

Barry gets out of Enlightenment and follows Planetary

133

Cliff the short distance to the camp. He isn't very happy about this instant easy identification of himself as one of Cliff's ilk, but he sees no reason to make a big fuss about it. He soon finds himself sitting around a smoking camp fire as part of a group of New Age breakfast eaters. Names are exchanged and Barry finds it hard to believe that these people really go around with names like Rune and Akio and Windowpane, but he knows too well to argue or to judge. A lot of children and dogs flit hyperactively around the edge of the group. A small, long-haired child of indistinguishable sex pokes Barry in the back of the neck with an old windscreen wiper, and nobody, except Barry, tells him or her to stop. The food is not wonderful. It is a form of grey porridge and it leaves Barry thinking longingly about motorway service station breakfasts.

'God, I hate society,' says Planetary Cliff. 'Don't you?'

Barry isn't sure whether the remark is addressed to him personally or to the air. In any case he says nothing and Cliff is soon speaking again.

'The thing is, I turn my back on society because society turns its back on me. I'm an outcast. I live on the margins. I'm poor, I'm hated by society, but what can you do?'

'Well,' says Barry thoughtfully, 'I suppose you could always get a job.'

Planetary Cliff looks at him fiercely and then breaks out laughing. The others round the fire join in. Barry isn't at all sure what they're laughing at, but at least the laughter feels quite friendly.

Planetary Cliff is still laughing as he says, 'I know what you mean. People call me a dole scrounger, right? But I don't scrounge. I do valuable work. I do a bit of fruit picking, a bit of scrap metal dealing, a bit of soft drug pushing. It's a living, isn't it? How about you?'

'Well,' says Barry, and he isn't at all sure how this is going to be received, 'I'm a librarian by trade.'

This information is received with a second outburst of

mirth. Barry still doesn't see what's so funny, but he feels it's necessary to add, 'I know I don't look much like one.'

'That's right,' Planetary Cliff starts again. 'People look at me and they say, oh yes he's an ex-hippie, he's a middle-class drop out, he's one of the homeless, and all right, to a certain extent that's true, I was middle class, I was a hippie, I am sort of homeless, but the thing is, you can't just look at people and make assumptions, can you?'

'Well,' says Barry, 'I think it might be fair to assume from looking at you that you're not a merchant banker or a barrister or a gynaecologist.'

'Well I wouldn't want to be any of those things would I?'

'I assume not,' says Barry.

'And people say we're dirty, and all right, we *are* dirty. But so what? You'd be dirty too if you lived in a campsite on the edge of a forest with no running water.'

'They do say cleanliness is next to Godliness.'

'Well, let God try living in a campsite on the edge of a forest with no running water. How would he keep clean *then*?'

Barry is aware that after a night in the back of Enlightenment he probably doesn't look his very best, but compared to his breakfast companions he looks positively spick and span. 'Well,' he says, 'God could always check into a travel lodge for the night and have a good scrub down.'

This is apparently the most hilarious thing he has said yet. Several of the travellers choke on their breakfast they find it so funny.

A skinny girl with a lot of tangled red hair and a jewel stuck in the middle of her forehead says to him, 'You're like one of those what you call its, aren't you? One of those idiot savants.'

'I might be a savant,' Barry replies, 'but I do my best not to be an idiot.'

They find that funny too, but something in the tone of their laughter tells him that they also find it wise and true.

135

'You like music?' Planetary Cliff asks him.

Barry is still well aware of the music issuing from the bus and he says, 'Some of it.'

'The way I see it,' says Planetary Cliff, 'the world is impelled by the Universal Sound, which is like emitted by the Original Being, and you know, it's proliferating towards material expression, but at the same time it's withdrawing towards chaos and noise.'

'Well, I'm very fond of Fleetwood Mac,' says Barry, and this completely brings the house down.

'Look Ishmael,' says Planetary Cliff between waves of laughter, 'why don't you join us? We need someone like you, someone with a good sense of humour. It's good to have that when you're travelling. We'll soon be moving on. There's a big shindig called the Gathering of the Tribes, sort of a New Age rave, going to happen up in Yorkshire at the end of the summer. We're on our way there. Why don't you come with us?'

The skinny red-haired girl smiles at Barry imploringly. He imagines there's probably a lot of free love to be had amid the New Age travellers, certainly if the number of children is anything to go by, but no, that isn't what he came on the road to find.

'It's a kind offer,' he says, 'but I have to say no. You see, I'm on a quest.'

'Really?'

'Yes.'

'In that case we understand. You have to follow your own impetus.'

'That's right,' says Barry. 'Also, I really dislike your music, your breakfast's really not very good and I don't like being laughed at all the time.'

Fat Les starts to work. He works long into the night, every

136

night. He strips down and reassembles. He reconditions and tunes up. He modifies and customises, spot welds and resprays. This is the biggest job he's tackled in a long while and it hasn't been easy. Getting eight donor vehicles of the required standard took some ingenuity in itself. But they're lined up in the workshop now, coming ever nearer to completion, being rapidly improved and changed, being made mechanically special and visually wicked. He is smoothing out the wrinkles, the differences, making all eight of them as identical as possible, giving them extra performance, extra pizzazz, making them better than Ferdinand Porsche and Adolf Hitler ever dreamed they could be.

As he works he plays Wagner, and indeed there are times when he feels like a strange, dwarfish creature who is forging something mythical and magical. But more often it just feels like hard work, work that is made harder because Les refuses to let any of his underlings work on these cars. The work goes on in secret behind closed doors. This is his project and he won't delegate this one.

Phelan proves to be a surprisingly easy employer. He is demanding but he doesn't interfere. He tells Les what's required and lets him get on with it. This job is not 'on the house'. Phelan pays in advance and pays a premium.

It amuses Les that Butcher's inspiration came from seeing a car that could only be Enlightenment. That vehicle was his masterpiece and none of these current eight machines will be nearly as special as that one. But if Butcher has seen it on the road then Ishmael must be in action again. Fat Les knows that must mean something but he isn't sure what.

He thinks of the time when he was, briefly, on the road with Barry and he thinks of the speed, the excitement, the rumbles, the scrapes, the battles, the feeling of being an outlaw, of being completely out there; wild and dangerous and very alive. It all makes him feel very old. Fat Old Les.

He wouldn't want to be the person he was back then: and yet he knows that person wouldn't have worked for someone like Phelan.

Les doesn't like Nazis, whether they're the old fashioned variety or whether they style themselves as neo. But work is work, money is money, he does have a business to run, and technology is neutral, surely. He balked a little at having to paint swastikas, iron crosses, death's heads and SS flashes on the doors and bonnets of the Beetles, but that's what it took to keep the customer satisfied.

Les works on using all the hours God sends. He is a man inspired, a man possessed. He puts in the hours, puts in a major effort, and eventually a time comes when all eight cars are ready, a shorter time than anybody but Les might have imagined.

He calls Phelan the moment the job is done, and although it is three in the morning, Phelan immediately comes to see the finished cars. He arrives wearing an all-encompassing black leather trench coat, a pair of jack boots and, as far as Les can tell, nothing else.

The eight Volkswagen Beetles sit in the workshop looking poised, dormant, dangerous. The black lacquered paint jobs reflect the strip lighting overhead, bending and distorting the bands of white light. Phelan surveys the scene. He is too sophisticated, too controlled, to allow himself a simple smile of pleasure, but nevertheless it is obvious that he's delighted by what he sees. In fact he is strangely moved.

'With vehicles like these,' he says to Les, 'a man might conquer the world.'

'Sure,' says Les.

'These are vehicles of the Apocalypse, make no mistake.'

'Okay, I won't,' says Les.

Phelan moves among the cars. He touches them lightly with his fingertips. At one point it looks as though he might bend over and kiss one of them. He opens the door of the

138

nearest of them and moves in behind the wheel. He is a man transported.

'Les,' he says, 'you're a superman.'

Barry doesn't feel so good. He feels that life on the road doesn't suit him nearly as well as it used to do. He isn't sure what's changed, whether it's him or the road. Certainly he still enjoys the driving, the opportunity to philosophise, the sense, albeit spurious, of freedom. But there's too much that he doesn't enjoy. He could hardly claim to have been bored on this trip, enough has happened to stave off ennui, but most of it has seemed somehow irrelevant.

However, the real reason he doesn't feel so good is that a fair amount of time has passed and these travels don't seem to be getting him anywhere, any nearer his goal. He hasn't found Charles Lederer yet, not even a trace, and he doesn't see how he's ever going to. He had begun by believing that instinct would get the job done, that he would find Charles Lederer because he *needed* to. He doesn't quite believe that now. He no longer knows where to look for him, in fact sometimes he isn't even sure that he'd recognise Charles Lederer even if he found him. What if he's changed his appearance? What if he's simply gone into hiding? He could be holed up in a hotel, in a squat, in a caravan site. All Barry's travels will be irrelevant if the object of his quest remains still.

For a long time Barry is too proud to abandon his mission, so he drives on and on, burning fossil fuels, pumping greenhouse gases into the air, wearing down his tyres and wearing out his engine. The milometer spins like the wheels of a fruit machine. The interior of Enlightenment becomes Barry's whole world. The dashboard, the seat, the steering wheel, the gear lever; these are the only landmarks on his mental map. The world passes before his eyes. He sees it through the windscreen, through a glass smokily, and he is completely detached and uninvolved. The world becomes something viewed on a screen, like a video or a made for TV movie.

He drives without direction and without will. Sometimes he will find himself driving down the quietest, most deserted country track at dead of the night. Sometimes he finds himself in dense, fast-moving motorway traffic in the middle of rush hour. In neither case does he have the slightest idea of where he is or how he got there. The only thing he knows for sure is that Charles Lederer is not there.

And then he hits the M25; one hundred and twenty-five miles of unbroken urban race track. There is something basic and elemental about it. He loves the symbolism, the symmetry, the fact that it is circular, continuous, endless. It seems to speak of natural cycles, of renewal, of the eternal return. Starting anywhere you would pass all possible destinations before returning to the place from which you started. Traffic revolves, comes and goes, uses the M25 as a way of avoiding London, of skirting the issues. Most drivers use only a part of its orbit, but Barry wants to go all the way.

He drives round and round the M25, and as he travels he feels less and less of anything, driving on automatic pilot, operating on pure instinct, overtaking, manoeuvring, becoming part of it all, experiencing a loss of self, an end of separation, experiencing a feeling of absolute unity, though he would be hard-pressed to say what he was becoming united with, possibly with an abstract notion of movement, with windrush, with road noise, with nothing human.

After a certain number of circuits it all becomes familiar, becomes his home territory, *his* motorway. The names on the road signs are his places. They read like a mantra: Swanley, Wisley, Leatherhead, Potters Bar, South Mimms. Passing through the Dartford tunnel, burrowing deep below the Thames, becomes a ritual of rebirth.

Days go by, nights go by. Barry goes on; not sleeping, not eating, not washing or shaving. He stops only to excrete and to take on fuel. He is a new man, a man possessed, a man in touch with a quite different reality.

Enlightenment eats up the miles. The pistons move in their cylinders, valves open and close, camshafts and crankshafts revolve, heat exchangers exchange heat. The wheels go round, the accelerator and clutch work in harmony. Slave cylinders and fuel lines and the wiring loom and carburettors and shock absorbers and spark plugs all operate in a state of mystical interdependence.

And then, without warning, it is suddenly all over. He crests the brow of a hill. He isn't exactly sure where he is – though there are road signs for Heathrow Airport nearby – when all at once Enlightenment dies under him. There is a brief, undignified spluttering, a slight judder and then nothing. Barry presses the accelerator, turns the key in the ignition, moves up and down the gears, but it makes no difference. The car drifts down the hill, slowing all the time. Other traffic pulls out around him to overtake. For Barry it is like waking from a dream. Now that he is out of touch with his mechanical carapace he is given back to himself. He blinks, looks around him, sees the world through new eyes, doesn't know what he's looking at. He steers the car onto the hard shoulder, brings it to a halt. He switches on the warning lights. He feels empty. He feels as though he is peering into some bottomless well. He slumps over the steering wheel, spent and hollow and exhausted. He falls into weird, edgy dreams about Marilyn; she is riding a Volkswagen trike, eating raw fish, transforming into a vampire, being chased by skinheads.

He is awoken abruptly some time later, though he doesn't know how much later, by a rap on the side window of Enlightenment. He is disoriented. Someone is looking at him through the window, a young black man who is saying, 'Need any help, man?'

Barry cannot deny that he does. He wonders if this stranger belongs to the police or is an AA man, but now he sees the car he's driving, and it's a metallic turquoise and peppermint green Beetle with suicide doors, not a vehicle much favoured by the AA or the police.

'My name's Zak,' says the young man. 'You want me to take a look at the car for you?'

'Well, yes, that would be very kind of you.'

Zak looks at the engine, tries to start it. He plays with this and that. After the briefest inspection he is able to tell Barry that he's run out of fuel. Barry looks surprised.

'Maybe you've got a leak,' says Zak. 'When did you last fill up?'

'I can't really remember.'

Zak looks at the state of Barry, at his half-closed eyes and his weary manner and says, 'When did you last get any sleep?'

Barry can't remember that either. Then Zak asks where he's going, and that's the hardest question of all.

Zak says, 'I can give you some petrol, but you've got to promise me you'll get off the motorway and have a rest.'

Barry nods helplessly and puts himself in Zak's hands. Zak siphons petrol from one Beetle to another. As he works he says, 'I always stop if I see a fellow Beetle-owner in trouble. And these days I find myself stopping more and more.'

'Really?'

'Yeah. They always seem to be breaking down.'

'Not this one,' says Barry. 'This one's different.'

'Well it looks different, that's for sure, but underneath they're all the same, aren't they? Sometimes I think I've had enough of mine really. I keep thinking I'm going to sell it. I think about taking it to one of those big Volkswagen meetings and selling it there. There's a big one coming up soon. Maybe you'll be there.'

'I don't know where I'll be,' says Barry.

After Zak has finished putting petrol into Enlightenment, they shake hands and continue their separate journeys. As he goes, Zak tells Barry to get some rest, but Barry has no intention of doing that. Now that the spell has been broken he realises he's been on a wild goose chase all along. He has been heading in the wrong direction. It has been a detour to nowhere. He realises that it no longer matters to him whether or not he finds Charles Lederer. It doesn't matter if a few Volkswagens explode. All that matters is love. All right, so he hasn't achieved his goal of finding her father; but that's no reason for Marilyn to spurn him. Goals can be changed. Itineraries can be revised. He will go to her, admit defeat, throw himself at her mercy, and if she's the woman he hopes she is, then she'll take him to her bosom and love him as he loves her.

Charles Lederer attempts to wander the roads of England. He is angry. He is mad. With his shaved head and his torn clothes he cuts a strange and disturbing figure, invoking, in some, both fear and compassion. He certainly doesn't look like the sort of person you'd want to give a lift to.

He stands at the roadside with his thumb held out but he no longer has high hopes. Hours pass, traffic passes, night falls. He continues to stand motionless. There is an awe-inspiring, almost religious stillness about him, yet inside his head there is turmoil. The mental images of exploding Volks-wagens have receded. They're now on the far edge of his field of vision. The foreground is full of images of slaughter, violent death, dismemberment. The hatred of Volkswagens set him on the right path, but now he knows who's really behind his confusion and pain. It's Ishmael. He is the engin-eer, the designer of this misery. If Ishmael can be found and destroyed then Charles Lederer knows that everything will be just fine. His life, he trusts, will then reform itself, be made whole again.

He continues to wait, looking for a sign, something that

will draw him across distance and history, deliver him to his fate. It arrives in the form of a lift in a double-decker bus painted with scenes from the Tarot. Who else would stop? Who would offer Charles Lederer a lift except someone who saw himself as an outsider, as a maverick? It is Planetary Cliff, and he stops for the old man. The doors open, Charles Lederer steps up and gets in without saying a word. He moves into an unfamiliar space, one of old leather and dirty curtains, of ancient wisdom and masses of amplifiers and speakers, one that smells of dogs and marijuana and petrol fumes.

The driver of the bus introduces himself as Planetary Cliff. He might once have appeared an appalling individual to someone of Charles Lederer's station and life experience, but things have changed. They both have partly shaved heads. They're both ragged and dirty. Planetary Cliff smiles and Charles Lederer smiles back. In some strange way the two men see each other as kindred spirits.

Some time later on a patch of waste ground between a scrap metal dealer and a secondhand tyre lot, at the travellers' latest camp, Charles Lederer is fed and given drink and a leather jacket to wear. The zip of the jacket is broken and one of the arms is falling off, but it suits him. He looks rather good in it, like some old, cherished witch doctor.

The travellers are at home here on the edge, on the margins, in a place of both waste and reclamation, of dispersal and recycling. They sit around a fire, though the night is not cold and the rainy spell is over. There are too many travellers for Charles Lederer to keep track of, so many children, so many dogs. He can't work out the relationships between people. There seems to be nothing so concrete as couples or families. They all appear to be friendly enough but nobody talks to him except Planetary Cliff.

'You feeling better?' Cliff asks.

'Yes, I am, actually.'

'You look like you've been in the wars.'

144

'Do I? I suppose I have.'

'We know the feeling.'

'Do you? I thought you young people would be terribly anti-war.'

'Oh sure. You try living in peace and see where it gets you. A lot of people feel threatened by the likes of us wanting to live in peace. That's why they try to kick the shit out of us.'

'Do they really?'

'Yeah. Like I'm into music as a shamanistic ritual, right? So I say to people, hey, harmony is a balanced fusion of all energies. It's a hermaphroditic power which acts as a central focus for the polarities which save us from the Abyss. But they just don't want to listen.'

'I see.'

Planetary Cliff hands his guest a can of lager. Charles Lederer chokes it down. He has never tasted anything quite like it. He wonders how long it is since he last tasted a good malt whisky. Years.

'Where are you headed for?' Planetary Cliff asks.

'I'm looking for someone.'

'Anyone in particular?'

'Yes. One of my old constituents.'

Planetary Cliff laughs at his use of the word 'constituent'. Charles Lederer doesn't want to tell lies. He feels curiously free to be honest with these new people.

'I used to be in politics,' he explains.

'Of course you did. Everyone's involved in politics. You can't avoid it.'

'That's true.'

'Why do you want to find this person?'

'Well, it's complicated, but I think basically I want to kill him.'

Planetary Cliff laughs nervously.

'I mean it,' says Charles Lederer, and Planetary Cliff can see that he does.

'It might be just as well if you don't find him, then,' says Planetary Cliff.

'Oh no, I'll find him all right.'

'What's he done wrong, this bloke?'

'Everything. You name it. For instance he drives a Volkswagen.'

Planetary Cliff can't help laughing at this strange, though distinctly oddball character he's picked up. 'Oh well,' he says, 'in *that* case.'

At the end of the evening the travellers return to their various tents and vans and buses. Charles Lederer feels wide awake. He sits by the fire, still looking serene and sage-like, still, by his own account, with murder in his heart. Planetary Cliff doesn't really think he's a wanton killer about to murder them all in their beds in the middle of the night, but the old guy is definitely weird and he'd rather have him where he can keep an eye on him. There's an ancient graffiti-daubed caravan at the corner of the site. It's full of waste paper, old magazines and newspapers that they have collected to sell for recycling, but there's just enough room left for one person to sleep in it. Planetary Cliff directs Charles Lederer there and once the old guy's inside, Cliff locks the door so he's secure in there till the morning.

Charles Lederer goes in willing enough but he still doesn't want to sleep, so he starts looking through the old news-papers and magazines. He has been out of touch for a long time, so that the pictures he sees and the articles he reads are like bulletins from another world; somewhere very strange and unwelcoming. The faces of the politicians, the names of the personalities, the newsworthy items, the lan-guage, the range of interests and obsessions are alarmingly unfamiliar to him. He feels a little frightened.

He picks magazines at random from the piles, browses through colour supplements, tabloids, women's magazines, until suddenly he finds that he has in his hands a copy of a periodical called *Volkswagen Universe*. He can barely believe that such a thing exists. It is a document of horror. It contains everything he hates and fears; page after page, photograph after photograph of Volkswagens in all their many appalling forms; lovingly, pruriently presented, in garish colours and fetishised states; the worst kind of pornography. His first urge is to burn the magazine but he keeps turning the pages, hypnotised by the thing he loathes. And then things get a lot worse.

He comes to an article about some famous Volkswagen collector, someone by the name of Carlton Bax. There are pictures of his house and his garage; room after room of the Volkswagen and all its terrible works; actual cars, models, representations, memorabilia, images and replicas, the whole sick, disgusting business. It makes him want to scream. And then things become intolerable. Right in the middle of this article, photographed right in the middle of one of these hideous rooms of Volkswagens, is his own flesh and blood, his own daughter, Marilyn. The caption reads, 'Zany weather girl Marilyn Lederer, Carlton Bax's other half says, "Volkswagens most definitely R us".'

When Planetary Cliff comes to the caravan in the morning, he sees that a superhuman effort, a hideous strength, has been used to break open the lock, and Charles Lederer is long gone.

Dawn. The sky is the colour of a washed out white T-shirt. The air is still, the day peaceful. There is a roaring sound: intense, fierce, but very far away. If you stand still and watch the horizon, the source of the noise will eventually appear, though not for a while. First the roaring becomes louder and more distinct, and reveals itself not to be a single sound, but an amalgam of eight similar though distinct noises; engine noises, a harsh metallic din of eight flat-four air-cooled

147

engines, throbbing inside eight all-black, wicked-looking Volkswagen Beetles, not that you would know that yet. It is a sound modified and processed by silencers and sports exhausts, changed and distorted by harsh gear changes and wild over-revving.

Soon they appear; in a haze of pale azure exhaust smoke, tyre noise and violent oversteer. They arrive at your premises, at your shop, your forecourt, at your warehouse or bakery or pub or restaurant. If you're lucky you'll still have time to run, to get the hell out of there.

They stop in a frenzy of skid and brake squeal and hand-brake turns. The engines are not switched off but the drivers' doors are thrown open and eight adrenalin-charged skinheads lumber out. They are armed with crowbars, base-ball bats, home-made Molotov cocktails. They are here to rob you, certainly, but also to terrorise, to create havoc and panic, and not just to you alone.

They are not entirely discriminating. They undoubtedly prefer it if the shop is run by Turks or Cypriots, if the ware-house contains saris, if the bakery is Jewish, if the pub is full of West Indians, if the restaurant has a gay clientele. But they don't allow themselves to get bogged down in ideology. They will attack white folks too if they don't like the look of them. They might say, if they were articulate, that they hate deviance from the racial and political status quo, but you know how it is when the feeling's on you, any port in a storm, beggars can't be choosers. If they're in the right mood they'll attack anything and everything, including each other.

After their raids and forays they return to Phelan with their loot and their stories. For Phelan it is a dream come true. His boys are now mobile and in action; tough, hard, clean-living lads driving across the country in the supreme flowering of Nazi technology. Phelan admires their capacity for improvisation. For example, after a raid on an Indian-run off-licence in semi-rural Sussex, they find themselves driving beside a village green on which a cricket match is being played. Without debate, as though with a single mind, they leave the road and perform various driving stunts across the centre of the cricket pitch, leaving it rutted with deep swirling tyre tracks. Phelan finds that wonderfully inventive, even if not entirely politically consistent, cricket, after all, being a beloved piece of the English heritage.

Butcher is enjoying his new lifestyle. It's all so much better since he stopped driving that poxy van, and especially since he doesn't have seven other drunken skinheads falling around in the back and distracting him. He has money, not serious money, but enough to pay for some new boots and new tattoos. But more importantly, now that he spends much of his time alone at the wheel of his own vehicle he feels so much sharper, more in control, so much more in touch with who he is.

Zak is filling up the petrol tank of his metallic turquoise and peppermint green Volkswagen when he see the eight Nazi Beetles, or rather when the eight skinhead drivers first see him. Zak can see there's something familiar about the cars. They look very much like that Beetle he stopped to help on the M25. But he thought that was a complete one-off. How come there are now eight exactly like it? There's something sinister and alarming about them, particularly about the way he can't see in through the smoked windows, can't see the drivers, and there's something positively threatening about the fact that they all pull into the petrol station and park behind, in front and beside him, so that he can't possibly drive his own car away. And he doesn't like the way none of the drivers has got out. The cars just sit there, engines revving, poised and predatory.

The tank of Zak's Beetle is now full. He clanks the nozzle back into its holder and goes into the office to pay. Perhaps, he thinks and hopes, by the time he's paid, everything will be all right, the other Beetles will have gone, or at least will have moved so as to give him room to make an exit.

149

It is not to be. When he returns to his Beetle, the other cars are still there, right where they were before, but the eight skinheads have now got out, and their appearance immediately tells him that things are anything but all right. They have not stopped for petrol, and in fact they are examining his Beetle with close attention. They're now scrutinising the exhaust system, looking underneath at the floorpan, checking out the wing mirrors, the doors, stroking the paintwork to feel its smoothness. Zak doesn't like this at all. They don't look like typical Volkswagen fans. They don't look like the kind of boys you can discuss technical tips with. He fears they might be planning to steal his car, or worse still vandalise it. He hardly relishes confronting a gang of skinheads but he doesn't see that he has any choice. He has to say and do something. He takes a deep breath.

'Hi,' he says in as unconfrontational way as he can manage.

Nobody returns his greeting but one of the skinheads says, 'We're just admiring your motor.'

'Well thanks.'

'Some work went into this. And some money.'

'I'll say.'

'I'm surprised you can afford it,' says Butcher.

'Well you know how it is . . . '

'Well no,' says Butcher, 'I don't. Because basically you're not the type of person we like to see driving a car like this.'

'Huh?'

'We tend to think that people like you aren't worthy to drive the Führer's car.'

'Hey,' says Zak, 'just let me get in my car and I'll be on my way.'

'No you won't.'

One of the skinheads blocks his path. Another grabs his arm, another thumps him in the kidneys. Before they've finished with him he's been kicked, punched, robbed and pissed on. They don't touch his car.

150

'I know why you're doing this,' he shouts after them as they walk away to their cars. 'It's because I'm black, isn't it?' 'Too bloody right,' says Butcher as he gets into his Beetle and drives away at the head of his dark convoy.

Davey has just about had enough. He's been on the road for a long time now and it looks as though he could arrive at the end of the summer without having made any friends at all in the New Age traveller community. It seems all too likely that he's never going to take Ecstasy, never going to dance in a field till dawn, never going to feel a sense of cosmic unity and an awareness of his place on mother earth. He's well cheesed off. Maybe he'll sell the van, get his old job back, then next year he can go on one of those singles holidays where everybody spends the whole time drinking and shagging, though with his luck he'll probably not make any friends there either.

He's sitting alone in a picnic area on the edge of Clumber Park eating a Cornish pastie and a tin of potato salad when he hears the unmistakable sound of approaching Volkswagen engines. They get louder and louder, unnaturally loud, and when he sees eight black Volkswagens weaving towards him through the trees, he knows that something is very wrong indeed.

He is extremely familiar with Ishmael's Enlightenment. He has even driven it. It was a great car. The eight Beetles he sees before him now appear to be strange, savage parodies of that vehicle. They have the form but not the essence. They park in a V formation not far from where he's sitting, but it's a while before any of the drivers get out. The moment one does, Davey knows it is time to get in his van and go. He has no reason to believe that the skinheads driving these Beetles are the same ones who attacked the New Age travellers in the lay-by at the beginning of his travels, certainly he

151

doesn't recognise any of them, but they still make him feel very uncomfortable. They lurch and tumble out of their cars, shouting and swearing at each other, throwing litter, spraying beer into the air. They look like people adept at finding and creating trouble.

Davey edges towards his van, hoping they haven't noticed his presence, but it's too late. They've caught sight of him and they're suddenly very interested. They're heading towards him and something tells him things will be even worse if he tries to run. He quickly shoves the last of the Cornish pastie into his mouth so as to be ready for the inevitable confrontation.

'Nice van,' says Butcher, who arrives first, a little ahead of his cronies.

'Yes,' Davey says through his full mouth.

'You live in it?'

'Sort of.'

'Like a gypsy or something?'

'Well, a bit,' Davey admits.

'We don't like gypos,' says Butcher. 'We think we'd be better off without them.'

'Yeah,' says another skinhead who has now joined the conversation. 'We reckon they're fuckin' parasites.'

'Well no, I'm not a *real* gypsy,' says Davey, swallowing hard. 'I'm more of a traveller. I'm more of a tourist actually.'

'Are you really?' asks Butcher.

'Yes, yes I am.'

'Well, let's put it this way,' says Butcher, 'if you were a real gypsy, or a Jewish gypsy or a Paki gypsy or a nigger or a queer gypsy, you'd seriously be in trouble right now. But as it stands, since you're more of a tourist, you're only *slightly* in trouble.'

Davey looks blank. 'What am I supposed to have done?' he asks.

Butcher dismisses it as an irrelevant question. 'Nothing,'

he says. 'That's why we're not going to knock three kinds of shit out of you.'

'That's right,' says another. 'We're just going to knock three kinds of shit out of your van.'

'Please, please don't do that.'

'We won't be doing too much damage,' says Butcher, 'because after all it *is* a Volkswagen of sorts, but let's face it, it's not *much* of a Volkswagen. It's just a van. It doesn't have that authentic Adolf Hitler flavour to it.'

'No, please,' says Davey again. 'Why are you doing this?' But even Davey knows that's a stupid question. They're doing it because this is what they do. Two of the skinheads grab him, one by each arm and they keep hold of him while the others get to work on the van.

They use chains and hammers and iron bars and cans of spray paint. They dent and scratch and smash every panel of the van. They spray obscenities all over the back and sides. The headlights are shattered, several windows have cracks like spiders' webs, engine oil is splashed furiously all over the roof and windscreen. Then the skinheads start rooting around inside the van, turning out the food cupboards, pouring milk, breakfast cereal and instant coffee granules all over the seats and floor, smearing margarine over the dashboard, handbrake and steering wheel.

Davey is forced to watch as his beautiful van is made ugly and wretched. He knows he can't fight these skinheads. He can't even break free of the grip of the two holding him. It doesn't take long for them to completely besmirch his van, at which point, well satisfied, they let him go. He walks towards the wreckage, tears rolling down his cheeks, his body shaking with misery and impotent rage. Butcher observes this and finds it a bit pathetic. 'Hey friend,' he shouts, 'don't be a pansy,' and he kicks Davey in the stomach. Davey falls over, and is still there on the ground, still trying to get his breath back, long after the skinheads have departed.

Time passes. Davey's misery does not, but he knows he

153

can't stay there forever, so at last he begins very slowly, very painfully to clean up his van. He knows it could have been worse. They could have beaten him to a pulp and set his van on fire for instance, but that isn't much consolation. The sense of invasion is total but he does what he can. He sweeps up and he wipes down, but the damage requires more than just a bit of cleaning. His pride and joy has been wounded. His van is all fucked up. How's he ever going to be able to get it back to its previous state of grace? Even a genius like Fat Les would have his work cut out to restore it now.

But oddly enough it's still drivable. The engine starts and the gears engage and even though it has no lights and is an obscene-looking, graffiti-splattered thing, and even though there's crud all over the seat and the steering wheel, he eventually drives it away. He doesn't know where he's going, but he needs to be somewhere else. As he drives, he knows that other drivers must be looking at him with alarm, and surely it can only be a matter of time before some passing police car spots him, pulls him over and arrests him for being in charge of an unroadworthy vehicle. Maybe that could even be for the best.

Then an extraordinary thing happens. Davey is still shaken, so he's driving a little slowly and unsurely along a quiet stretch of dual carriageway when he becomes aware of an unusual vehicle closing rapidly from behind him. He expects the vehicle to overtake but instead it slows right down and starts tailgating him.

'Oh God no,' he thinks. 'Not more trouble.'

The vehicle is a double decker bus painted with scenes from the Tarot, and it begins flashing its lights, and the driver waves for Davey to pull over. Davey can see that the driver's a wild, dangerous-looking character, pierced and tattooed, bare chested, with a top knot and the sides of his head shaved. Strange as it may seem, he looks a little familiar, though Davey can't quite place the face. Then he realises this is one of the New Age travellers who declined to offer him hospitality. Now however, the driver looks decidedly friendly, and Davey pulls in at the nearest lay-by. The bus pulls in behind him and Planetary Cliff leaps out.

'Hey! All right!' he shouts to Davey enthusiastically. 'What a great looking van.'

Davey looks at him suspiciously, thinking he must be mocking him.

'Yeah,' Planetary Cliff continues. 'The moment I saw it I knew you were one of us. Are you on your way to the Gathering of the Tribes? Why not come and join us?'

Davey looks at Planetary Cliff's rough but open face and sees that he really means it. Once again tears stream down Davey's face, but this time they're tears of joy.

* * *

The first problem the police have with serial murders is determining what constitutes a series. Boy meets girl, boy gets her in his car, boy takes her to some lonely spot, beats her over the head, strips her, rapes her, mutilates her; so far so commonplace. So far this is an everyday story. The fact that more or less similar events are happening all the time in any number of locations, is not enough to suggest that a pattern is taking shape. Before police are prepared to admit that a serial killer is on the loose they want something a little more concrete, more decisive, a particular quirk, an idiosyncratic way of working, the fact perhaps that the murderer has a taste for handcuffs, has a savage way with a speculum, or even perhaps that he drives a Volkswagen Beetle.

Here is Ted Bundy, comparatively early in his life of crime. He is an accomplished shoplifter, though in general he is fastidious about stealing only what he has use for. But today

155

he is in a garden centre in Seattle, Washington and suddenly he gets an uncontrollable urge to steal an eight foot tall potted Germanica plant that is for sale and is positioned tantalisingly close to the exit. So he simply picks it up as though he owns it, walks out of the garden centre and heads for his car, a light brown Volkswagen Beetle. So far so good. But he's still got to stash the plant in his car and make his escape. How's he going to get an eight foot plant into a Volkswagen? Dead easy actually. The car's a 1968 model, the kind with the canvas sun roof that peels right back. He inserts the plant through the roof so that it rests in the passenger seat and Ted Bundy drives away unchallenged.

It must have been an unusual sight, seeing this Volkswagen bowling along the freeway with three feet of Germanica foliage sticking out of the sun roof, but people who drive Bugs are the sort of people who do that kind of thing. They're fun guys, individuals, mavericks. Nobody bats an eyelid.

'Christ,' says Ted Bundy to himself, 'I love this car.'

Here is Ted Bundy at Sammaville Beach in Seattle, Washington. It's a holiday afternoon and the place is crowded with people. He's dressed in all white sports clothes and he's got his arm in plaster. He cruises the beach, stopping girls from time to time with a line that goes something like, 'Hey babe would you help me lift my sailboat onto the roof of my Volkswagen? You can see I've injured my arm. How about it?' So they go to the car park. The Volkswagen's there but the boat isn't. 'Oh, I forgot to mention,' he says, 'my boat's up at my parents' house, just a few miles up the coast. Get in the car and I'll take you there.'

Ted tries this line on a lot of girls. Most of them don't fall for it, but three do. Later they are raped, violated, murdered.

It is said that Bundy had college boy good looks, that he was charming, intelligent, and a law student. On the one hand this is supposed to explain his ability to pick up girls. On the other it is supposed to surprise us; how strange that a good-looking, charming, intelligent, law student should be the one to murder thirty or more young women. Wouldn't it make life easier if people who are serial killers advertised the fact a little more?

But what did the girls think, the ones who agreed to drive up the coast with this stranger? Certainly they might have thought that he didn't 'look like a murderer', and perhaps they thought that a man with an injured arm wouldn't be able to attack them. But more than that, it seems somehow likely that they thought a sex killer would be driving a dirty old pick up truck, or a beat up muscle car, or one of those vans with the murals and the padded interior and the bed with the mirrors. Maybe they thought that only nice guys drive Volkswagens.

And here is Ted Bundy in Utah in 1975. He has a dozen or so killings under his belt by now. He is stoned on marijuana and is driving his Volkswagen for the sheer hell of it, noticing how sharp and clear all the sounds and colours are tonight. And perhaps he's too stoned to notice that he's driving well over the speed limit, and too stoned to notice that there's a police car behind him. And perhaps he doesn't even see the red stop light that he drives through, but the officer in the car certainly does, and the siren starts sounding and there's a brief chase before Bundy is forced to come to a halt in a gas station.

The officer gets Bundy out of the car and checks his ID, which appears to be perfectly in order. However, he looks into the car, sees there's no front passenger seat and that there's a jemmy lying on the floor. The officer calls for help. More police arrive. They search the car and find an ice pick, a mask made from silk stockings and a pair of handcuffs. Bundy is hauled in, and a more thorough investigation of the car's interior takes place. They gather up all the dirt and fibre and debris, and send it off for analysis. Eventually they will discover a human hair from the head of one of the

157

murder victims, and, curled at the base of the gear lever, a pubic hair belonging to another dead girl.

But all this takes time. Initially all they can charge Bundy with is the possession of tools that might be used in a burglary. Bundy is let out on bail and one of his first acts is to sell his Volkswagen. It must have broken his little heart.

The police are gradually putting two and two together. With Bundy in the frame they have the opportunity to see if there is evidence to link him to the murders. They find a girl whom Bundy tried to lure to her death. She identifies him. The charge changes from possessing tools to aggravated kidnapping. Bundy is in trouble, the heat is closing in, but he is determined to go down in a blaze of blood, death and car theft.

Here is Ted Bundy managing, on two separate occasions, to escape from jail. Here he is hiding in the hills, stealing cars; a Cadillac, an MG, a Toyota, a Dodge van. Here is Ted Bundy the fugitive stalking the corridors of the Chi Omega sorority house, committing two more murders and numerous acts of brutal mutilation. It's the real thing for Ted, but it's not the same without a Volkswagen.

On Sunday February 12th in Tallahassee, Florida, he finally gets lucky. He's walking down the street looking for another car to steal and he comes across a Beetle sitting there with the keys inside. He gets in and drives a few miles. But the car is heavily customised, all fancy body work and dressed up and chromed, and Ted, a Republican at heart, fears the modifications may have impaired the car's essential reliability. So he ditches it. And then he finds another Beetle. This is a stock 1972 model, painted orange. He decides it's the car for him. This too turns out to be a clunker. If he drives over fifty miles an hour the wheels shake as though they're about to fall off, but he decides he'd better stick with it.

It's real film noir stuff by now. He steals credit cards, tries to use them for food and accommodation but they've already been reported stolen. Ted drives up a dirt road to lie low for a while and finds himself on an airforce base, then the wheels of his Volkswagen get stuck in the soft earth. Bundy tries to steal handbags in a shopping mall and is bounced by the security guards. Finally the police recapture him, not because they recognise him as Ted Bundy the serial sex killer, but because he's at the wheel of a stolen Volkswagen.

In January 1979 the trial of Ted Bundy begins. He is found guilty of murder, and on January 23rd 1989 he will eventually be executed.

While on Death Row he receives a lot of mail. There are a lot of love letters, women who want to marry Ted Bundy, give him their love, have his children. There are packages containing all kinds of tokens both of love and hate. One contains a bottle of barbecue sauce for when Bundy is 'fried'.

But the oddest of all comes from a man who bought Ted Bundy's Volkswagen, the one he sold after his first arrest. The writer of the letter says he hates Bundy and he'll never drive a Volkswagen again. He's had the car taken to the scrapyard, but he's kept the gear lever as a grim souvenir and now, for reasons he only dimly understands, he wants Bundy to have it back.

Of course, the prison authorities open all Bundy's mail and if they consider the contents unsuitable then Bundy never gets to see them. They never give Bundy the gear lever of his old Volkswagen but it is often rumoured that it found its way into the collection of Carlton Bax, one of the items kept in the famous locked room.

159

VII

Volkswagen Descending a Staircase

Inside Carlton Bax's gentleman's residence, Marilyn Lederer pours herself another whisky and lemonade. It is the latest in a long series and she doesn't expect that series to end for a while yet. The drink tastes sweet and harmless but is nevertheless numbing, though not quite as numbing as she would like. She still feels so unhappy. She feels so lost and alone and on the margins. She doesn't see how things could possibly get any worse, and yet things are about to.

Behind the house, in a spot without street lamps, a red van draws up. An old man gets out, thanks the driver for the lift and the van drives away. It wasn't so difficult to find this place. The magazine article gave a number of clues, but if it had taken forever he would still have got here.

The old man walks up to the high garden wall that surrounds the property and attempts to climb it. The would-be intruder is, of course, Marilyn's father, but he is weak and weary and the walls are designed specifically to prevent people climbing them. He investigates the walls for a long time, looking for some other means of entrance. It looks completely hopeless but then he sees something that stirs his blood, something that makes him very angry, and yet something that seems almost magically ordained.

As he watches, a black Volkswagen Beetle draws up outside the locked, wrought iron security gate of the house. It is Barry Osgathorpe in Enlightenment. Barry gets out of the car and pulls the metal knob that rings the bell next to the gate. As he does so he is watched by a security camera which transmits his image to a monitor screen in the hall of the house. Upon hearing the bell Marilyn gets up, staggers a little, and goes to inspect the screen. She feels neither optimistic not pessimistic. By now she feels that nothing, no phone call, no sudden discovery, no unexpected arrival, can possibly make any difference to her. She sees that it's Barry ringing the bell. Even that doesn't particularly surprise her and it certainly doesn't appear to promise anything. Indifferently, she presses the button that opens the gate to let him in.

Barry gets in Enlightenment and drives into the grounds, but in the brief moment before the gate automatically closes, Charles Lederer sees his chance. He makes a dash for the gate and, unseen in the darkness, just manages to slip in before it clangs shut and electronically locks itself again. He stands in the garden, breathing heavily, and decides to hide in the bushes until the time is exactly right.

Meanwhile, not so very far away, eight more or less identical Volkswagen Beetles, each of them modelled on Enlightenment, are en route to Carlton Bax's gentleman's residence. The eight skinhead drivers plough their fierce, lonely furrow through the mean night streets, travelling in V-formation when they can, working to a firm, well thought-out and extremely vicious plan.

Barry parks neatly outside the front door of Carlton Bax's gentleman's residence, although, of course, he doesn't know it is Carlton Bax's, Marilyn hasn't told him that. He simply thinks that Marilyn must have some very rich friends indeed; but then that is no great surprise. He bounds out of his car, his heart fit to burst with love and enthusiasm for Marilyn. She has left the door unlocked and he takes that to be a good, welcoming sign. 'Marilyn!' he calls cheerily as he enters, but there's no reply. He goes into the living room and there she is, drunk, bare-foot, bleary-eyed, her legs splayed, her hair all messed up. She has never looked lovelier to Barry.

However, even Marilyn's presence cannot distract him from the strangeness of this house. Even a cursory glance at the hall shows that the place is littered with Volkswagen treasures, and that seems very strange indeed. He would question her about this but she gives him no opportunity.

'Oh where have you been my blue-eyed son?' she says, being more or less incoherent by now. 'Oh where have you been my darling young one?'

Barry doesn't catch the reference, but he's rather pleased that she's calling him darling.

'I've been all over the place,' he says, 'but my heart's always been right here.'

'Oh dear. I don't suppose you found my father?'

'No, but I found something more important.'

'What's that?'

'I found my heart's desire.'

'Well, that must be very nice for you.'

'It is. Because I've found you.'

'No you haven't Barry. Really you haven't.'

'What do you mean?'

'Isn't it obvious what I mean? This house, this whole arrangement.'

Well no, it isn't, and then Barry sees a console table at the foot of the stairs on which is a framed photograph. It shows Marilyn and some stranger, an older man, and they're standing beside an extremely exotic looking Beetle. They're holding hands and they're gazing into each other's eyes. They seem to Barry to be nauseatingly fond of each other.

'Are you trying to tell me something?' he says.

'Oh Barry, don't be so thick.'

Barry doesn't understand, doesn't even want to. He can't believe that his love is going to be spurned like this. He would like the chance to discuss this with her at greater length, to state his case, to melt her heart. However, it never happens. There are suddenly noises off; footsteps, a scrabbling, breaking glass, some coughing and grunting. Then the door to the living-room is thrown open and Charles Lederer stands before them. No longer weak and weary he now looks wild and mad as hell. His hair has grown back a little but not uniformly, and its patchiness adds to his demented look. The eyes are raging, the chin is jutting forwards nobly, and there is a definite mushy drool trickling down from the corners of the mouth. Most alarming of all, he is armed with the chrome bumper from a 1952 American specification Beetle. It has all manner of sharp points and hard edges and he's waving it around menacingly, the menace being all the greater because he is so unfocused and uncoordinated.

'Oh Dad,' says Marilyn joyously, and without thinking she runs to embrace him.

'Keep away!' he shouts and she stops in her tracks.

'But what's wrong?' she asks.

'My daughter!' he shouts. 'And my worst enemy, here together plotting against me.'

'No Dad,' says Marilyn. 'Barry isn't your enemy, and we're not plotting against you. We're on your side.'

He doesn't like the sound of that at all. He thrashes the bumper savagely against the glass front of a wall cabinet containing rare tin plate Beetles. Glass splinters and pieces of dented metal spew from the cabinet. Charles Lederer wants it to be known that he means business. Marilyn and Barry get his message and edge away, but Marilyn still wants to be placatory.

'We've been looking for you,' she says.

'Oh really?' Charles Lederer says with unbelieving disdain.

'Well, Barry here has at any rate.'

'And now he's found me,' snarls Lederer.

'Yes,' says Barry. 'It's quite a Zen thing really. You go on a long voyage looking for something or someone, but only after you've abandoned the search do you find it.'

'Shut up,' says Lederer.

'Okay,' says Barry, and he shuts up.

Charles Lederer turns towards his daughter, and asks, 'Why were looking for me?'

'Because I love you Dad. I knew you were out there lost and alone and I wanted you to come home. Also I didn't want you blowing up any more Volkswagens.'

Charles Lederer looks uncomprehending. A part of him would like to believe that his daughter still loves and cares for him, but in that case why is she standing in a room full of Volkswagen tat conspiring with his arch enemy? He circles the room, looking at all the Volkswagen memorabilia on the walls and in the glass cases, and it's as though he's walked into the jaws of hell.

'I never thought it would come to this,' he says. He turns towards Barry, looking positively homicidal, and lunges at him.

Barry looks desperately for a means of escape. There are some French windows that open onto the garden. They look as good a way out as any, and they start to look better and better as Charles Lederer gets closer and closer. The only problem is that they're locked, but as Lederer gets closer still, even this problem doesn't seem insuperable. Barry wraps his arms around his head and charges at the windows. They burst open in a shattering of glass and splintering of wood, and Barry finds himself sprawling in a flowerbed. He is stunned by the impact, and if Charles Lederer were quick enough he could certainly beat Barry to a bloody pulp there among the geraniums, but something is preventing him. Barry looks over his shoulder into the room and sees that Marilyn is his saviour. She is gripping her father's legs in a sort of rugby tackle.

He soon dislodges her, but the moment's delay gives Barry some respite. In that time he manages to get to his feet, get out of the flowerbed and start running. Quite where he will run to is uncertain. As Charles Lederer knows, Carlton Bax's house is surrounded by a high and unclimbable wall, and

164

the wrought iron gate can only be operated electronically by someone in the house. Barry knows there's no way out.

The grounds are dark, in places there are dense bushes, and there are several outbuildings. Barry thinks that together these might provide him with enough places to hide, at least until Charles Lederer calms down or wears himself out or until, with any luck, Marilyn summons the police. Charles Lederer realises this too. He doesn't want to spend the whole night playing hide and seek. He just wants to get the job done, and he knows what it will take.

It is some years since he drove a car, and the idea of sitting in a Volkswagen Beetle is chillingly repellent to him, but desperate times need desperate measures, and the keys are sitting there conveniently in the ignition.

Charles Lederer grits his teeth, summons up his strength, and gets into Enlightenment. He settles himself in the driving seat, starts the engine and revs it ruthlessly. Over the far side of the garden Barry hears that familiar mechanical noise and is filled with panic. Someone is stealing his car, not just anyone, but someone who hates him and appears to wish him dead. And not least of Barry's worries is the fact that given all the modifications done to the car, it is now something of a beast to drive. If a complete madman like Charles Lederer tries to drive it, there's every chance he'll wreck it completely. He has to do something, and just as Lederer hoped, he comes running out from his hiding place, running towards the car, waving his arms in a gesture of supplication and surrender. But Charles Lederer is taking no prisoners.

There is the noise of gears being stripped as the car is forced into first. The engine roars as though in pain. Enlightenment bounces on its suspension and then goes into a wheelie as Charles Lederer puts on the power, and launches the car through the air, aiming straight for Barry.

Barry dives out of the way of the advancing car. He survives. Enlightenment has missed him and clipped a nearby

165

birch tree. Barry lies face down on the gravel drive, panting and fearful.

Charles Lederer in the meantime has brought the car to a halt and, by means of a tyre-destroying handbrake turn, spun it round so that it is ready to run over the flattened Barry. The car springs forward, a dark, dangerous mass, a black bullet with Barry's name written all over it. Barry tries to get to his feet, starts to run, slips, finds himself on the ground again, and instinctively rolls over as rapidly as he possibly can to avoid the advancing wheels.

The front of the car misses him by millimetres and smashes instead into a stretch of garden balustrade. He gets to his feet. Lederer whips the car round, ready for another attack. There is no escape this time. Barry braces himself for the crash, ready to feel the hideous coming together of car and flesh. But perhaps his instincts are better than he knows. Having no time to leap out of the way, he relaxes, jumps, falls forwards and somehow finds himself safe and alive and adhering to the bonnet of Enlightenment.

His hands grip the wing mirrors and his feet lodge on the nerf bars that have replaced the front bumper. He resembles an oversized, and decidedly misshapen mascot, a misbegotten Spirit of Ecstasy, though he feels anything but ecstatic at present.

Charles Lederer is more furious and more demented than ever, but now he sees a chance to destroy Barry once and for all. He hurls Enlightenment round so that it's pointing down the drive, away from the house towards the metal security gate. He builds up the revs, making the engine scream, toying with the clutch pedal so that the car frets and twitches, and then he feeds in the power and the car leaps forward, eating up the drive at incredible speed, heading straight for the locked gate. He allows himself a giggle as the car picks up speed and the gate looms ever larger in front of him.

And then an odd thing happens. The car is only inches from the gate and Barry has given up any hope of survival, he's just hoping the result will be instant and final, when the gate suddenly flies open. The expected impact never comes, and Enlightenment sears out of the open gateway onto the road outside and does not stop.

Marilyn, who has helplessly watched this weird little battle, this bizarre manifestation of male conflict, from an upstairs window and not even thought of calling the police, has finally found a way to be of help. It is she who, in the nick of time, presses the electronic switch that flings open the metal gate and saves Barry. It is the least she can do. She staggers back from the window, shocked, relieved, tearful and desperately in need of another drink. She takes a swig straight from the bottle, then begins to sob uncontrollably, and she sits down in a big leather swivel chair, one of Carlton's favourites, eventually adopting a foetal position and clutching the whisky bottle to her as a comforter.

Enlightenment roars off into the night. Charles Lederer at the wheel, Barry on the bonnet: and not long after it has gone, eight more black Volkswagens, each one a dead ringer for the departing car, arrive at Carlton Bax's gentleman's residence. The skinhead drivers are surprised to find the front gate open, although however secure the gate had been, it would not have delayed them long. The eight cars move into the drive, slowly, sedately, until they come to the front door of the house where they park, arranging themselves into an intricate, formal pattern which if seen from the air would be clearly visible as a swastika.

Charles Lederer drives on and on, with Barry clinging to the bonnet for all he's worth. His knuckles are white and knotted, his feet are starting to develop cramp. He looks up towards the windscreen, hoping he'll be able to look into the face of Charles Lederer, but the smoked glass prevents that. He feels that he's being propelled backwards into the future. His sense of time is dislocated; a minute spent on that bonnet seems like an age, nevertheless, he is aware that Charles Lederer really is driving a very long way. Perhaps he has realised that sooner or later Barry's aching hands and feet are bound to lose their grip, then Barry will slide forwards off the car and then he'll be finished.

But the way Lederer's driving, it's as if he's forgotten all about Barry and has set off on some wild journey of his own. He is driving very swiftly if erratically, accelerating fiercely round bends, whipping through amber lights, scraping the occasional bollard or parked car as he goes, weaving dangerously in and out of traffic. But in a way Barry is pleased to see other cars. Surely, he thinks, this offers him a chance. Either the traffic will force Charles Lederer to slow down or stop in which case he can leap from the bonnet, or else a passing police patrol car might spot them, or maybe even some public-spirited motorist will see Barry's plight and attempt to stop the car.

It's a long time coming, by which time a great many miles have been covered and a lot of time has passed, but eventually a big white car, a BMW, begins following Enlightenment, flashing its lights and sounding its horn to persuade Charles Lederer to pull over. This, of course, does not work, so the white car starts to overtake Enlightenment and as soon as it's past, the driver brakes hard, forcing the Volkswagen to swerve and stop in a screech of brakes and tyres.

Barry's position doesn't allow him to observe much of what's going on, but he can see the white BMW has no police markings and that the driver is a woman, not that he's giving these things a lot of thought. There are other things on his mind. The moment Charles Lederer stops Enlightenment, Barry throws himself blindly off the car and lands, rather fortuitously, on a soft grass verge. It is such a relief to be detached from the car. He feels broken and his heart is still beating as though it wants to escape from his chest, but he feels better and more secure than he has for a long time.

Charles Lederer's drive has been brought to a halt, but that doesn't mean he's ready to come quietly and let bygones be bygones. Despite the presence of the other car, he throws Enlightenment into reverse and tries to back up, with a view to subsequently driving forward and running Barry over as he recovers on the verge. But fate finally smiles on Barry. Enlightenment stalls, or rather Charles Lederer stalls it. There is a moment of hesitation, in which time the female driver has swiftly sprung out of her own car, approached the Volkswagen, ripped open the driver's door and yanked the key out of the ignition and out of Charles Lederer's grasp. Enlightenment is immobilised. Barry is saved. It is an act that required considered bravery and presence of mind, but perhaps one would expect nothing else from Detective Inspector Cheryl Bronte.

Barry scrambles to his feet and recognises his saviour. 'Thank God,' he says.

'I said I'd see you again, didn't I Barry?'

'I believe you did!'

Cheryl Bronte takes an unwarranted pleasure in being proved right on this point, but then she turns to Charles Lederer and says, 'Is this your car, sir?'

'You know it's *my* car,' says Barry.

'Can't the gentleman answer for himself?' and then she looks inside the car and sees that he can't. Charles Lederer is slumped over the steering wheel, exhausted, spent and quite incapable of speech. So Barry says, 'Don't worry, I can explain everything.'

Cheryl Bronte looks at him with a pained expression, as though she's far from sure that she wants to have everything explained, but Barry has an unstoppable need to tell his story, and he does so. The story takes a considerable amount of time to unfold, and only some of it is of immediate interest to Cheryl Bronte. However, she does prick up her ears when Barry tells her that the old man in the Volkswagen is Charles Lederer, ex-Member of Parliament, father of late night weathergirl Marilyn Lederer, and the man most likely to be res-

169

ponsible for the spate of exploding Volkswagens. However, she still needs convincing of this last proposition.

'What makes you think he's our man?' she asks.

Barry considers the question for a while and in the end can only say, 'Well, that's what his daughter told me.'

'I wonder why she told you that.'

'Maybe because it's true.'

'I think we'd better all go and have a word with this daughter of his,' says Cheryl Bronte.

That suits Barry very nicely. Charles Lederer is decidedly reluctant to move, but he is eventually lifted into the back seat of Cheryl Bronte's car. They head back to Carlton Bax's gentleman's residence, with Charles Lederer maintaining a profound and mournful silence for the entire journey.

Charles Lederer has driven a long way and it's some time before they arrive at the house. The metal security gate is open, but that doesn't surprise them so very much. There's no sign of neo-Nazi Volkswagens, but then they would have no reason to expect them. Neither is there any sign of Marilyn but it takes some time before they realise that.

Cheryl Bronte drives in through the open gate and parks. She sees the tyre tracks that have carved up the lawns and flowerbeds, then she sees the smashed French windows through which Barry made his original exit. She does not look best pleased.

'I can explain all this too,' says Barry.

'Not now,' says Cheryl Bronte. 'Please not now.'

She goes to the front door, finds it open and cautiously steps inside. Barry and Charles Lederer follow her in. There is no sound in the house, and no human presence. All three of them sense that something's terribly wrong here. They look into the first room they come to, Carlton's study. It is in a state of chaos. Drawers have been pulled out of desks, cabinets and glass cases have been smashed, displays torn from the walls, furniture has been overturned and cushions slashed open. The room has not been so much ransacked as

170

completely demolished. And as they move on they see that the whole house has received similar treatment; floorboards have been lifted, and in places even the wallpaper has been scraped off. Something demonically thorough and systematic has been at work.

'Do you know what's going on here?' Barry asks.

'Do you?' Cheryl Bronte asks in return.

'Well of course not,' says Barry. 'Is it a burglary, or what?'

'What do you think?'

'I don't know anything, do I?'

'I don't know what you don't know, Barry. But I think this was only a burglary in a very specialised sense of the word. I think whoever did this was looking for something very specific.'

'Like what?'

'I don't know, but I'd surprised if it wasn't a Volkswagen in some shape or form.'

'And do you think they found it?'

Cheryl Bronte offers nothing but a shrug. At her side Charles Lederer looks around him at the mess and destruction of all the Volkswagen parts and models and badges, and although he still says nothing, his face looks quite satisfied by the spectacle. Then Barry panics. 'What about Marilyn?' he demands. Again Cheryl Bronte says nothing so he runs madly from room to room, calling Marilyn's name, searching for her amid the debris; but he doesn't really expect to find her. He knows she has gone.

It is in the bathroom, where the shower has been wrenched from the wall, where tiles have been smashed and towels torn to ribbons, that he at last sees the message that tells him what he feared most. The message has been written on the wall-sized mirror in shocking pink lipstick and it says, 'We took Carlton Bax. We've taken Marilyn Lederer. When we get what we want you can have them back.'

Barry calls to Cheryl Bronte who comes running, reads the message then nods sadly as though this is exactly what she

171

has been expecting all along. 'Who is that message addressed to?' Barry asks but by now he has learned not to expect a reply. Charles Lederer then arrives in the bathroom and having read the words begins to weep.

'You stupid old bugger,' Barry yells. 'If you hadn't spent half the night trying to kill me, we could have been here to protect Marilyn. Don't you see, we were on the same side all along.'

Cheryl Bronte is unimpressed by this. 'There's nothing more you can do here,' she says to Barry. 'Leave this to me. Just go home.'

'And what about him?'

Charles Lederer is now sobbing his heart out, shivering, shaking, making a deep bovine noise.

'Why don't you take him with you?'

Charles Lederer opens his mouth and lets out a blood-chilling wail of epic, mythical proportions, and suddenly all the mania and the anger is stripped from him, and Barry can suddenly see him as a kind of tragic hero, as a fond and foolish father, as a flawed human being, worthy of pity and compassion, as Oedipus, as King Lear.

'Okay,' says Barry. 'You're right. I'll take him home with me.'

*   *   *

Some time ago now I wrote a short story about a man who believed he could do motor repairs by the laying on of hands. As you may imagine, it was an ironic sort of piece. At the time I wrote it I was living in a village in Kent about twenty miles from London. When my wife and I first moved there we decided we wouldn't be like the other commuters, we'd try to be part of the community. So we took out a subscription to the local parish magazine. It was called *Trident* and it was full of births, marriages and deaths, ads for local butchers and builders, and a lot of short articles where locals described what Jesus meant to them.

I admit that as a way of participating in community life this was fairly limited, but I read the magazine avidly enough, especially the Jesus pieces which always had just the right blend of naivety, humourless sincerity and bad grammar to send a cynical agnostic like me writhing on the floor with derisive laughter. Then one day the following piece appeared:

Just over three years ago I set off for Greenbelt (a religious pop festival) with three Christians, one of whom was my cousin. On the first night in the tent the girls sat down to pray before going to sleep. One of them spoke in tongues (a spiritual language) and one gave the interpretation. It was talking about things that had and were about to happen in my life that none of them could possibly have known about, and telling me how to give my life to Jesus so he could sort out the mess I had made of it so far. On the way home the car broke down. The other three laid hands on the car and it started again.

Well, this was the long arm of coincidence and no mistake. Of course, I didn't know what kind of car they'd been driving, and for that matter I didn't know what drugs – if any – they'd been on, but I filed the information away and thought I might use it somehow if I ever wrote a sequel to *Street Sleeper*.

A couple of weeks later I drove the few miles to the nearest supermarket in Swanley, bought groceries and loaded them into my Volkswagen. The car was enjoying one of its more reliable phases, so it was quite a surprise when I turned on the ignition and absolutely nothing happened. I kept turning the key and pumping the accelerator but got absolutely no result. I got very depressed.

It was winter, late afternoon and it was getting cold and dark. I had a look at the engine and could see nothing amiss.

I tried to start it again, but still nothing. I decided to call the AA. I undertook a long circular walk on which I discovered that every phone box in Swanley had been vandalised. It looked as though I'd have to ask somebody in one of the local shops if I could use their phone. I didn't particularly want to do that but I couldn't see any alternative. However, I thought I'd have a final attempt to start the car before I did so.

I went back to my Beetle, looked at it sadly and laid a hand on the front, nearside wing. I didn't say 'be thou whole' or anything like that, but I was definitely hoping for a bit of divine intervention. But then I thought I'd raise the stakes a little. I said to myself, 'Okay, if this Volkswagen now starts then there *is* a God. If it doesn't there isn't.'

I got into the car, turned the ignition key, and it started first time. Only just, and the engine wheezed and coughed a little at first, but start it most certainly did. I was genuinely and appropriately amazed.

Now, the mechanically minded among you may say that I had simply flooded the engine, and the time it took me to do a circuit of the vandalised phone boxes was time enough for the excess petrol to evaporate. I'm happy to accept that this is absolutely the case. You'll be glad to know that I don't really believe I can repair cars by going around and laying my hands on them. And, of course, this incident wasn't enough to absolutely convince me of the existence of God. However, I have to admit that it was all a little bit peculiar.

It sometimes occurs to me that I should have raised the stakes higher still and asked God to prove himself by ending war, or pain or global pollution. Something tells me that proof might not have been so readily forthcoming. But that's okay. I have always known that God moves in mysterious ways, and it seems only common sense to me that if there is a God, then he must surely be a Volkswagen enthusiast.

VIII

A Book of Common Volkswagens

Barry collects Enlightenment from the grass verge where Charles Lederer abandoned it, and begins a long, slow, melancholy drive back to the caravan site in Filey. The car is still drivable despite the thrashing Charles Lederer gave it, although it is no longer the car it once was.

The man who did all the damage sits beside Barry as he drives. For a long time he has nothing at all to say for himself, but that's all right with Barry who has plenty to occupy his mind. One of the things he thinks about is that he'll have to get in touch with Fat Les again in order to get Enlightenment repaired, and his last meeting with Les was hardly cordial. But he spends far more time thinking about Marilyn. A part of him feels he should be out there searching for her, trying to find the villains who have kidnapped her, trying to free her. That certainly ought to make her feel good about him, and yet he knows this is a quest he will not be making. Basically he's had enough of flogging round the country in a Volkswagen, not knowing where to look or what to look for. He found Charles Lederer when he stopped looking for him, and perhaps it will be possible to find Marilyn by not looking for her at all. It's a long shot, but it's all he's capable of right now. Besides, what's the point of searching for someone who doesn't love you, who's in love with some rich swine who collects Volkswagens.

They are nearly home before Charles Lederer finally speaks. 'I've been a fool,' he says.

'Yes,' Barry agrees.

'I thought you were my problem. I thought that if I destroyed you, I would be destroying all my problems.'

'Is that what psychiatrists mean when they talk about transference?' Barry asks.

'I don't know. Maybe it was just displacement activity.'

'And no doubt you felt the same way about Volkswagens.'

'What do you mean?'

'You felt that if you couldn't destroy me, you'd destroy a few Volkswagens instead.'

'I never destroyed any Volkswagens,' Charles Lederer says, sounding puzzled.

'Ah,' says Barry, 'now I think you're demonstrating what the psychiatrists call denial.'

'I feel so lost,' Charles Lederer says. 'I can't see what's at the end of the road.'

Barry peers through the windscreen and although visibility is less than perfect, he can still see the road ahead quite clearly.

'Huh?' he says.

Charles Lederer continues, 'I can see only the scrap dealer, the breaker's yard, the crusher.'

'Not necessarily,' says Barry, and he remembers something the Ferrous Kid told him. 'Quite a lot of recycling goes on. There's a big demand for secondhand parts. A lot of metal gets melted down and used again. It's a bit like reincarnation I suppose.'

'Is it really?' says Charles Lederer, and then he resumes his silence.

At last they arrive at the caravan site. Barry has mixed feelings about this return. Certainly it's good to be home and not to have to spend any more days and nights on the road, yet he is not returning on the terms he would have wished. He would have liked to be the returning hero, bringing home Marilyn, his true love. That was not to be, and frankly he can't ever see Marilyn wanting to live with him in a caravan when she has the chance to live in Carlton Bax's gentleman's residence. So instead of bringing home his true love, he's bringing home his true love's father. He feels humbled.

He also feels there's going to be a little difficulty in accommodating Charles Lederer. They can hardly share one caravan, if for no other reason than, as Barry has found out in the course of this return trip, the old man has a disturbingly ripe odour about him. Perhaps that ought to be irrelevant to an aspirant to wisdom such as Barry, and certainly he knows he can't leave a fellow traveller stranded on the sliproad of life, but he thinks life will be much easier if he can get the old boy set up in a one man tent, preferably on the far side of the site.

The old place looks familiar enough, and yet Barry senses immediately that there's something different about it. There's something in the air. There's a feeling of hussle about it, an animation among the holidaymakers, a hint of anxiety.

The moment Enlightenment appears outside Barry's caravan, a tiny, familiar figure comes running. It is the Ferrous Kid and he's extremely excited. He's glad enough to see Barry, but that isn't the major cause of his excitement. Barry gives him a cheerful wave but after his long drive he thinks he isn't quite ready to cope with the kid's boundless and exhausting energy. However, he needn't have worried.

'I took your advice,' the kid says happily. 'I don't joyride any more.'

'Oh good,' says Barry.

'Not even responsibly.'

'I'm very glad.'

'Who's the old guy in the car?'

'Don't ask,' says Barry.

The kid shrugs then says, 'Anyway, you got back just in time.'

'In time for what?'

'There's a big meeting going on at the site owner's house. Everyone's going.'

Barry says he can't be bothered to go to any meeting with the site owner. How could it possibly be of relevance to him? But the kid is insistent and he grabs Barry by the elbow and hurries him along. As he goes Barry looks back at Charles Lederer, still seated in Enlightenment, and he hopes he'll not get into trouble before he gets back.

As he walks along with the kid, he sees that people from all over the caravan site are heading in the same direction, and by the time they get to the house they're part of a crowd. It isn't a vast crowd, perhaps only a hundred or so strong, but the people look hostile and angry and Barry asks the kid what this is all about. The kid assures him it will be obvious soon enough.

Sam Probert, the site owner, lives in a pleasant but modest stone-clad house only a few hundred yards from the caravan site. There is a white fence and a carefully laid out and tended front garden with a decorative miniature windmill and an ornamental pond. The crowd however, has no respect for the niceties of garden design. They clamber over the fence and trample all over the lawn and flowerbeds. The arrival of such a mob would bring most proud house owners running to their front door demanding to know what they think they're doing, but this particular house owner knows exactly what they're doing. They ring his doorbell and hammer on the glass of the bay window, but Sam Probert declines to appear.

This only maddens the crowd. They become increasingly restless and vocal, and then someone, probably deliberately, knocks over the miniature windmill, which tumbles into the ornamental pond and shatters into plaster fragments. This is quite a crowd pleaser, and one or two people pick up lumps of the plaster and hurl them towards the house, and it is this action which finally brings out the owner. He doesn't come to the front door, that would be far too risky, but his face does appear at an upstairs window. He looks out nervously and slowly raises the window, fearing that further lumps of plaster might be aimed at his head.

Barry's dealings with Sam Probert have always been brief and pleasant enough. He has never appeared to Barry to be the sort of man who would provoke such passion and hatred in his neighbours and caravanners. Certainly his appearance placates the crowd a little, but after a while, when he simply stares out and says nothing, they soon become rowdy and incensed again. This is not Barry's idea of a 'meeting' as promised by the kid, rather it provides an opportunity for the crowd to abuse the man at the window. Someone calls him a money-grubbing bastard, and someone else shouts something about forty pieces of silver, but Barry can't follow this at all. Not surprisingly, the crowd's antagonism only provokes defiance in Sam Probert, and after listening to a few more insults he's definitely had enough.

'They're my bloody fields and I'll do what I want with them,' he bellows back.

'It's a disgrace,' says one of the more articulate protesters. 'It'll be chaos. There'll be noise and smells, and dogs and children, and people revving their engines and loud music and drugs, unprotected sex and people peeing in the street.'

'I've hired quite a few chemical toilets,' Sam Probert protests weakly, but this does not satisfy the crowd at all.

Things look as though they might turn decidedly ugly, and Barry wants no part of that, so he manhandles the kid away from the house, to safety.

'I still don't have a clue what this is all about,' Barry says.

'I think it's brilliant,' says the kid. 'You know the old bugger also owns two fields adjacent to the site?'

'No, I didn't,' says Barry.

'Well anyway, he's rented them both out for this weekend. He's rented one out to a Volkswagen enthusiasts' club for some shindig called Bug Mecca and he's rented the other

179

one out to a bunch of New Age travellers for a Gathering of the Tribes. It should be hell on earth. I can hardly wait.'

The same old scout hut but now with some new Nazi regalia; flags and banners, medals and uniforms, and a more intense air of aggression and stupidity and casual destructiveness emanating from the skinheads. Phelan appears before his boys, his disciples. Tonight he is feeling expansive and he gives them a brief tour of his favourite obsessions; that the Jewish Holocaust was a myth, that Adolf Hitler in fact had a full complement of testicles, and that AIDS can't be such a bad thing if it kills off gays, drug users and Africans. He can feel his power growing, a strange potent energy that passes from his boys to him.

The skinheads are feeling good too. Thanks to Phelan they have more money than they know what to do with, and they now appear in a stylish, not to say positively mannerist, array of cherry red DMs, Ben Shermans, Crombies and Harringtons. Butcher has even taken to wearing a bowler hat. Phelan is faintly disappointed by this. He was hoping to steer them towards a more paramilitary look, but he doesn't want to push them too far too fast. There is money for any amount of extra strong lager, for Oi records and for new tattoos of staggering scope and complexity.

Tonight there is almost a party atmosphere, something helped along by the presence of Renata Caswell. She has told Phelan how turned on she gets by a good collection of skinheads and that's an interest he wants to encourage. She is dressed in the shortest of leather skirts and a Luftwaffe bomber jacket, hardly skinhead gear, but the lads are nevertheless juiced up by her presence. Only Butcher seems to be less than one hundred per cent sanguine. Something is bothering him, and it does have something to do with a woman.

180

'What happened to the girl?' he asks Phelan.

'What girl would that be?'

'Come on. Don't fuck about. The one we found in that house. The one we kidnapped for you.'

'She's being taken care of,' Phelan says.

There is much dirty laughter from the other skinheads, though not from Butcher.

'What's that supposed to mean?' he insists.

Phelan says nothing, just looks across at Renata and smiles. But Butcher won't be shaken off that easily.

'I mean did you fuck her, or beat her, or kill her, or what?'

'What do you think I am?' asks Phelan. 'A monster?'

Even Butcher has to laugh at that.

'Seriously though,' says Phelan, 'I'm not sure it's any of your business.'

Butcher isn't sure either. He already suspects that Phelan gets up to all kinds of things that he'd rather not know about, and the fate of Marilyn Lederer might very well be in that category. But if something terrible's happened to her then he was a part of it, an accessory, and it's all very well Phelan saying they're a new breed of hero and above the law, but the fuzz might see it a bit differently. Till now all he's really been involved with is fisticuffs and a bit of nicking. Phelan seems to want to push him into some whole different world.

'And anyway,' says Butcher again, 'what were we doing in that house anyway? What were we supposed to be looking for?'

'If I told you that,' says Phelan, 'then you'd know as much as I do.'

Given time to think about it, Butcher would have realised that remark was neither true nor relevant, but Phelan doesn't give him any time.

'What does it matter?' he says. 'You enjoyed yourself didn't you, Butcher?'

'Yes,' Butcher admits.

'You enjoyed smashing things up. That's your talent, your forte.'

'Yes,' says Butcher.

'That's what I need you for. All of you.'

Phelan's face adopts a look of fatherly love which both flatters and embarrasses them. Then he gets them to tell him stories of their recent exploits; raiding petrol stations, doing over tobacconist's shops, video stores, off licences, provoking fights in pubs and clubs, nicking cars, beating up a few Pakis and Jew boys. It does him good to hear it. He glances frequently at Renata to see how she's reacting to these accounts, and he thinks he sees the patina of sexual arousal on her face.

Even Butcher joins in with the stories and before long he's much more like his vicious old self, but he still remains more thoughtful than the other skinheads and he says, 'Do you know which rumble I enjoyed best?'

'Tell me,' says Phelan, genuinely interested.

'Beating up them New Age travellers.'

'Yes?'

'Yeah,' says Butcher. 'There was something really good about it. I think it was because they were like hippies, all dirty and long-haired and spiritual. And like they think they're better than everybody else, like they've found something special and got all the answers. Only they haven't. It's not right. It's not British.'

'Well, I'd agree there,' says Phelan. 'What do the rest of you think?'

The rest gradually agree that there was indeed a certain frisson in knocking hell out of the New Age travellers, and the general consensus is that they'd like to do more of it.

'Now,' says Phelan, 'I just may be able to help you there. It appears there's going to be a so-called Gathering of the Tribes in the not too distant future.'

'How many are going to be there?'

'Thousands I understand.'

182

'Bloody hell.'

The eight skinheads realise that even they might have a little trouble putting fear into thousands of New Age travellers.

'You have friends don't you?' asks Phelan.

They admit that they do.

'So let's say you bring in some new blood. Let's say each of you recruits four more like-minded individuals. Each of you will then be a leader of your own quasi-autonomous force. A force that, at a pinch, can be accommodated in a Volkswagen Beetle. Five of you per car makes forty. That ought to be enough, surely. That's a lot of aggro.'

The skinheads give it some thought. They obviously want to agree with Phelan. They want to believe they are an elite force, a match for a number of old or new hippies. They also like the idea of being leaders.

'Remember,' says Phelan, 'that they have no discipline, that they won't be expecting you, that they'll be high on drugs, and that they're racially inferior.'

Butcher says, 'All right, you're on.'

Phelan looks across at Renata so that she can acknowledge how wonderful, how powerful he is. Then he looks back at the skinheads.

'You may be Nazi scum,' he says, 'but you're *my* Nazi scum.'

Phelan drives home, Renata beside him, his hand playing absent-mindedly on her upper thigh. He doesn't drive a Volkswagen Beetle, of course. He prefers the plush, solid certainties of a Mercedes, the make of car Adolf Hitler usually chose to travel in, whatever his feelings about the Beetle.

'They're a wild bunch,' says Renata, referring to the skinheads.

'They're the future,' says Phelan.

183

'The future's going to be dumb but sexy?'

'There are worse futures.'

'That boy called Butcher, he's interesting,' she says. 'He's not quite like the others.'

'Do you want to fuck him?'

'I want to fuck them all,' she replies, in a manner that might or might not be serious.

'It can be arranged.'

'I bet.'

For now, however, there is other work to be done. They arrive at Phelan's home. He lives in a strange, grey, bunker-like industrial building, on the edge of London, in a location that might have been chosen for its appalling proximity to roads and traffic. Its entrance is off a giant roundabout, around which cars and lorries swirl at high speed all day and all night. Six lanes of traffic scream past the back of the building, while overhead a flyover carries vehicles to and from the start of the motorway. Exhaust fumes hang over the area. Tyre noise and engine roar and the deep vibration of Juggernauts make the place alive with infernal sound and fury. There are no pavements, no public transport, no place for pedestrians. Phelan says he would live nowhere else. It feels modern and technological. It keeps him sharp and in touch, and it's also extremely private. If you kidnapped, say, a Volkswagen collector and kept him locked in your base-ment here, nobody would ever find him. If you then kid-napped his girlfriend, or rather got eight of your followers to do so, you could stash her there too. You could keep them both in captivity, play one off against the other, tease and coerce and torment them until they told you what you wanted to know. Not that they've told Phelan anything yet. Marilyn Lederer is being every bit as uncooperative as Carlton Bax; pleading ignorance, admitting nothing. And that's where Renata comes in. He thinks that a woman's touch may be just what's needed, that Marilyn will tell her things that she'd never tell him. And in a sense he's right.

184

Once inside the bunker, Phelan goes to the trophy room, the place with the flags and the bed and the military Volkswagen that he uses as a prop for their couplings. Meanwhile Renata goes down to the basement, to the locked room where Marilyn is being kept, to see what confessions she can wrest from her. But Phelan is hardly surprised when Renata returns half an hour later looking disappointed, though not, in fact, as disappointed as Phelan thinks she ought to look.

'She says she doesn't know anything,' Renata reports.

'And do you believe her?'

'You know, I think I probably do.'

'Well, if she doesn't know anything then she's no use to me. I'll have to get rid of her. Maybe I could throw her to Butcher and his friends.'

'Some girls have all the luck,' Renata says and she goes over and kisses Phelan. He grabs her by the hair, with a studied roughness. She smiles through the discomfort. They go to bed, their minds so full of perverse images that tonight they do not even need to use the Gestapo Volkswagen.

Next morning Phelan gets up, washes and cleanses himself with a thorough, military precision. Renata remains in bed, looking worn out, used, satisfied. Phelan dresses, studying himself closely in a number of full length mirrors the whole time. Finally he's ready to go about his business. He gets the Mercedes and is ready to drive away from the bunker, leaving Renata to her feigned sleep.

Amid the road noise she listens for the slamming of doors and the start of the engine and when she's sure that he's gone, she springs from the bed, dresses quickly and carelessly and runs out to her own car, the yellow Volkswagen that Fat Les smashed and then repaired for her. She drives fast and determinedly through the patterning and interplay of traffic until she arrives at Carlton Bax's gentleman's residence.

185

The gate is closed and there is some police tape tied across it to forbid entry, and yet it is unlocked and it moves and opens easily enough at her touch. The front door of the house and the broken French window have been hastily and clumsily boarded up, and entry wouldn't be too much of a problem, but she isn't going into the house, she's going into the garage where Carlton Bax houses his full-size Volkswagens.

She gets out of her car, opens the boot and removes a tool kit. She uses a crowbar to break open the garage door and once inside she heads straight for the state of the art, electric-blue Baja Beetle. Its doors are open and she positions herself in the passenger seat. The car has a modified dashboard of very cool-looking brushed aluminium. It seems a shame to wreck it but that's what she's here to do. She takes a hammer and chisel from the kit and knocks the chisel in behind the dash so that it tears away from the frame of the car. She pulls back the metal until there's just room enough for her to slide her hand inside. She feels around until her hand touches something small, square and plastic. She grabs it, pulls it out, and sees that she's holding a piece of buried treasure, a computer disc containing the catalogue of Carlton Bax's Volkswagen collection.

She pockets the disc, gathers up her tools and heads back for her car, then she drives to her own flat, a place she doesn't get to very much since she's been involved with Phelan. She is no computer buff and she hopes the information on the disc isn't encoded, but since Carlton Bax went to the trouble of physically hiding the disc, she imagines the catalogue will give up its secrets easily enough. She hopes her own limited skills and her own PC will be enough. Then, if this catalogue tells her what she thinks it's going to tell her, she'll be able to get out, to write her big article or series of articles, expose Phelan and make a big name for herself as the daring and feisty investigative journalist who infiltrated and cracked a neo-Nazi gang.

She slips the disc into her computer, and sure enough, she was right. The disc gives up its information without too much of a fight. The problem is, there's so much information and most of it is so desperately dull. She spends hour after hour searching through menus and files, through directories and spreadsheets, peering through windows, scrolling through bleak, dry entries that list and describe innumerable items of Volkswagen memorabilia in exhaustive, obsessive detail, complete with dimensions and colours, date and source of acquisition, and value. There are listings and groupings and cross references, and endless footnotes. Only a nut like Carlton Bax could possibly be interested in this stuff, and then she remembers that a nut like Phelan would be very interested in it too. The day passes. She is drowning in data. There are over 300 entries on Volkswagen key rings alone, and she needs to read each one, just in case the item she's looking for is hidden there. From time to time she calls up the Help function on the menu, but each time it tells her, 'No help is available here.'

Day turns into evening. Her eyes are hurting and her back aches from being perched on the edge of her chair. She's falling asleep. She's ready to call it a day. It's all so maddening, so frustrating, and maybe she was wrong, maybe she's been wasting her time and the information she needs isn't even here. Then suddenly it is one in the morning, and she realises she must have dozed off, must have slumped down on the keyboard, but in the process she has somehow, inadvertently, given the right command. A really Zen piece of computer operation. She has summoned up a directory called LOCKROOM, a name that even in her weary state she can see is highly promising. She plunges into it. The directory contains a list of files with weird names like PRESLEY, MANSON, BUNDY, none of which she can quite understand, and then she sees it, the entry that makes sense of everything; a file called HITLER. DOC. She calls it up. The entry appears:

Item: Volkswagen automaton

Date of construction: 1938
Dimensions: 300 x 115 x 140 mm
Country of manufacture: Germany
Constructed of wood, metal, glass, semi-precious stone, human bone
Maker: Paul Löffler
Previous owner: Adolf Hitler
Value: priceless.
Location: Mrs Lederer

She almost swoons with pleasure.

Here, finally, is Adolf Hitler in the Spring of 1938 in a timber cabin in the woods of Bavaria. He is here to relax from the affairs of state. Eva Braun sits beside him on a Biedermeier love seat, sipping Apfelwein and nibbling Mohnstriezel.

And here is Paul Löffler, one of Germany's finest, most inventive makers of clocks and automata, and one of Hitler's favourites. He is here to entertain the happy couple, to amuse and amaze them with his latest wonderful creation. In the past he has made cuckoo clocks out of which pop extinct or mythological creatures – cerberus, a gryphon, a tyrannosaurus rex, a dodo – or an automaton the size of a wedding cake on which lovingly hand-carved figures enact scenes from Wagner's *Ring*, synchronised to music played on gramophone records.

Löffler enters carrying a large carpet bag which he places on a small occasional table in front of the Führer. He releases the clasps and opens the neck of the bag before reaching in and producing what looks like a small model of a Volkswagen Beetle, though at that time, of course, he would only have known it as a KdF-Wagen. It is carved from smooth, polished mahogany, with brass fittings for the hub caps, windscreen wipers, door handles and headlamps, and although it has a fabric sun roof, the windows are opaque, made of black glass. It is no more than a foot long.

Löffler holds it out to Adolf Hitler who takes it from him and eyes it carefully. He does not smile. He can see that it is a well-made and skilfully executed model of the car, but somehow he had expected more from Löffler.

Then he notices that there is a small brass winder protruding from the rear of the car, like a cranking handle, that just cries out to be turned, and Hitler duly turns it. Slowly and smoothly the sun roof rolls back to reveal the interior of the car. There are seats and a steering wheel and a metal gear lever and foot pedals, but there are also two small figures, a man and a woman sitting beside each other on the rear seat.

'They're carved from real human bone,' Löffler says confidentially.

Adolf Hitler peers at the two tiny figures. They are beautifully carved and they are articulated. They are able to move thanks to an intricate system of threads, wires and armatures, and as the handle turns, they begin to perform. But there is something disturbing about them. First, they are naked, a forgivable artistic licence perhaps since it shows off Löffler's fine carvings of muscles and flesh; but what seems unforgivable, what in the circumstances would have previously been considered unthinkable, is the fact that the two white figures have been given the faces of Adolf Hitler and Eva Braun.

As Hitler continues to turn the handle, the female figure lowers her head towards the male figure's crotch where a penis, flatteringly out of scale and disproportionately large, rises towards her mouth. The two bone automata mime an act of vigorous fellatio until, in a sudden rapid conclusion, the female pulls back her head and a shower of sparkling powder – 'Genuine diamond dust,' Löffler explains – jets out of the automaton's penis and coats the face of the miniature Eva Braun. Instantly the sun roof springs back over the car and conceals the two figures. Again it looks like a harmless model of a KdF-Wagen.

189

Paul Löffler looks extremely pleased with himself, but Adolf Hitler shows a more complex, more equivocal response. His face is not inert, rather it seems to be searching for an appropriate expression. Beneath the moustache, his lips twitch in an uncertain manner that Löffler certainly hopes will turn into an expression of uncontainable pleasure, and sure enough, at length, the Führer does allow his lips to bend into a thin, taut smile.

Later that same day, Paul Löffler is taken out into the woods and, in a spot well screened from the cabin by a row of silver birches, he is shot by a Gestapo officer called Hans Krauss. Adolf Hitler shows his appreciation by giving Krauss an early version of a Kraft durch Freudewagen, a full size one, a car that will eventually find its way, not into Carlton Bax's locked room, but into Phelan's bunker.

Renata continues to stare at the entry on the screen. Now she understands. So this is what Phelan has been looking for so hard and so long, why he kidnapped Carlton Bax and Marilyn Lederer; because Bax had got Adolf Hitler's toy Beetle, and because Phelan wanted to play with it. Ah well, boys will be boys. But what Phelan obviously didn't know was where to find it, and frankly she's not sure she's much wiser for having seen this file. What on earth does 'Mrs Lederer' mean as a location? Could that be Marilyn's mother, Charles Lederer's wife? Would Carlton Bax really have left his priceless Volkswagen with his girlfriend's mother? Why not just leave it in the famous locked room?

And then she turns around, away from the screen, and she nearly jumps out of her skin as she sees Phelan is standing behind her, and may have been watching her for who knows how long. His hands are folded casually in front of him and he looks controlled and serene.

'I hate it when people lie to me,' he says.

'I haven't lied . . . ,' she starts to say.

'Yes you have. You said Marilyn Lederer had told you nothing. It looks like she told you more than enough.'

'She didn't . . . I was . . . .'

'It's all right Renata. I've known for some time that you weren't exactly what you appear to be.'

'I always intended to tell you where Hitler's Volkswagen was.'

'What you intended doesn't matter at all. You've found out what I wanted to know. You see, I want that Volkswagen rather badly. I believe it's the final thing I need. Once I've got it I'll be ready. I believe it contains serious magic, Renata. It's my Grail, my lost ark. And thanks to you, Renata, I now know where it is. I ought to be grateful to you.'

Renata stands beside her monitor screen, trying to back away from Phelan. He moves towards her, raising his hand as he approaches. He could be about to slap her, but in fact the hand comes to rest harmlessly on her shoulder. He squeezes her flesh, firmly but not harshly. In other circumstances it might seem affectionate.

'You don't have to worry about me,' Renata says. 'You don't have to do anything about me.'

'Personally I'm not going to do anything to you at all.'

He reaches into his jacket pocket and takes out a pair of heavy duty handcuffs. He picks up Renata's right hand and places one cuff around her wrist, gently as though it was a piece of jewellery, then locks it. He shepherds her into the bedroom and pushes her face down onto the bed. He loops the handcuffs through the metal curves of the brass bedhead then locks in her other wrist. He gets up, walks to the bedroom door. She can hear footsteps and male voices and she turns her head to see Butcher and four other skinheads enter the room. She hasn't seen these others before. They are Butcher's friends, his new recruits.

'Do whatever you like to her,' says Phelan. 'But make it

191

permanent and don't be too long about it. Remember there's a gathering of the tribes you have to get to.'

* * *

In some sense I suppose an author is all his characters. I am, I suppose, both Barry Osgathorpe and Fat Les. I am both Charles and Marilyn Lederer. I am the New Age travellers and the neo-Nazis. I 'am' these people to the limited extent that I need to impersonate them and live inside their heads for the amount of time it takes to write them. I become them but yet I don't have to become *like* them; and this is a blessing. However, there is an important sense in which I am somewhat like Carlton Bax: I'm a Volkswagen collector.

Obviously I'm not in the Carlton Bax league. I don't claim to be a great or even a very serious collector. I have no garage or warehouse full of classic and historic Beetles. I certainly have no locked room. In fact I don't own any 'real' Beetles at all at the moment, but my flat is littered with hundreds of toy and model Beetles, Beetle clocks, mugs, egg cups, books, magazines, a few T-shirts, that kind of stuff.

When people ask me 'How come?' I usually say it all started as a joke and it subsequently got out of hand. I imply that I bought myself a couple of toy Beetles when I first owned a real Volkswagen and that it has grown from there. I say that well-meaning friends are always giving me Volkswagen stuff and that the collection has grown of its own volition without any guidance or interference from me.

This is almost entirely untrue. It's obviously true that there was a moment when I had no model Beetles at all, and there must have been a moment when I suddenly had one or two. However, as soon as I had two or three it became entirely obvious to me that this could be the first step towards a vast and significant collection. This may not have been

192

entirely rational. One or two friends have given me Beetles as presents, but I am a difficult person to buy for. Once a collection has reached a certain size the chances are that I already have the more common examples that people are able to buy for me.

From the beginning I have tried to explain and justify the collecting urge, and I tend to say that I collect Beetles, rather than, say, E type Jaguars or Morris Minors, because the Beetle has such an archetypal form. It has penetrated so many countries and cultures. It is ubiquitous and instantly recognisable. I am no great traveller but over the years I've been in the United States, France, Morocco, Egypt and Australia, and in every place there have been real Beetles on the roads and model Beetles for sale in the shops or at markets.

Some of the items in my collection become a form of travel souvenir. In Cairo I bought a couple of Beetles moulded out of recycled plastic, out of what looks like shredded and melted down detergent bottles. The moulds must have been too hot, so that the plastic has scorched and turned a slightly revolting shade of blue/brown. I remember clearly the Egyptian man who sold them to me, how he seemed to think I wanted to haggle over the price when in fact the price he'd asked was so cheap I just wanted to be sure I'd understood him correctly. They cost so little that I sometimes wish I'd bought dozens of them, taken them home and turned them into some sort of sculpture. I remember being in a gas station in Yuma, Arizona and trying to buy a couple of toy Beetles they had for sale at the counter, but they didn't know what I was talking about when I asked to buy 'those Beetles over there' since they, of course, only knew them as Bugs.

Some of the models in my collection are extremely good, beautifully detailed, made by real craftsmen. Others are very crude, mass produced, designed to be thrown away. But they are all welcome. One of the thrills of these crude representations is to see just how inaccurate a model of a Beetle may be and yet still remain, recognisably, unmistakably, a Beetle.

Quality is not a matter of complete indifference to me, but the essential concern is variety and diversity. And this must surely be the reason for collecting anything; a means of asserting difference in a world of mass duplication.

The twenty-odd million real Volkswagen Beetles that have been produced clearly resemble each other in all the important ways; their lines, their profile, their layout. Despite changes in engine capacity or window shape or headlight design, they have far more similarities than they have differences. A Beetle standing alone is one thing, but whenever two or three stand side by side we are able to compare and contrast, to see the different interpretations and patinas wrought upon the cars. Even if the owner doesn't actively personalise or customise the Beetle directly, it becomes unique by virtue of dents, scrapes and resprays. This is a means by which we humanise a machine.

In 1992 I was telephoned by Catherine Bennett of the *Guardian* who was writing an article on collecting and collectors. When the article appeared she quoted me as follows:

'I think collecting's a weird thing, a very uncreative activity,' says Geoff Nicholson, though he has a growing heap of toy Volkswagen Beetles. 'I suppose in the real world I'd quite like to collect real Volkswagens, and having models of them kind of puts you in control of a very tiny world. It sounds sort of pathetic and twisted doesn't it?'

I think I'm prepared to stand by this. However, several things need to be said. First, I'm not sure I *do* want to own a collection of real Volkswagens. Owning real cars is a demanding, frustrating and expensive business. They go wrong, they need constant attention, and even when looked after properly they still deteriorate and decay. A collection of models or memorabilia doesn't. It remains intact and, with a modicum of luck, becomes increasingly valuable. Secondly, being in control of a tiny world seems to me exactly what a novelist does so perhaps it isn't so pathetic and twisted after

194

all. And thirdly, it is an outrage to suggest that my Beetle collection is a 'growing heap'. My Volkswagens are cherished, loved, kept on shelves, in boxes and display cabinets, so that my flat, it might well be said, looks like a still life with Volkswagens.

IX

Bonfire of the Volkswagens

Mrs Lederer moves around her apartment, plumping a cushion here, making a minor adjustment to a flower arrangement there. She wants the room to look right. Somehow she knows he's about to arrive. She doesn't know his name or what he will look like, but she wants to be absolutely ready for him. She hears tyres on the gravel and she looks out to see a Mercedes pulling into the drive. The car stops and a man gets out, a complete stranger, and yet there is no mistaking him. It could only be Phelan. He looks strong and determined, eager but not hasty.

He rings the front doorbell and she waits a moment before going to answer it. She checks herself in the hallway mirror then opens the door wide and invites him in. He had imagined that he might have to use persuasion, coercion, even force on Mrs Lederer but her manner is entirely open and cooperative. It looks like there will be no problems here.

'Mrs Lederer,' he says. 'I'm very pleased to meet you.'

She smiles and nods but says nothing.

'You have something I want,' he adds.

'Yes,' she says. 'I think I do.'

'Have you been expecting me?'

'You or someone like you.'

He nods sympathetically, a family doctor making a house call. 'And you know why I'm here.'

'I can guess. Long before Carlton Bax disappeared, he gave me a package. I thought it was a slightly odd present at the

196

time but I tried to look grateful. When Marilyn disappeared too, I made one or two deductions and suspected that someone would be coming to reclaim that present sooner or later.'

'I think you're being very sensible about this,' he says. 'Now show me the Volkswagen.'

'It's upstairs,' she says and she leads him from the living room up to her bedroom. The bed is unmade and the room smells of bodies.

She goes over to a carved oak chest at the foot of the bed and lifts the lid. She tries hard to be casual. She reaches inside and pulls out an old but innocuous looking cardboard box, no more than a foot long. It is scuffed, discoloured and it has some indecipherable German writing on it. She hands it to Phelan. He takes it from her as though it might explode. His hands betray a slight tremor as he places the box on the dressing table and carefully opens it. Within is a small glass case with a wooden base, and set on that base is the object of all his needs and fascination; Paul Löffler's automaton, Hitler's Beetle.

He removes the cardboard box, takes off the glass case and stares fixedly at the naked reality of the model. He glances up at the angled dressing table mirrors and sees three reflections of the car and himself, multiple images that project through time and history.

He touches the handle delicately, just the way Adolf Hitler must have done all those years ago. He knows it is only his imagination, and yet the brass of the handle feels hot, as though there is some potent electric current coursing through it. He begins to turn the handle and gently, slowly, the sun roof of the Volkswagen rolls back. He sees the naked figures of Adolf Hitler and Eva Braun, delicate, absurd, utterly obscene. He can hear the whirr of tiny gears and cams moving effortlessly inside the car. The operation is smooth and reassuring. With every turn he can feel his powers growing. Now that he has this, nothing can stop him.

He prolongs the sequence, savouring each movement of

197

the model figures, each turn of the mechanism, until both he and the automaton of Adolf Hitler can delay no longer and the tiny shower of diamond dust sprays from Hitler's over-sized bone penis and the sun roof snaps shut.

Phelan is aware that he has an erection, but it is not because the pornography of the automaton has aroused him. It has more to do with power, with the anticipation of conquest and domination. He is also aware that his skin feels like sandpaper, that the light in the bedroom has become thickly luminous and that he may be about to sob.

He tries to collect himself. Swiftly but lovingly he returns the Volkswagen to its case and then to its box. He picks it up, holds it firmly in both of his big, beringed hands.

Suddenly Mrs Lederer slaps him across the face with all her might. It is a spiteful and shocking blow, delivered with a strength that comes from some fierce, surprising place deep inside her.

'If you've done anything to my daughter . . . ,' she says.

'Your daughter is just fine,' he says. 'She's with her boy-friend.'

She says nothing.

He rubs his cheek, at least partly in admiration of her power.

'You've done well, Mrs Lederer,' he says. 'You've done the right thing in handing over the automaton. When this whole business is over, I could have a need of someone like you.'

She stares at him coldly, a little contemptuously, and yet there is something in her face that tells him that their needs might not be entirely at odds.

On Friday afternoon they start to arrive. They come from everywhere, with their different hopes and expectations and modes of transport. The New Agers come in their buses and vans and converted ambulances, and some even on foot.

The Volkswagen enthusiasts arrive in their campers and Bajas, their splits and ovals, their Karmann Ghias and Jeans and Super Beetles, some Cal look, some Resto-Cal, some customised, some completely standard. The camp followers arrive too. For the New Agers there are vegetarian food stalls, tarot readers, astrologists, vendors of crystals and aura goggles. For the Volkswagen enthusiasts there are the sellers of dress-up engine parts, customisers, engine tuners and rebuilders, dealers who specialise in Volkswagen toys and collectables.

Inevitably there is some confusion. Sam Probert has organised a few stewards to direct people as they arrive, but the stewards themselves are not organised at all, and so, especially at first, some Volkswagen fans end up in the New Age field, and vice versa. But gradually the build up of Volkswagens in one field and of New Age culture in the other, ensures that a moment comes when no such mistake can be made. There is a small police presence, and they do their best to remain friendly yet formal.

Both crowds are surprisingly diverse. Among the Gathering of the Tribes there are many genuine full-time New Age travellers, but there are also plenty of old hippies, crusties, punks, a few bikers, and more than a smattering of clean and healthy looking youngsters who seem to have borrowed Mum's hatchback and are playing at being New Age for the weekend. There are even one or two skinheads, though not of the neo-Nazi variety.

Those attending Bug Mecca are also varied in their own way. Some are family groups out for a weekend's camping, while others are history buffs and are driving thrillingly authentic antique Volkswagens. Some are trendy young things in immaculate, restored Beetles, while others try to look like California surfers.

Moreover, a certain number of visitors are interested in both events. Some old hippies are interested in Volkswagens. Some Volkswagen enthusiasts are into things New Age. Fans of rave culture are at home in either camp. People pass back and forth between the two fields, sometimes in Volkswagens, often not, and they are able to partake of both Volkswagen and New Age worlds.

One or two locals are happy enough to welcome the visitors; mostly the owners of the local garages, supermarkets and off licences, who do a brisk trade. They tend to welcome the Volkswagen people more than the New Age travellers because, in the main, the former spend more money, but when Planetary Cliff arrives at the petrol station in his double decker bus and fills it up with diesel, he's made to feel very welcome indeed. Nevertheless, the people who said it was a disgrace, that there would be chaos, noise and smells, dogs and children, people revving their engines and loud music and drugs, unprotected sex and people peeing in the street, still feel they're going to be proved absolutely right.

In fact Planetary Cliff is one of the first to arrive, naturally enough, since he's the one providing the music for the Gathering of the Tribes. Many hours are spent unloading his bus and setting up his vast sound system in a corner of the field furthest from the caravan site. Cliff tries to be considerate.

A stage is rapidly constructed out of scaffolding and old boards, and it has a navy blue back cloth with suns, moons and holy symbols painted on it. A lighting rig will illuminate the stage at night, and there is a row of microphones so that Planetary Cliff, or anyone else, can address the crowd and share some cosmic wisdom with them.

Cliff never has any shortage of helpers on these occasions, and the most enthusiastic helper here by far is Davey.

'Looks like I'm finally going to do it,' says Davey.

'What's that?' Planetary Cliff asks.

'Get to dance in a field till dawn, out of my head on Ecstasy.'

'Well,' says Cliff, 'whatever gets you through the night.'

'Think it'll be easy to get some E?'

'I dare say.'

'You know, I was talking to a girl a few minutes ago and she said the Earth Goddess is talking to us in our dreams. What do you think about that?'

'I think she might be a very good source of drugs,' says Planetary Cliff.

In Barry's caravan site a siege mentality has started to take hold. Most of the inmates have declared that they're not setting foot outside the site until this whole sordid business is over. Thus they will avoid all contact with, and risk of pollution from, the invading hordes. A sort of road block has been set up at the entrance to the site and teams of men are working as sentries to vet anyone who attempts to enter. Another small team of vigilantes patrols the perimeter. This does not make for a pleasant or relaxing atmosphere.

Even Barry has thought of going away for the whole of this festive weekend. Fond though he is of Volkswagens he doesn't want to spend the whole weekend watching them come and go, seeing and hearing them being put through their paces, listening to the sound of their air-cooled engines, their sports exhausts, their in-car stereos. And he certainly doesn't want to have to put up with an all night New Age rave on the other side.

So he thinks of going to Southend for the weekend to renew contact with Fat Les and to get him involved in repairing Enlightenment. He rings Fat Volkz Inc but fails to speak to Fat Les. Instead, an extremely young boy answers the phone and says he can't be of any help because he's just there holding the fort and everybody else has gone to the Bug Mecca being held near Filey. Fat Volkz is having a trade stand there and if he's absolutely desperate to speak to Fat Les he could always go there. Once again Barry is amazed by the extent to which the world seems to bring him what he wants when he wants it. This has saved him the problem of driving to Southend. However, there is still the problem of Charles Lederer.

The old man has settled into his new environment rather well. Barry has not succeeded in organising a tent for him. More precisely, he found a tent without any trouble, but Charles Lederer is refusing to sleep in it. By the time Barry had returned from the angry meeting with Sam Probert, Lederer had installed himself in Barry's caravan and he now shows no sign of budging. The old guy is still obviously in a state of shock and distress, and Barry doesn't want to be hard on him, so for the time being Barry has returned to sleeping, and indeed living, in Enlightenment.

Charles Lederer spends a lot of time asleep and Barry has no objection to that. He thinks, in fact, it might be very much for the best if the old man could remain unconscious for the whole weekend. If Charles Lederer wanders out of the caravan site and finds himself standing in a field with a couple of thousand Volkswagens, then Barry fears the worst.

Fat Les arrives at Bug Mecca early on Friday. The Fat Volkz trade stand is extremely impressive. It consists of a small marquee in which there are display boards showing before and after photographs of some of the best Beetles he's restored or customised. A bank of video screens shows these same cars in action, though neither photographs nor videos show Enlightenment nor any of the eight neo-Nazi Beetles. In the centre of the marquee is a wretched looking, rusty, dented pale blue Beetle that a couple of the lads will be knocking back into shape and giving a tricksy paintjob over the course of the weekend.

Les has some very flashy lines of Volkswagen accessories for sale; louvred wings and running boards, pink and black leather replacement door panels, a gear lever encrusted with diamantes and turquoise. But what he prefers to offer is a total service. He says he wants his customers to put them-selves entirely in his hands, to free their minds and to dream up their wildest Volkswagen fantasies, and then he will make those fantasies a reality.

At least that's what he says to his more gullible customers. Now, as he stands in this flat, dreary field surrounded by Volkswagens, their owners and their drivers, he once again feels overwhelmed, bored, satiated, nauseated by their insistent presence. He wouldn't mind seeing the whole bloody lot of them blown up.

Sure enough, Phelan's skinheads also arrive that Friday evening; forty of them, five per car as demanded by Phelan. Of course, they had no idea that there would be a Bug Mecca in the field adjacent to the Gathering of the Tribes, and they are more than surprised to find themselves the subject of considerable curiosity and attention from Beetle fans. They are directed into Bug Mecca even though that's not where they want to go, and once inside, a small crowd gathers around the cars. There's a general admiration for the work that's gone into their Beetles, though several people make disparaging remarks about the presence of swastikas and SS flashes on the paintwork. At first the skinheads find all this hard to take, but Butcher points out to his cohorts that a Volkswagen meeting is just about the perfect place from which to launch their attacks on the New Agers. It provides them with a reason to be there and a lot of cover. If their victims report that they were beaten up by somebody in a Volkswagen, that isn't going to tell anybody very much, is it?

Friday night passes off more or less peaceably. There is some scattered rowdiness and partying in both fields. There is no doubt a little drug and drink abuse, and certainly there is music and dancing. But the partying remains non-violent, the intake of drink and drugs remains moderate, and Planetary Cliff's sound system, vast though it is, stays quiet enough to avoid complaints from police or locals, and it is turned off before midnight. Not long after that, both fields become calm, quiet and dormant. Camp fires burn here and there, and the occasional Beetle cruises the local roads, but there is nothing going on here that need frighten or threaten the local community. But then again, this is only Friday night.

It is Saturday morning before reports begin to circulate that several New Age travellers have been beaten up and robbed in the night. These attacks are declared to have been cowardly and unprovoked, carried out anonymously, viciously and under cover of darkness. Unseen fists, boots and baseball bats have emerged from the darkness, and none of the victims is able to describe the attackers, certainly none could specify that he was beaten up by Volkswagen-driving neo-Nazi skinheads.

Saturday morning. Dawn breaks. Pale sunlight moves over the fields and the caravan site, over Volkswagens and caravans and tatty old buses, over holidaymakers and New Age travellers and Beetle drivers alike. Slowly things come to life. At the edge of Bug Mecca a group of skinheads is seen performing exercises, martial arts moves and occasional Nazi salutes. It is quite clear to those camping nearby that these boys are up to no good, but so far their misdeeds have been entirely clandestine and they have created no cause for concern. Furthermore, the campers reason, any group of lads that drives such a tasty set of Volkswagens can't be all bad.

, This is to be the big day of the Bug Mecca. There will be an engine changing competition, a concours d'élégance, and a Miss V-Bug competition, although so far there are only two entrants for that. There will be continuous showings of the Herbie movies in a darkened marquee for the children. There will be an autojumble and swapmeet, and a display of Beetle dragsters, although they won't be allowed to drive anywhere, and there is the promise of an 'engine destruct' – an event where an old Beetle engine is over-revved until it destroys itself.

It will be a big day for the Gathering of the Tribes too. There will be any number of workshops and seminars on Tai

204

chi and water divining and on how to spot a spiritual vortex. There will be chanting and meditation. There will be demonstrations of tattooing, massage and reflexology. All good stuff. But it is hoped that at some point the tribes will not only gather, but actually merge, so that there will be a loss of self, to be replaced by a feeling of oneness, a blending into the group mind. To this end Planetary Cliff will be playing some extremely loud music and everyone will dance and take a lot of drugs; just as Davey dreamed. However, since these activities will take place throughout a long, sleepless night, things are a little slow to get moving in the New Age field; everyone is resting up for the rigours ahead.

Fat Les is up bright and early. A lot of potential customers will need to be chatted up in the course of the day and he has to be ready for them. He has to appear civil, friendly, welcoming, enthusiastic. None of this will be easy for him, so he takes his first big drink of the day at a little after nine-thirty.

Barry wakes early enough too; not surprising, given the level of comfort to be found sleeping on the back seat of Enlightenment. He gets up, goes across to the shower block and ablutes. There's a perfectly good shower unit in his own caravan but he doesn't want to risk waking Charles Lederer. He knows the old guy is hardly likely to sleep solidly for the whole of the next two days but Barry intends to spend the afternoon and evening with him in the caravan, talking about life and death and other Zen topics, and thereby ensuring that he doesn't see the hordes of Volkswagens. With this in mind he plans an early visit to Fat Les, so that with any luck he'll be back before Lederer even stirs. Nevertheless, just to make sure, he locks the door of his caravan before departing.

He goes on foot to the Bug Mecca, since there is already a traffic jam forming along the roads surrounding the caravan site. He comes to the entrance gate and pays the exorbitant entrance fee. He wanders between the rows of parked Volkswagens and the trade stands for a good spell before he finds Fat Les. He sees the Fat Volkz marquee and as he enters he sees Les holding court with a group of enthusiasts. He comes up behind him and says loudly, 'I've got a Volkswagen I'd like you to take a look at.'

Fat Les turns to see who's talking to him, and when he sees it's Barry, he turns back in disgust.

'It's Enlightenment,' Barry persists. 'It needs some attention.'

'Yeah?' sneers Les. 'Take it to your approved dealer.'

'Please,' says Barry. 'Why this hostility?'

'If you don't know . . . '

'Please tell me. Please express your anger. Get it off your chest.'

Les doesn't need asking twice.

'You let me down, you bastard. I asked you for help. I asked you to help clear my name. I asked you to find Charles bloody Lederer, and you wouldn't.'

'But I would. I did.'

'What?'

'I looked for Charles Lederer. I found him. I caught him.'

'Did you hand him over to Cheryl Bronte?'

'No, he's locked up in my caravan.'

'Are you serious about this?' Les asks. 'You're not just winding me up?'

'I'm serious,' says Barry. 'He's at the caravan site not two hundred yards from here. Of course the old guy swears he never blew up any Volkswagens but I must say I don't believe him.'

'I may have misjudged you,' says Fat Les. 'Have a drink.'

Fat Les gets rid of his customers and Barry tells him about the various adventures he's had while finding Charles Lederer, although he omits the stuff about Marilyn apparently being in love with someone else, and he tells him about the damage that was inflicted on Enlightenment. Fat Les is sorry to hear about the damage but he's confident that Fat Volkz

206

Inc can make it as good as new. In fact he's come up with one or two new modifications that he thinks might fit very nicely into the existing structure of the car. Barry is thrilled. They're soon talking like the friends they once were. They begin to reminisce, to discuss the old times and this takes them several hours.

It is mid-morning when Phelan arrives in the nearby village and starts chatting to the local inhabitants. Has there been any trouble yet? Have there been fights, robberies, drugs and sex? When people tell him there haven't, he begins to wonder whether his boys have been slacking. Outside the caravan site he encounters the Ferrous Kid.

'Have you seen signs of trouble?' he asks.

'No,' says the Kid.

'Don't worry, there'll be trouble soon enough.'

'Will there?' asks the kid. 'All the ones I've met have been peaceable enough.'

'Well that's precisely the problem, isn't it? People aren't always what they seem?'

'You mean that you might really be a hippie in disguise?'

'I mean,' he says sternly, 'that people may look like good solid Englishmen but they turn out to be cosmopolitan riff raff. Someone ought to teach them a lesson.'

'What are you?' the Kid asks.

'I'm sorry?'

'Well I thought you must be a journalist or something, but you don't ask enough questions.'

'I'm just an interested party,' he says.

'But for all I know, given that people aren't always what they seem, you could be cosmopolitan riff raff, couldn't you?'

'How old are you?'

'Nine and a half.'

'Well let me assure you child, there's nothing cosmopolitan about me,' he says proudly and makes a dignified withdrawal.

207

The Ferrous Kid thinks this may turn out to be one of the great weekends of his young life. He sees all these Beetles arriving, in all their myriad styles and finishes, and his heart feels big within his chest. He stands at the edge of the Bug Mecca, watching all those gorgeous Beetles, and he feels spoiled for choice. Which one will he steal first?

Phelan needn't have worried about his boys. The gang of skinheads are soon on the job of causing localised outbreaks of casual aggro. They enter the Gathering of the Tribes, split up into small groups and start creating trouble. Some of them pinch girls' bottoms and squeeze their breasts. Some start pissing very conspicuously onto a row of tents where people are still sleeping. Others get into a fight over the price of food with the owner of a vegetarian food stall. A fortune teller's tent gets turned over. A couple of skinheads go up to Planetary Cliff and say that if he knows what's good for him he'll play a lot of music by the Upsetters in the course of the day. Planetary Cliff, of course, has plenty of reasons to hate and fear skinheads, especially since they beat him up in a lay-by at the beginning of the summer, but the ones who speak to him, being new recruits, weren't part of that attack, and besides, Cliff isn't averse to a bit of reggae now and then, so he doesn't argue.

The skinheads move through the crowd, knocking food and drink from people's hands, pushing people out of the way, and if anyone protests they threaten serious violence. None of this is exactly evil, and much of it isn't even directly confrontational. The threats so far remain just threats, and when resisted the skinheads tend to back down. They don't want a pitched battle, not yet. But word soon gets out that they're around and looking for trouble, and even though they're few enough in number, they still manage to create a feeling of unease and distrust, and that is exactly as intended.

And still they come. Zak arrives in the late morning in his

metallic turquoise and peppermint green Beetle with the suicide doors. He'd been contemplating bringing it along to Bug
Mecca with a view to selling it, but since his brush with the
skinheads he feels it's his duty to keep the car. If he got rid
of it now, that would be as good as letting the neo-Nazis win.
But he has a much better reason for coming. The memory of
his sexual encounter with Mrs Lederer is still very vivid, and
that encounter seemed to take place entirely because of the
car he drives. He could handle some more encounters like
that one, and if the kind of women who melt at the sight of
a man in a cool Volkswagen are to be found anywhere, they
are surely to be found at an event like Bug Mecca. He has
high hopes for the weekend.

Eventually Barry realises he ought to get back to his caravan
site and to Charles Lederer. He's been away longer than he
intended. Fat Les says he'll come over and have a look at
the damage to Enlightenment when he gets a quiet moment,
though that probably won't be till the early evening. Barry
says he'll look forward to it. Fat Les also seems extremely
keen to cross-question Charles Lederer about exploding
Volkswagens, although Barry assures him it will be hard
work to get much sense out of the old man.
    Barry hurries back. In places the crowds and traffic are
now so dense he has to fight his way through. He notices
that the music coming from the Gathering of the Tribes is
getting louder all the time, but he supposes that's the way it
is with tribal gatherings. He gets to the caravan site, nods to
the two caravanners who are manning the roadblock at the
gate and tries to enter.
    'Here, what's your game?' the first of them says.
    'Game?' asks Barry. 'I'm going to my caravan, that's all.'
    'Your caravan? You don't look the type to be enjoying a
caravan holiday.'
    Barry scratches his stubble, considers his blue leather
motorcycle suit and realises this is true.

'I'm not on holiday,' he says. 'I live here.'

'Then why haven't we seen you around?'

'I've been on the road. On a quest.'

'Oh sure.'

'I do live here. Really.'

'It's all right son, we know what you're up to. You're trying to get into the site to do a bit of thieving so you can support your drug habit, aren't you?'

'No,' Barry protests. 'I live here. Be reasonable.'

They laugh at him.

'Okay, I'll tell you what we'll do,' says one of them. 'We'll stand here blocking your way and if you try to get past us we'll break both your legs. How's that for reasonable?'

Barry can tell they mean it. He slinks away, smarting with the unfairness of it all, and wondering how and when he'll get back in to the site. He's more concerned than ever about Charles Lederer. He has to think what to do next but can't think of anything better than going back to Bug Mecca. He reasons that if Charles Lederer does leave the safety of the caravan and go there, then at least there'll be a chance of spotting him and calming him down, although the crowd is so thick by now he knows it will be all too easy to miss him.

In mid-afternoon Charles Lederer does indeed wake up. The inside of the caravan looks totally alien to him, though the fact that the door is locked seems curiously familiar. Still, caravan doors don't present much of a problem. He breaks open the lock and steps outside. In the days when Charles Lederer was a Member of Parliament, caravan sites were hardly his stomping ground, and he finds his current surroundings extremely charmless. He decides to leave. The two men on the gate look at him curiously as he walks past them, but they are too busy keeping people out to be concerned with keeping anyone in.

Once in the road Charles Lederer is thrust into a seething if good-natured tumult; people coming and going, dodging in and out of traffic, and he notices that far too many of the cars are Volkswagen Beetles. Different parts of the crowd are heading in different directions, some to the Bug Mecca, some to the Gathering of the Tribes, and although he knows it will cause him pain, he finds himself being irresistibly drawn towards the field of Volkswagens.

He gets to the gate of Bug Mecca where a steward demands an entrance fee, but Charles Lederer gives him a look so wild and demented that the steward waves him in. He moves through the field, past dune buggies and Bajas and convertibles, past T-shirt stalls and club stands. He hears the noise of flat-four engines, he senses the love of Volkswagens, and he becomes completely disorientated. It all gets too much for him. He doesn't know where he is or how he got there, but a part of him thinks it quite likely that he has died and gone to Hell. He sees a row of chemical toilets and heads for them. He enters a cubicle and locks himself in. He remains there for the rest of the afternoon, thereby making the already inadequate toilet arrangements even worse.

Phelan eventually catches up with some of his skinheads. They are standing in a crowd watching a performance of gamelan music. They are predictably unimpressed and offer up a barrage of loud, sneering comments, mostly to the effect that they'd prefer to hear something by Skrewdriver. Phelan takes Butcher aside and asks how things are going. Butcher notices that he's carrying a briefcase.

'Things are all right,' says Butcher.
'The new recruits?'
'They're fine.'
'The Volkswagens?'
'Yeah, they're fine too.'
'Did you take care of Renata?'
'Yeah we took care of her.'
'One day you'll have to tell me all about it.'
Butcher shrugs non-committally.

211

'So, no problems at all?' says Phelan.

'Well I don't know,' says Butcher. 'I think we could be just pissing in the wind here.'

'How's that?'

'I mean okay, so we can cause a bit of aggro. We can even get into a full blown rumble. But there's thousands of these New Age buggers. There's no way we can kick the shit out of all of them.'

'Of course not,' Phelan agrees.

'So what are we doing here?'

Phelan smiles. This is precisely the question he wanted Butcher to ask.

'Physical violence is all very well,' says Phelan, 'but it's far from being the only type.'

Butcher is confused by this notion and looks to Phelan for an explanation. The explanation is forthcoming, and as it unfolds, as Phelan reveals his latest plan for mayhem, Butcher gets a really good, evil feeling. When he has finished explaining, Phelan opens his briefcase to reveal endless bags full of anonymous white pills, the pharmaceutical medium by which his plan will be realised.

Butcher smiles and the briefcase is handed over. Butcher spends the rest of the afternoon distributing the white pills. Some people accept them readily enough as free samples, as though Butcher was some Owsley de nos jours. Others will only accept them when Butcher asks for money, believing they only get what they pay for. Butcher smiles a lot, acts friendly, assures them all that it's very good stuff. He tells them it's acid or Ecstasy or amphetamine depending on what they appear to want to hear. Other pills are crushed and the powder gets secretly dropped into batches of fruit juice, into pulse and bean salads, and in one case into a large tank that connects to a tap from which people are drawing drinking water. It is a long, hard afternoon's work, and Butcher prefers not to delegate, but before long he sees, with great satisfac-

212

tion, that a lively trade has started in the drugs. Somebody even offers to sell *him* some.

A couple of the tablets eventually get to Davey via a bare-foot hippie with tiger stripes painted on his face, who assures him that this is the very highest quality Ecstasy. Davey has spent most of the day in a vain search for consciousness-changing chemicals and he doesn't need asking twice. He eagerly swallows a couple of the tablets and waits for astounding results.

As the warm, sunny afternoon fades, and as Planetary Cliff pumps up the volume of the music, many members of the various tribes begin to feel a strange, unfamiliar edginess that has very little to do with loss of ego or the formation of a group mind.

Barry spends a long and not unenjoyable day at the Bug Mecca. He becomes engrossed in the many pristine Beetles on display. He becomes fascinated by the range of products and services that are available for Beetles. He enjoys the atmosphere. He finds it friendly and good-natured. There is a feeling that nothing bad will happen here, and he is reassured by the fact that he sees no sign of Charles Lederer.

Zak does not enjoy the day nearly as much as he had hoped to. He parks his metallic turquoise and peppermint green Beetle with the suicide doors in a conspicuous place and stands leaning against it in a cool but heroic pose, and winks at women as they go past, trying to engage them in chat. It doesn't work. The only people who want to talk to him are other young, male Volkswagen enthusiasts. Zak doesn't want to be unfriendly but that's not what he's here for. He thinks things are getting completely silly when some nine and a half year old kid tells him this is his favourite car in the whole Bug Mecca.

'If you were ten years older and of a different sex I'd offer to take you for a ride,' says Zak.

The Kid says, 'That won't be necessary.'

Zak decides to circulate, that'll be the way to meet girls.

213

But even that doesn't work. A lot of the girls are only there because their boyfriends are, and after an hour or so of being snubbed by girls and glared at by boyfriends, he decides to go back to his car and go home.

In fact he can do neither. At that very moment his Beetle is being driven along the A64, away from Filey, by the Ferrous Kid. He drives responsibly and really rather well for a nine and a half year old, and he has every intention of returning it undamaged to its rightful owner when he's finished with it. But that won't be possible either. Zak has had enough of Volkswagens for the time being. He leaves Bug Mecca, goes to the Gathering of the Tribes, and when someone offers him some drugs he takes them willingly enough. Getting totally zonked feels like the best way of dealing with this rotten day out.

At the end of the afternoon Barry returns to the marquee belonging to Fat Volkz Inc. Les is there looking overworked and a good deal the worse for drink, but he welcomes Barry like a long lost pal. Barry explains that he can't get back into the caravan site and Les assures him that if the worst comes to the worst, he can always kip down in the marquee. Les also plies him with drink and Barry accepts readily enough. He is starting to feel quite merry, and when Les suggests that they go and check out what's going on at the Gathering of the Tribes it doesn't seem like such a bad idea at all.

They walk there. It's almost dark now. At the edge of the field Fat Les spots one of the neo-Nazi Volkswagens but he chooses to ignore it. Barry, however, can't believe his eyes. He wants to go over and investigate it but Les restrains him.

'Is somebody making replicas of Enlightenment?' he asks.

'Yeah, me.'

'How come?'

'I'll tell you when I'm drunk enough.'

That isn't a good enough answer for Barry but they press on into the crowd. The music is loud and the beat is rapid and all around them people are dancing. They are a strange lot. Whatever tribe they belong to it's clearly one that doesn't include Fat Les and Barry Osgathorpe. The dancers are wild-eyed and frenetic. They're certainly into the rhythm but they don't exactly look as though they're having a good time. Les and Barry press on. They feel out of place, as though they're moving through a madhouse, a freak show.

When fires start at the perimeter of the field they, like many others, assume this is all part of the show. At first it looks like a series of harmless camp fires, but as time passes the fires start to spread and combine, and before long there's a continuous band of flame encircling the whole field. Barry can see this is going to make it hard to leave but at the moment he has no desire to leave at all. He isn't enjoying himself exactly but the spectacle around him is extremely compelling. One or two women are now dancing topless and he has never been averse to seeing topless women dancing. Fat Les passes a bottle of whisky back and forth and although they are now feeling drunk and a little out of it, they are clearly feeling out of it in a very different way from the rest of the crowd.

Skinheads move through the crush, kicking and punching people as they go, but many of the victims are in so trance-like a state they hardly notice. Unseen by most of the crowd, half a dozen skinheads pull Planetary Cliff from his position on stage from where he operates the sound system. He disappears in a rapid and efficient flurry of fists and cherry red leather and the skinheads take over the music. At first there isn't much of a change in the sound but gradually the beat gets faster and harder and it is overlayed with the sounds of machine gun fire, explosions, and clips of the voice of Adolf Hitler.

This has a gradual but increasingly dramatic effect on the dancers. If they were wild before, they now become posi-tively possessed. A disturbance starts not far from where Barry and Les are standing. A young man is dancing with

215

more than usual verve. He is naked and his body is covered in thick, chocolate-coloured mud. He is jerking his limbs and swirling around with a manic, not to say self-destructive, energy. His sense of rhythm is uncertain and his movements are uncoordinated, but there's a kind of deranged grandeur to his hyperactivity. The crowd parts to let him through and suddenly he is shaking and thrashing just a few inches away from Fat Les and Barry. They make eye-contact and Barry and Les see that the dancer is Davey, a much-changed old face from a long time ago. In the circumstances nobody quite knows what to say, then Davey yells, 'Are *you* here?'

'Well yes,' says Barry. 'How are you?'

'Oh,' Davey replies, 'I've completely lost the plot,' and then he cavorts away into the mass of people.

'You know,' says Fat Les, 'this isn't a bit like Butlins.'

They drink some more. They listen to the music and they watch the dancing. A few of the revellers are looking exhausted, but that doesn't slow them down, and a few are crying, though whether that's because of the agony or the ecstasy it's hard to tell. Then Barry feels a hand on his shoulder. That's not so strange. The flailing of limbs around him leads to all sorts of involuntary contact, but the hand tightens, becomes painful, and starts to pull him round. Barry turns to protest and sees Butcher's big ugly face staring at him in delighted disgust.

'You know me, don't you?' says Butcher.

'Er no, I don't think I . . . '

'Yes you do. You're the lad who's so handy with a pot of coffee.'

Barry is about to insist that he knows nothing about any pot of coffee. However, before he can speak, Butcher grabs him by the collar and raises his other fist.

'Hey,' says Fat Les, who has, of course, had some previous dealings with Butcher, 'leave him alone. This is Ishmael.'

'I don't care what his fuckin' name is.'

'He's a good lad,' Les insists. 'Let go of him.'

216

'Stay out of this you fat git. He's got a beating coming to him, and you can have one as well if you want.'

'Who are you calling a git?'

And suddenly fists are flying. Barry tries to hit Butcher in the face but that only sets him off on a frenzied attack in which he tries, with surprising success, to kick, punch and headbutt Barry all at the same time. Barry holds him off as best he can, but this conspicuous flurry of violence brings other skinheads running to the fray. Barry is knocked to the ground where he is given a damned good kicking, and the skinheads only stop when Fat Les points out that Barry's white and English and a Volkswagen driver, and if they really want to do some kicking there are more satisfying targets at hand. The skinheads grudgingly accept this, regroup and walk away looking for fresh prey. When he's sure they're gone, Barry staggers to his feet, and with Les's help manages to get to the comparative safety of somebody's empty teepee not far away. He falls in and sits down, speechless, nursing his wounds.

'They shouldn't have done that,' Fat Les says.

The teepee looks like an increasingly good place to be. Outside, the music is getting more demonic and intolerably loud, and something, maybe the drugs or maybe the music or maybe a dangerous combination of the two, is having a pretty weird effect on the crowd. Some of them are throwing up, some are sobbing uncontrollably, some are crawling on their hands and knees, some have adopted a foetal position.

Then the sound of engines starts; a familiar roar, flat-four, air-cooled Volkswagen engines. The sound comes from all directions, rising and falling, fierce and threatening, and then the skinheads' Volkswagens are in action, driving at terrifying speed into the mass of people. The crowd panics, tries to scatter and part, but there's nowhere to go. The low black Nazi Beetles drive them back and forth like sheep being herded by mad dogs. People are terrified; the fires, the noise, the bad drugs, the strobes, the lasers, the killer Beetles coming

217

at them from all directions. They scream and stampede. They rush back and forth in ragged waves, but they're constantly driven back; there's no escape, nowhere to run to. The cars demolish tents and stalls. People get hit by the speeding cars, knocked over, run down. Exhaust smoke and terror hang in the air. The skinhead drivers think it's the best fun they've ever had. They've produced total chaos, total fear and hysteria; a suitable atmosphere and backdrop, an appropriate warm up act.

The cars suddenly cease their attacks. The drivers head for the edge of the field, where they park their vehicles and get out, leaving their Volkswagens to stand like mechanical sentries, silhouetted against the ring of flame. The music stops dead, leaving an awesome silence, and the light show finishes. The stage is in darkness for a long time until a spotlight hits the back cloth and picks out a lone, dark, powerful figure. It is Phelan. His hands are raised in a victory salute. His whole posture says Obey me, Worship me. All the crowd's attention focuses on him, all their eyes, all their minds full of weird visions, full of strange, hard-edged colours. They are compelled to watch. Now he has something in his hands, what looks like a toy Volkswagen, and he holds it out as though giving it to the crowd. He picks up a microphone and speaks to them, his voice full of metallic reverb. He says, 'This is my talisman. This is the source of all my power,' and he begins to speak about Adolf Hitler and white supremacy and ethnic cleansing. This is all going to take some time.

In the teepee Barry is starting to get his senses back. He feels pretty terrible but oddly enough, Fat Les looks to be in even worse shape. They can hear Phelan's voice. They can tell something terrible is happening.

'What the Hell's going on out there?' Barry asks.

But Fat Les doesn't give him an answer, he simply repeats, 'They shouldn't have done this.'

'You're telling me.'

218

'No, I mean they *really* shouldn't have done it.'

'What do you mean?' Barry asks.

'I've done some terrible things,' says Les.

'Haven't we all?'

'Not like me,' says Les. 'I have a profound need to confess.'

'Is this really the time?'

'Yes it is. You see it was me who blew up all those Volkswagens.'

'You?'

'Yeah. I did it. I did it all.'

'Why would you do a thing like that?'

'I don't know exactly, but I think maybe Cheryl Bronte was half right. I guess I just got sick of Volkswagens. You know, there was a time when I lived and breathed Volkswagen Beetles. They were my work and my play, my hobby and my profession. They were good years and I wouldn't have had it any other way, but as time went by I started to change. I suppose basically I started to get a bit bored. I started to think there might be more to life than Volkswagens. But I didn't give them up. How could I? I was Fat Les the Vee Dub King. How else was I going to make a living? So I carried on, but the magic wasn't there any more. I didn't resent it exactly but you know, whereas it had once been an obsession, maybe even a love affair, it turned into just a job.

'Then as time went by I *did* resent it. I started to get fed up. I started to get cynical. I got to the stage where the mere sight, or sound or the mere mention of a Volkswagen Beetle made me feel sick. But still what could I do? By then I'd got the place in Southend. I had a business to run. I'd got debts and responsibilities and people working for me. I couldn't just jack it in. But something had to give, otherwise I'd have gone completely bonkers. I had to do something to express this pent up anger and frustration. So I started blowing up Volkswagens.'

'But you kept telling me it was Charles Lederer who did it.'

'Of course I did. That's what I wanted everyone to believe. It suited me just fine. And when his daughter started believing it too, that was even better. And if they caught him and put him inside for being a raving old nutter that would have been better still. I'd have got away with it completely.'

'Oh God,' says Barry. 'This is going to play terrible havoc with your karma.'

'I realise that. It was all so simple. I'd get Volkswagens coming in to Fat Volkz Inc from all over the country; needing a new petrol tank here, a new dashboard there, a new wiring loom somewhere else. I did the work as asked, but while I was at it, it wasn't so difficult to hide a little explosive device somewhere in the car, with a timer to make sure it was a long way from me when it finally blew up.'

'Les, that's just terrible.'

'I know. I know. But the thing is, I did it with those neo-Nazi Volkswagens too.'

'You did?'

'Yeah,' and he pulls a little black box out of his pocket, a thing that looks not unlike a remote control for a television set, though this one has more switches and LEDS, a few loose wires and one very big red button.

'I press that,' says Les, 'and it's bye-bye to eight wicked-looking black Volkswagens.'

Outside they can hear Phelan ranting on about the Aryan race, world domination and the triumph of the will. It's very eloquent, very compelling and grand, and even if it might be construed as a little overdramatic and dictatorial, he undoubtedly has the crowd where he wants them. They are hanging on his every word, applauding and cheering, and here and there his name is being chanted.

Barry says, 'You mean you press that button and the cars all blow up.'

'Yep. Just like that,' says Fat Les.

'I think we have to do it, don't we?'

'I think we do.'

They leave the teepee. This is something they want to see with their own eyes. Phelan is no longer speaking, just basking in the adulation of his new followers, holding Hitler's Volkswagen aloft. Then someone appears on the stage beside him. It is a bedraggled old man with a skinhead haircut, Charles Lederer, looking his wildest to date.

Phelan does not want to share the stage with anyone and yet he hesitates for a moment, perhaps thinking it's a fervent supporter who's got a little carried away with enthusiasm. Certainly he thinks the old man looks harmless and unthreatening. Charles Lederer approaches, gets very close, and his hands are extended as though he wants to congratulate Phelan. But what he actually wants to do, what he succeeds in doing, is lay his hands on Hitler's Beetle. Phelan is caught off guard. Charles Lederer's fingers make contact with the model, but the laying on of hands is not enough for him. He grabs the Volkswagen and dashes away across the stage, and even as Phelan lunges after him, even as he summons a few skinheads to deal with the situation, Charles Lederer winds back his throwing arm and flings the Volkswagen hard and high away from the stage, up over the heads of the crowd.

It is a mighty throw. The model rises and rises in the air. It reaches the top of its parabola of flight and seems to hang there, crystalline and perfect, showing itself to the multitude, spinning like a tiny lost planet. Phelan yells through the mike, 'Catch it. But gently.' Thousands of eyes look up. Dozens of pairs of hands steady themselves ready to catch the falling Volkswagen if it comes their way.

Fat Les holds out the remote control to Barry.

'Would you do me the honour?'

'I certainly would.'

Barry presses the button, there's a pause, and then, at the edges of the field, eight black, wicked-looking Volkswagens, each one more or less a replica of his own Enlightenment, explode in banks of searing flame.

The synchronised noise is terrifying, and this crowd has a

great talent and propensity for terror. Black smoke rolls across the field. A huge, multivoiced scream goes up. It's as though a war's started. They stampede again, bouncing off each other as they go. The wall of fire surrounding the field no longer seems like such a great obstacle, and they run so fast through the flames that they don't even feel the heat.

The falling Volkswagen, formerly property of Adolf Hitler and Carlton Bax, is totally forgotten. It drops unnoticed into a scrum of frenzied hippies, hits someone on the back of the neck, then falls to the muddy ground where any number of running feet crush and destroy the beautifully-made automaton.

On the scaffolding stage Phelan drops to his knees. Beside him Charles Lederer stands tall and firm, and seen a certain way it might look as though Phelan is kneeling at his feet in prayer. Charles Lederer looks out over the field. He doesn't exactly understand what's been going on here, nor what his part in it was, but he feels extremely, peculiarly pleased with himself, as if the simple laying on of his hands was enough to destroy all his demons.

Barry and Fat Les stand and watch. They are stunned but gratified, and they watch with renewed amazement as a white car emerges from the smoke and mayhem. It is a white BMW and it makes slow, stately progress through the running crowd, avoiding bodies and tents and the burning wrecks of Volkswagens. It looks serene and other-worldly.

As the smoke clears a little the driver is revealed to be Cheryl Bronte. Beside her sits Renata Caswell, and in the back of the car are Marilyn Lederer and Carlton Bax. They are holding onto each other for dear life. They look wretched and traumatised, and yet they look totally, hopelessly, in love. Barry has seen some strange sights today, but this is one thing he cannot bear to look at.

X

I Beg Your Pardon, I Never Promised You a Volkswagen

The noise of twin carburettors and stinger exhausts screams across the sky. There is a curl of blue smoke, the smell of multigrade and four star and teen spirit, the sound of radials on loose gravel, a squeal of overheated brake pads. Here they come, a procession, a danse macabre, something stately and dangerous, new-fangled yet elemental. They come in different styles and colours, in different specifications, with or without optional extras. They suit different personalities, satisfy different needs, are the products of different obsessions, but in the end, one size fits all.

Here they come, the heroes and the bad guys, the lovers and killers, the good, the bad, the pranksters and fugitives and collectors, the winners and posers, the hippies and cops, the postmen, the surfers, the ravers; all driving Volkswagen Beetles, always crashing in the same car. Everyone has a Volkswagen story. Everyone is a driver or a passenger.

Here are some Disney executives at the boardroom table having a brainstorming session, some time in the late sixties. 'Hey it's freaky out there. Everybody's taking drugs, marching on the Pentagon burning their draft cards, what we need is some mawkish sentimental crap for the family audience. And sure, we've made plenty of mawkish sentimental crap about wildlife and children, but hey, let's face it fellers, the times they are a changing. How about this for a concept?

223

Let's make some mawkish sentimental crap about an anthropomorphic Volkswagen!!!!! Far out or what?'

In fact they get through about thirty different Herbies in the making of *The Love Bug* and the true Beetle obsessive will spot that the cars used vary from 1966 through to 1969 models. These days, only one Herbie stands in the Volkswagen museum at Wolfsburg, with the number 53 on its doors and bonnet, and the legend 'Gross in Fahrt' painted along its sides. But, of course, since the car has to be seen to race and beat Corvettes and Ferraris, most of the stunt cars have to use a Porsche engine. But that's okay, that's authentic enough, that's just the nature of film, that's just showbiz.

Here is Ralph Nader, pioneer of consumer safety, the man who nixed the Chevrolet Corvair, and he isn't at all happy about this Bug mania that's sweeping the country. They're strange and foreign and popular as Hell and it sure wouldn't do his profile any harm if he could prove they were rolling Germanic death traps. So he looks at them and drives them and takes them apart and crashes them, and in the end all he can find to complain about is the fact that in the event of a serious collision, the petrol cap cover might, you know, fly off and hurt somebody.

Here is Ivan Hirst, the man who brought the Wolfsburg factory back to life after the allied conquest of Germany, the man who more than anyone else was responsible for the post-war rebirth of the Volkswagen Beetle. It is 1989 and he is living in the village of Marsden in West Yorkshire, a Volkswagen Golf GTi in his garage, and a neighbour asks him is it true he used to work for Volkswagen.

'Well actually,' he says, 'Volkswagen rather used to work for me.'

Here is Peter Weir in the Australian Outback filming *The Cars That Ate Paris*, using a Volkswagen Beetle as the 'monster'. Spikes jut out from every panel of the car and are supposed to look scary and lethal. In fact they look like they're made from thinnish cardboard.

224

Here is Woody Allen with *Sleeper*, where a Volkswagen Beetle that hasn't been used for centuries still starts first time. And serious students of Allen will note that when Susan Anspach leaves him in *Play it Again, Sam* she too drives away in a Beetle.

Here is Philip K. Dick in July 1964, driving a Volkswagen Bug; Philip K. Dick, a man with a taste for Tri-Chevvies and Jags. Here he is, paranoid and speeding, seeing angels and devils, crazy as a hoot-owl in the opinion of his girl-friend, fearing he is being persecuted by the CIA and the FBI as well as by some nameless neo-Nazi organisation. He powers the Bug into a corner, completely misjudges its capacity for understeer, and he flips the car over. He has to wear a body cast and has his arm in a sling for the next two months. Even the Volkswagens are against him.

Here is Liberace making a grand entrance in his new Las Vegas show. He is driven on stage in a mirrored Rolls-Royce, gets out, displays himself to the audience, lets them thrill to the sight of his latest outfit which consists of a cape of pink feathers. The Rolls-Royce departs. He removes the cape to reveal the drag underneath and just for a moment he looks as though he has nowhere to put the cape; at which point a mirrored, open-topped 1971 Volkswagen Beetle with a Rolls-Royce grille, double headlights and uniformed chauffeur drives onto the stage. Liberace tosses the feathered cape into the back of the Volkswagen and the chauffeur drives it away again.

Here, on some New England campus in the early nineteen-sixties, are a whole bunch of young students engaged in the sport of 'jamming', in which they attempt to cram as many people as possible into a Beetle. Bodies press together, hands, faces and erogenous zones are brought into unlikely and intimate contact. It just wouldn't be the same in a Cadillac.

Here are the Beastie Boys, white rap group and general funsters wearing VW logo badges on chains round their necks like pieces of jewellery. And not long after a few media appearances, it's impossible to leave any Volkswagen on any street in England without fearing that the badge will have been ripped off by the time you get back.

Here are the guys at Doyle Dane Bernbach, the advertising agency that's landed the account for Volkswagen in America. Thing is, some of these guys are Jewish, and naturally they have a few qualms. Hey, they say, Adolf Hitler was responsible for the Volkswagen. Adolf Hitler killed six million Jews. I'm a Jew. So is it ethical for me to help sell the Volkswagen? Big decision.

With the integrity for which advertising agencies are famous, they decide it *is* ethical and they go on to create one of the most respected and successful and talked about advertising campaigns there's ever been. The campaign doesn't mention the war, doesn't mention Adolf Hitler, scarcely even mentions the fact that the car is German; but they sure feel better for having had the qualms.

And here are the factories in Nigeria and South Africa, in New Zealand and Belgium and Singapore, in Australia and Portugal and Yugoslavia and Brazil; all closed now. Only Mexico still makes them. Mexico, a country where the Beetle is known as the Navel, because everybody's got one. Not quite true in the case of the car; demand far exceeds supply.

And where are they going, all these fellow travellers? What's the destination? Why, they're heading for the vanishing point, following the yellow brick road towards the darkness at the edge of town. Are you there Dean Moriarty?

And here am I, writing this novel in a room full of Volkswagen books and Volkswagen clippings and Volkswagen models and Volkswagen memorabilia. I could pretend it's all just research material, but who would believe me? Here I am skimming through biographies and running through indexes, looking desperately for material. Did the Yorkshire Ripper drive a Beetle? Did Jeffrey Dahmer? And if they did then that's great, that's another chapter I can write. Or is there something from my own life, some anecdote or coincidence that I might have forgotten about? Did Clint Eastwood drive a Beetle? Did Billy Connolly? Did Eddie Van Halen? Did John Paul Getty II? Well yes, as a matter of fact they all did, but what exactly can I do with that?

And sometimes I ask myself 'Why a Beetle?' and sometimes all the stuff that the Ferrous Kid says to Barry back in the first chapter about blankness and ubiquity seems like reason enough, and other times it doesn't. Sometimes I think I might have chosen some other familiar, cultish, man-made object. Why not the Luger or the Zippo Lighter or the Fender Strat? But that's another story, another obsession, another novel.

* * *

'I can't believe I'm doing this,' says Barry Osgathorpe. 'I can't believe I'm sitting in a 747 about to fly to Los Angeles with a woman I hardly know.'

'You know me,' says Renata Caswell. 'And you'll get to know me even better now that I'm your ghost writer.'

'I don't know that I need a ghost writer.'

'Yes you do, Barry. You have a story to tell. I want to hear it and I want to write it down for you.'

Barry has never flown before. It is all very strange and yet surprisingly mundane. The interior of the plane is so cheap and plastic, the muzak so dreadful. His fellow passengers look so ordinary and they're taking this all so easily in their stride. None of them seems to be experiencing the same blend of excitement and uneasiness that he is.

'But why do I have to tell it you in America?' he asks.

'Because Barry, dear heart, having just been central in a national scandal involving an ex-Member of Parliament, a television weathergirl, neo-Nazis, New Age culture and exploding Volkswagens, it makes a lot of sense to get away for a while. A lot of very unsavoury hack journalists will be after you if you stay home. I'm here to protect you. Besides, you signed an exclusive contract with my newspaper, didn't you?'

'It seemed like a good idea at the time.'

'It *was* a good idea. It still is.'

'But you've got the story already. Why do you need me?'

'You're the story. You're the human angle.'

'Am I really?'

The prospect doesn't make him happy. He feels a ripple of tension building up inside him, and he's not sure whether it's fear of flying or fear of being a human angle.

'Besides,' says Renata, 'you'll like America.'

And yes, he thinks he believes her. He thinks he probably will enjoy the friendly people, the open roads, the big skies, the food. At least he thinks he will. At least he hopes he will. He is no longer sure what does and doesn't give him pleasure. Somewhere back there, like Davey, he fears he may have lost the plot.

'So let me get this straight,' he says, 'were you only ever involved with Phelan so that you could get a story?'

'Of course.'

'But you slept with him and everything.'

'I didn't *sleep* exactly. I did what I had to do to get a story.'

'That's dedication, or something,' says Barry. 'So does that mean you're not a neo-Nazi?'

'Come on Barry. Surely you can see that I've got old-fashioned liberal written all over me.'

He looks at her. He isn't at all sure what's written on her. She feels the need to assert her credentials again.

'You know me,' she insists.

'I know sod all.'

'What don't you know?'

'Well, for a start, where was Carlton Bax's locked room?'

'There was no locked room, Barry,' she says with exaggerated patience. 'That was the point. Quite a Zen thing, really,

Barry. I thought you might have appreciated that. The locked room was in the mind of the beholder. Carlton Bax knew that certain people wanted to get their hands on his prize exhibit and they believed, because Bax had made them believe, that the Hitler Volkswagen must be in the locked room. Therefore they were searching for that room, searching for something that didn't exist. It was a good scam. Meanwhile the Beetle in question was sitting quite happily in Mrs Lederer's bedroom. He gave it her ostensibly as a present, but in fact for safe keeping. The last place anyone would think of looking. Not even Marilyn knew it was there.'

He prefers not to think about Marilyn. It only brings him pain. In fact, when he gets right down to it, he realises that she has never really brought him anything else. He tries not to think about her and Carlton Bax, not to dwell on the fact that they're probably together right now, probably in a suite in some swanky hotel, between the sheets, having a long celebratory sex session, all hot mouths and swelling parts. He feels ill, and it definitely isn't fear of flying. Like she said, sex is a funny business.

'And what about Butcher?' he asks. 'Did he really rape you?'

'Ah well, Butcher is an interesting case. Right from the beginning I knew there was something different about him, but I wasn't sure what. Eventually I worked it out. The difference is, he's gay. Phelan sent a gay boy to do a man's job, and Butcher didn't want any part of it. He set me free, told me to make myself scarce, then he and the rest of his gang went off to the Gathering of the Tribes. That was fine by me. Left alone, knowing that Phelan was away too, I was able to go back to the bunker and release Carlton Bax and Marilyn, and then we went to Cheryl Bronte and told her the whole story. It took a while, but she finally believed us. Then we piled into her car and headed for the Gathering of the Tribes to exact our retribution on friend Phelan. But in a

229

sense we got there too late. You'd already done the job for us.'

'I'll bet Carlton Bax is pretty pissed off. The non-existent locked room business may have been very clever but he still lost his whole collection one way or another.'

The thought gives him considerable pleasure.

'Well, maybe Marilyn can afford to buy him some new toys,' says Renata. 'She's been offered her own television show. "Marilyn After Midnight". It's not prime time but it's a start. In fact things are looking up for the whole family. I gather Marilyn's mother and father are having a trial reconciliation. And I hear that old man Lederer's about to be given his own newspaper column – the voice of reason type thing.'

Barry shakes his head. He wants to say again that he can't believe it, but these days he can believe just about anything.

'I bet Fat Les is pretty pissed off too,' he says.

'Why do you say that?'

'Well he's going to end up in jail isn't he, given the number of Volkswagens he blew up.'

'Very probably, but I don't think the sentence will be all that long, and in any case, a little spell inside probably won't do him too much harm. You know, I think Les is one of those people who has a need to be punished. He feels guilty. He knows he's done wrong. He wants to pay his debt to society.'

'Spare me the pop psychology,' says Barry, sharply.

'Okay, I'll save it for my readers.'

'And what about Phelan? Is he going to go to jail?'

'Who knows? It's my experience that people like Phelan don't go to jail. It doesn't agree with them.'

'But wasn't that the whole point? Isn't that why you were trying to expose him?'

'I was trying to get a story, not be an avenging angel, but I certainly slowed him down a little.'

'He deserves worse than slowing down.'

'Come on Barry, don't be naive.'

230

'I just don't understand why he isn't rotting in a cell somewhere.'

'Could it be that he has a special relationship with the police?'

'With Cheryl Bronte?'

She nods.

'Maybe your next exposé should be of her.'

'Maybe be it should, but as it happens, I've been employed to be your ghost writer.'

The plane is full now. The doors are being closed. The overhead storage lockers are being slammed shut.

'I've never been to America,' says Barry.

'I know that.'

'I've never been out of England.'

'It's time you did.'

'I find it all incredibly scary.'

'It's brave of you to admit it.'

'Really?'

'Don't worry. I'll be there to protect you.'

Barry looks at her carefully to see whether she's mocking him. She doesn't seem to be. She really seems to mean it. Barry feels better already.

'You know Barry, this could be the start of a beautiful friendship.'

'Really?'

'I've told you. I do what I have to do to get a story, but some of the things I do for myself.'

She squeezes his knee in a gesture of unfathomable ambiguity. Barry thinks he might as well enjoy it.

It is now that part of the pre-flight charade when the cabin crew wave their arms in the direction of the emergency exits and demonstrate how to strap on a life jacket. It only adds to Barry's anxiety. He watches but he doesn't really see. They look like mime artists. Then he notices that one of the air stewardesses looks oddly familiar. The hair and the uniform are unfamiliar but as she shows the correct way to inflate a life jacket by blowing down a small, transparent, plastic tube, Barry realises it's Debby. She was as good as her word. She's found a way to travel. Barry sinks down in his seat, puts a hand over his face, and pretends to be fascinated by the in flight magazine.

Much, much later the plane touches down. Barry and Debby have managed to spend the whole flight without admitting to each other's existence. Not a glance, not a word, not a gesture has been exchanged. Renata has found all this screamingly funny and she has been very tempted to interview Debby to get extra background.

Renata and Barry go through passport control and although a huge, sandy-haired official with a walrus moustache gives him a hard time and says he looks like a mass murderer in his passport photograph, they are soon out of the airport and collecting their rental car from one of the lots. The light is harsh and glaring. Everything looks bright and hard, and Barry feels as though he's on another planet.

'Sorry we can't rent a Volkswagen Beetle,' says Renata. 'The rental fleets don't use them.'

Again he checks to see whether or not Renata is sending him up, but again she seems to be sincere. They take charge of a Ford Thunderbird and he can immediately see its advantages, its solidity, its comfort, the sense of sitting in someone's office. It is not at all what he's used to, but Renata looks perfectly at home with the power steering and the automatic gearbox and she sails the car out of the lot into the easy swell of American traffic.

Almost immediately they pass a small workshop selling secondhand tyres and hubcaps, and Barry sees his first American Beetle parked outside it. The car too looks very at home here, basking in the California sunshine; a candy purple convertible with Porsche alloy rims and lavender upholstery. Barry and Renata are soon on the freeway, heading towards a superior motel that Renata just happens to know. Barry is still not sure what the sleeping arrangements are going to be and he's far too polite to ask. Renata drives swiftly, and she has the radio on, and consequently they have no idea that moments after they pass the purple convertible it blows up in a geyser of flame and, like many before it, is reduced to a tangle of blackened, burning wreckage.